SUGAR
MIA BALLARD

MIA BALLARD

SUGAR
MIA BALLARD

SUGAR

SUGAR

For my mother,

Even though you wouldn't approve of most of the things in this book I hope you're still proud of me up there.

MIA BALLARD

ORANGE COUNTY, CA. 1978

MIA BALLARD

PRESENT DAY

The plan to kill Dean unfurled in my mind like a dark bloom in the midst of an otherwise idle Tuesday evening, the kind where the air tastes like spent fuel and the sky bleeds orange, stubbornly holding onto the last dregs of daylight. It was a whim, really, until it wasn't. Until it became the kind of necessity that gnaws at you, a secret you nurture in the darkest recesses of your heart.

The revelation came shattered into a million shards of betrayal over plates of meticulously arranged sushi at our usual spot—the one with the dim lighting and the waitstaff who knew not to ask for our orders because we had settled into the kind of comfortable predictability that couples often mistake for happiness. Lilah was there, happy to be a third wheel. Lilah Patrick had always been the cornerstone of my sanity, the one I clung to when the world seemed too slippery to navigate alone. She was the kind of friend who didn't need to fill silences, her presence alone was enough. Quiet, yes, but her stillness was the sort that commanded attention. She was a force rendered in soft strokes, her brilliance sometimes overshadowed by her beauty—or perhaps it was the other way around. And then, between bites of salmon nigiri and shared laughter that now felt like a performance, I saw it—the look. It was a fleeting thing, a mere second where Dean's gaze held Lilah's a beat too long, a silent exchange that crackled with an electricity that was unmistakable.

I had been suspecting Dean of cheating for a few months now. I wanted to get proof first, and something in me told me to set up this night, to study them. All those times Dean and Lilah conveniently went out of town around the same time, the way Dean would barely meet her eye and lock himself in our bedroom whenever she visited. The perfume on Dean's sweater that smelled exactly like Lilah's after coming home from a work dinner. I have never heard of doctors having a work dinner. It seemed my intuition was correct.

The realization gutted me, an implosion that left me gasping for air in a room that suddenly seemed too small. The betrayal was a visceral thing, a punch to the gut that left me reeling. And so, the plan to kill Dean was born not of vengeance, but of survival. It was the primal scream in the face of an existential crisis, the decision to cut off the tumor that threatened to consume me from the inside out. It was, in its essence, an act of reclaiming my dignity from the ashes of our crumbling relationship, from the lie that had become my life.

I excuse myself to use the bathroom. I can't let them see me angry. I can't let them know that I know. Not yet. As I slip into the bathroom, the walls pulsate—a breathing, confining witness to my anger. The air is dry but fragrant, laced with lemon disinfectant and the faint, earthy smell of cheap floor cleaner. I catch my reflection in the streaked mirror, my face flushed as if I've been slapped by the discovery. It's strange how anger morphs my features, twisting them into an unfamiliar landscape.

I place my purse on the cold, granite edge of the sink, the metal zipper a harsh, resonant sound that breaks the room's sterile silence. I dig through it with the fervor of a treasure hunter who finally sees the glint of gold, but mine is not made of precious metal. My shaking hands scrape against lipstick tubes and crumpled receipts until they reach the ziplock bag, that clear plastic pouch holding my escape. With fingers that do not seem like my own, I wrestle the tab out. It is small and innocuous looking, but I know its power. It shimmers slightly under the flickering fluorescent light, a gateway to another reality. I place the tab under my tongue, feeling its familiar bitterness dissolve. My eyelids flutter close, and I lean against the sink, the coolness seeping through my blouse. The euphoria doesn't creep in; it crashes over me like an inevitable wave. Tension begins to untangle from my muscles, the anger seeping out through my skin like evaporating sweat. The bathroom tiles beneath my feet start to ripple, veins of grout seeming to flow as if the floor itself has become unmoored from the earth.

Colors bloom and stretch, a kaleidoscope weaving its way through the once mundane space. I open my eyes, and the mirror isn't just a reflection anymore—it's a portal to something vaster and forgiving. In this moment, I am no longer contained. The silver faucets stretch and morph into liquid metal vines, spiraling upward into infinity. The walls melt away, leaving me suspended in a universe punctuated by distant stars and vivid streams of light. Anger is a distant echo now, swallowed by the boundless tapestry unfolding before me. I am free.

The meticulous nature of my planning was not born of malice but of necessity. It was a declaration of independence, a refusal to be the victim in a narrative where I had always seen myself as the heroine. The plan was my salvation, my catharsis, a way to sever the rot before it consumed me whole. Killing Dean, in theory, was not about ending his life; it was about reclaiming mine. It was about staring into the abyss of my own despair and choosing, instead, to rewrite the ending.

After dinner we drive home. Dean has had too much to drink, so I drive. It's a silent drive. I'm surprised when he grabs my hand as we stumble to the door. His hand in mine feels like a plea, a desperate attempt to cling to a narrative that has long since unraveled. I lead him to the bedroom, but it feels more like leading a lamb to slaughter, only this lamb has wronged me in ways that have left scars too deep for time to heal. His drunken stumble up the stairs is almost comical, an absurd pantomime of lust that once drove us those first couple years of marriage. That goofy half-smile, an attempt at seduction, now only serves as a stark reminder of how far we have strayed from each other. I can't help but think of how the man I once found irresistible has morphed into this stranger I barely recognize—a stranger with whom I share a mortgage and a web of lies.

I study the man I had planned to love for the rest of my life. I find myself lamenting not the impending loss of him but the loss of myself. The vibrant woman who once took pride in her appearance now mirrors his unkempt, subdued existence. My transformation wasn't for love; it was a sacrifice on the altar of compromise, a slow, insidious erasure of my identity. The realization of his infidelity is a perverse liberation, a permission slip signed in betrayal that frees me from the self-imposed shackles. I no longer feel the need to dim my own light to match his dull glow. The pain of betrayal is sharp, but it cuts the ties that bind me to this charade of a marriage. There's this thing about descent—it's quiet, almost imperceptible, like the slow fade of sunlight at dusk, until you're standing in the dark wondering where the day went.

That's how it was with Dean. Our love—or whatever it was that passed for love, had dulled, faded from the brilliant hues of new passion to the drab, washed-out colors of routine. He smiled at me, that smile, frayed around the edges, no longer a symbol of mutual desire but a relic of what we used to be. Ironic, how the very things that once drew me to him had become the markers of our mutual decline.

That fucker.

He stumbles up the stairs, looking back at me with his half-hearted attempts at seduction, he doesn't realize he's going to die. The promise of sex is a currency devalued by his infidelity, each dalliance a withdrawal from the bank of my patience, until now, when I'm overdrawn and bankrupt of fucks to give. As I descend back down the stairs to grab a knife, I feel the weight of our history, distorted and frayed at the edges, pressing down on me. It's an odd sensation, this clarity. I'm not fueled by rage, not really. It's something colder, more precise. His voice floats down to me, a sing-song invocation of my name, dripping with an intimacy we no longer share. *"Sataraaa."* It feels like a taunt, a reminder of all the ways we've failed to truly know each other. I walk up the stairs, slowly.

Entering the room, the scene before me is almost comical in its mundaneness. There he is, sprawled expectantly, that goofy grin plastered across his face—the same grin that once made my heart flutter was now nothing more than a grotesque caricature. Maybe it was the acid but as I look down at him all I see is a sentient puppet. Half human, half doll, made of plastic. His skin is shiny, and his mouth is dark and cavernous as he opens it. I straddle him, the knife hidden behind my back, and as I reveal my intent, the shift in his expression is a slow dawning of horror. It's a look I'll remember forever, a fractured snapshot of the man I thought I knew.

His Adam's apple bobs against the cold blade. "Satara, what are you doing?"

There's a power in naming your suspicions aloud, giving them form and substance. "Are you sleeping with Lilah?" The words taste like bile, poisoned and acidic on my tongue. His denial is immediate, a reflexive spasm of self-preservation, but his eyes, those windows to a soul I've never truly seen, flicker with something unreadable. There's a raw, unfiltered brutality in the moment. My emotions sprawl across the spectrum, vibrant and violent in their expression.

The air between us is charged with electricity that's palpable, the kind that precedes a storm. "Out of all people. You choose my *best friend*."

His response, a frantic denial, a feeble attempt to stitch up the gash his deceit has left in the fabric of our lives, does little to staunch the hemorrhage of trust.

"Do you love her?" The question hangs between us, heavy with the weight of implications yet unexplored. His hesitation, a gaping chasm into which my last vestiges of hope plummet. The silence stretches, taut and expectant, until his denial, fervent and imploring, shatters it.

"No. I love you, Satara."

But love, that fickle, traitorous beast, proves inadequate to the wound festering between us. His proclamation, meant to sooth, only fans the flames of my indignation. The taste of betrayal is bitter; a noxious brew of hurt and disbelief that coats my tongue and thickens my blood with anger. I raise the blade, a glinting symbol of my resolve. Anger propels my arm, a righteous fury that seeks an eye for an eye. He stops me. Our movements become frantic. There is an urgency in every gasp, in the widening orbit of our struggle. Dean's grip on my wrists, his sudden surge of strength, is a revelation that jolts through the turmoil.

Our bodies collide with the ground, and our mutual scream is a symphony of frustration. He pins me down, momentarily victorious, but the pain I inflict upon him, a knee to the groin, is a reminder of the resilience of my resolve. As he is doubled over in pain I grab the blade. His attempt to thwart me, a pull at my leg, is a last desperate bid for control.

But the knife finds its mark, a slash across his leg. I must have cut an artery, blood spurts from the wound. His scream is a raw, ragged thing that fills the space between us with something primal. "You always were the weak one in the relationship," I say standing over him, the words tumbling out, dark and heavy. His gaze is suddenly fixed on our bedroom window, which is slightly cracked open.

"Help! Somebody help!" he yells.

My heart hammers against my ribcage. With swift, deliberate movements, I run towards the window and shut it. As I do, I'm aware of Dean's movements, a slow crawling progression towards the stairs. I reach him quickly, placing my foot on his back. I raise the blade, and bring it down on Dean's back. The first impact is rough, the resistance of flesh and bone momentarily shocking. I do it again, and again, each thrust a desperate plea for finality. He keeps moving, keeps trying to get away, but my determination is a tidal wave cresting. I stab until he stops, until there's no movement, just the unsettling quiet of a body relinquishing its grip on life. I turn him over, needing to see his eyes, to witness the final spark leave them. His blue-green gaze goes dark, vacant; the light snuffed out like a candle. Blood spills from his mouth. The blood is technicolor, a rainbow spilling out his chest. I stare at it like a painting. It is beautiful.

My beloved Dean is gone, and with him, any semblance of the life we once knew. I hadn't expected it to be this hard. Dean had never been strong. But he fought me off well, desperation lending strength to his otherwise weak frame. Still, I had the upper hand, driven by a fury that burned hotter and fiercer with each passing second. As I stand over him, the adrenaline begins to ebb, replaced by a tidal wave of conflicting emotions. I look at the blood-stained knife, then at Dean's lifeless form, the room spinning.

The weight of what I've done presses down on me, a physical force that threatens to break me apart. His features are slack now, peaceful in a grotesque mockery of sleep. I can't help but trace the contours of his face with my eyes, remembering the moments of tenderness, the times when his smile was genuine and his touch warm. The sense of finality is suffocating. There's no undoing this, no going back. The man I loved, the man who betrayed me, lies still and cold; a chapter closed with brutal finality. The echoes of our last conversation ring in my ears, his last words now etched into the fabric of my mind. The rage, the betrayal, the twisted love—it all led to this moment, this stark, unyielding end.

SUGAR

* * *

After burying my beloved Dean underneath the lemon tree in our backyard, I did the only reasonable thing left: I bake a cake.

But first, the house, tinged with the metallic scent of blood, needed scrubbing. So, I clean; each wipe and wash a step toward absolution, a motion to distance myself from the finality now resting beneath the soil. A long, scalding shower follows, the water scorching away layers of dirt and blood from my skin, cleansing me so thoroughly I wonder if it could reach deeper, into my marrow, into the parts of me that had become irrevocably tainted.

Sleep didn't come, so I fell into the rhythm of baking, an act of creation to offset the destruction I'd wrought. I chose a vanilla cake with pink strawberry frosting. The ritual of sifting flour, cracking eggs, and measuring sugar is hypnotic, a trance that blocks out the night and replaces it with sweet precision. I take deliberate care, spreading the frosting in sumptuous waves and placing fresh strawberries in perfect symmetry.

The women in the neighborhood love my baking, often dropping by to taste whatever I happen to make that day, or commissioning desserts for their special occasions. The kitchen is usually my sanctuary, where the oven's hum and the scent of vanilla and sugar create a haven untouched by the outside world's chaos. Today, however, my sanctuary is a stage for my twisted sense of triumph. By the time the cake is complete, it is a beautiful, therapeutic masterpiece. Each meticulous step has guided me through the haze of shock, and as the clock hits seven a.m., its beauty is punctuated by a cold reality. Life didn't pause for grief or guilt, and despite everything, it was still a normal day, with the demands of daily routines waiting impatiently.

Dean and I didn't have children, just two adorably rambunctious cats that we've owned since we got married, Whiskers and Avocado.

They are the persistent soundtrack to my mornings. Feeding them was autopilot work. Their eyes, large and conspiratorial, often led me down hallways of what-ifs. If we had kids, would I have played the role of the dutiful, long-suffering wife, or would I have snapped like I did last night? Maybe I would have put a pillow over his face in the dead of night and say he just died in his sleep so they wouldn't feel abandoned? Or perhaps I'd just paint Dean as the deserter, the man who loved his career more than his family, setting them up with a lifetime of unresolved daddy issues.

I had floated the idea to him many times. I'd known the script by heart: suggesting children over countless dinners, in bed, during commutes. The answer was always a gentle yet firm *not yet*. Another year added to my internal clicking clock. "I'm almost halfway to forty, I will be old and withered by the time you finally say yes," I'd say, desperation a bitter edge in my voice. He, the well-respected doctor, deeply ensconced in his world of white coats and accolades, never seemed wounded by the idea of a childless legacy. I was supposed to be the love of his life; wasn't procreation a natural expectation, a testament to that love? But his passion lay in medicine, the kind of single-minded dedication that edged out any room for sticky fingers and bedtime stories. And with each growing year, the hurt calcified. The realization that his ambition eclipsed any desire for children painted him as a selfish prick, varnished with dedication.

The thought of lying to protect my hypothetical children from their father's illicit affair with the neighbor and the woman I called my friend would have been a hell I am glad to have not had to experience. Whiskers and Avocado were simpler. Their needs straightforward. They didn't give a damn about legacy or moral dilemmas. They didn't care that Dean was gone.

SUGAR

The mortgage company I work at is nestled in the heart of Orange County, a place where the sun kisses every surface with an almost mocking indifference. It's another day at Weinman and Weinman, another cycle of monotony that neither excites me nor breeds contempt. The half tab of acid I take every day helps.

I make my way inside. As a secretary, my days are a litany of phone calls, filing, and scheduling—the kind of tasks that are designed to obscure the hours but not enough to blur the edges of an unforgiving reality. The men I work with maintain an air of casual cruelty, their laughter hanging in the air like cigarette smoke, curling around my spirit, poisoning it slowly. On those days, the ones where their words are sharper than scalpels, slicing through the fragile armor I've built, it's harder to find comfort in my day-to-day tasks.

There's a rhythm to the office, a predictable cadence of paperwork and passive aggression. Each keystroke, each click of a stapler, is a small act of continuity in a life that feels perpetually fraught. The clock ticks with an almost oppressive precision, dragging me through to the end of the day. The men revel in their power games, their jokes about my body, my intelligence, or lack thereof—each comment a calculated strike. *"Hey, sweetheart, can you manage to bring me those files without tripping over your own feet?"* I've learned to armor myself in silence, letting their words batter against my defenses without breaking through entirely.

There's a lull in the late morning and I escape the office and take a smoke break. I sit on a bench at a park near the office, the comfort of my own thoughts disrupted by the sight of a couple on the bench across from me. I blow out a thick plume of smoke and watch them. They're sipping coffees with that casual, radiant charm you only see in movies, the kind that feels too polished, too perfect for ordinary lives.

Then my thoughts drift, unbidden, back to Dean—my beloved, my almost-forever. Six years we had, each one, a chapter of gradual erosion. We should've had more good years—more years before the familiar weight settled in, before he stopped looking at me as if I were his world. The aching need for another husband gnaws at the edges of my resolve. It's a practical need, almost clinical, a gaping hole I must fill to keep society's whispers at bay. I already have someone in mind—a potential suitor who doesn't yet know he's been chosen.

The couple at the park is obliviously radiant. I watch them, my heart clenched around the remnants of what could've been, my mind already strategizing the next step. Love, for all its beauty, is fragile. It can slip through your fingers or be buried under the lemon tree in your backyard.

An hour later as I'm sitting at my desk and Chris Stiles, the object of my affection, strides into the door. He's incredibly late, but for someone of his status, that doesn't matter. From the moment he first joined the team as a broker two years ago, I found myself captivated by his presence. Unlike the other assholes here he carries himself with a decency that sets him apart. Though he mostly ignores me, his indifference is a respite compared to the rudeness I often encounter, and that was enough for me.

He's clad in a royal blue suit and a red tie. His black wavy hair glistens, evident of a recent shower. But it's his distinct features that hold my attention captive. His giant nose is unapologetically prominent; sits proudly on his face. Above it, his bushy black eyebrows frame his eyes that are way too far apart. He's a contradiction, an enigma. His ethnicity is ambiguous in a way that makes him simultaneously everything and nothing. And yet, despite his unconventional aesthetics, or perhaps because of them, I find myself helplessly drawn to him. There's a magnetic quality in his ugliness—an allure that defies explanation. He possesses a raw, unfiltered sexiness that defies societal norms and expectations. I can't fully comprehend why I'm so infatuated with him. It's a maddening puzzle, an obsession that consumes my thoughts. He holds a power over me, captivating my mind and arousing my deepest fantasies. He's completely ordinary and yet I still think about him every night as I touched myself, his face flashing behind my eyes, his body clad in whatever suit he wore that day. I couldn't picture him naked for the life of me. He's always in a suit in my fantasies. And I was okay with that.

My dearly departed Dean and I were rarely having sex anymore, the once electric connection between us was reduced to a flicker. It left me marooned on an island of unsatisfaction, where desire gnawed at me like a persistent itch that could never quite be scratched. Nights spent in separate corners of the bed felt like eons, the chasm between us widening every night. Of course, now I know Dean was getting his fill elsewhere. The knowledge settled into my bones with a cold, dispassionate relief.

There I was, feeling abandoned and guilty for the afternoons spent lost in fantasies about my coworker, admiring his easy laughter and the way his shirt hugged his chest. My guilt dissipated. The fantasies about my coworker had been a desperate clawing for connection, a way to remind myself I was still alive, still capable of wanting and being wanted. And now, with Dean's betrayal exposed, those daydreams felt less like infidelity and more like reclamation. There's something almost poetic about it—a bitterness that loops back into itself until it becomes sweet. As I watch Chris from across the room, I allow myself a small, victorious smile. Of course, I know he's married. The ring on his finger is a glaring reminder, and to make matters worse, his wife, Elizabeth—or "Lizzie" as she insists everyone call her—is a member of the book club I reluctantly attend.

Lizzie.

The nickname grates on my nerves, not just because she's married to Chris and they share a child, but on pure principle. A 30-something-year-old woman masquerading under a relic of youthful nicknaming feels ridiculous. It would irk me even if she weren't married to Chris.

The book club started a year ago, initiated by Cynthia Bailey, one of the agents who used to work at Weinman & Weinman. She left six months ago, due to the relentless sexual harassment she received by the men at the office that upper management left unchecked. I remember the whispery, guarded conversation between Chris and Cynthia in the lobby. "My wife is a stay-at-home mother and she's feeling trapped. Getting out of the house and going to a book club once a week could be good for her."

It ignited a spark within me, a sudden surge of interest in joining the club, a pressing need to infiltrate Lizzie's space. I yearned to dissect her, to understand the woman who held the enviable privilege of seeing Chris naked, to memorize the curves and quirks of her that Chris must treasure in their intimate hours. Imagining her moans as he entered her late at night, his mouth silencing her as their child lay blissfully unaware nearby, sent shocks through my bloodstream. Their soft, hushed cries melding into a symphony, the potent scent of sex hanging thick in the air—these visions consumed me.

Entertainment of these thoughts brought waves of jealousy crashing down, a tsunami of rage that rose from the pit of my stomach and clawed its way up my throat. The violence I turned on myself in those moments was both punishment and catharsis. My fingers would weave through my hair and tug relentlessly, my palms slapping my face, my mouth spewing the vilest insults at the reflection staring back at me in the mirror. It was a gut-wrenching acknowledgment that it would never be me. I would never experience the raw, primal pleasure of his touch.

So, every week in that book club, sitting across from Lizzie, listening to her opinions on the latest novel, I become a quiet observer, soaking in her every word, every gesture. She became the subject of my study, my intricate dissection of everything she is and everything she has that I do not.

This is my penitence, my relentless reminder that the universe has ordained me as an outsider to the intimacy I crave. The thought festers, tangible and sour, a reluctant companion to my unfulfilled dreams.

* * *

The weight of the day has soaked into my bones. My mind is set on the pre-made lasagna in my fridge, the one I had planned to cook for Dean and me tonight. Thoughts of it have occupied my mind since noon. Instead of eating lunch I stayed in the office, finding weak excuses to haunt the break room where Chris was consuming a burrito that looked like it could feed a small village.

Each time I entered, he seemed embarrassed, hastily covering his mouth and wiping stray bits of sour cream and tortilla from his lips. I fixate on this small, human action as if it were a Morse code of his feelings. Was this a sign that he liked me? Why would he care if I saw him messily devouring a burrito?

The first time I swept in, I pretended to need something from the fridge, bending down far more provocatively than necessary, ensuring my ass was at eye level. "Someone took my drink," I lied, willing some kind of reaction from him.

He stayed silent for what seemed like an eternity, chewing slowly, his eyes not meeting mine. Finally, he swallowed and muttered a disinterested, "Wasn't me."

Frustration gnawed at me as I stormed out of the break room, my face hot with a mixture of anger and humiliation. I returned a second time, busying myself with brewing a fresh pot of coffee. "Never too late for coffee." He remained silent. I left again, pride bleeding out of me with each step.

Two whole minutes later, I was back, clutching the cup of coffee like a lifeline. "Forgot sugar, silly me," I said, forcing a lightness into my voice that cracked around the edges. This time, Chris seemed visibly irritated, stuffing the rest of his burrito into his mouth with grim determination. He rose abruptly, his chair scraping loudly against the linoleum floor. A knot formed in my throat as he left the room, tears threatening to spill.

Two years of being coworkers, and yet he showed no interest in cracking the surface to get to know me. There's a perverse desire that grips me, a longing so visceral it feels like a wild animal trapped within my chest. I wanted to unhinge my jaw like a snake and swallow him whole.

As the day closes to an end, I round the corner and make my way to my car, and I notice the same couple from earlier. The Bench Couple. They walk lazily, gazing into each other's eyes, the man's arm wrapped across the woman's back, guiding her towards a high-rise apartment building. Something possesses me and I find myself following them. I keep my distance, but close enough that when the man takes out his key to unlock the front door, I slip in before it softly closes, narrowly making it inside.

I feel a sense of audaciousness as I slink along, shadowing their every move. The woman's cheeks are rosy, her eyes bright, while the man remains grinning from ear to ear. Never have I seen a couple so infatuated with each other, completely lost in their own world, oblivious to the fact that a random woman was following them. They step into the elevator, and I cautiously join them. The woman finally notices me as she leans into her boyfriend's embrace. She's young and stunningly beautiful, perhaps in her mid-20s, but there's a maturity in her demeanor. She has a short brown bob, thick almost black eyebrows and stunning green eyes, her lips are pink and plump, a sign of youth. She was the kind of beautiful that women found enviable— high fashion, editorial. Slightly androgynous.

The man is older, probably around my age. He's handsome; debonair and tall, with perfectly coiffed black hair and a movie-star smirk. Of course, he's dressed in a very expensive-looking charcoal grey suit. He switches his black leather briefcase back and forth to whatever hand that isn't busy groping his girlfriend. I retreat to a corner of the elevator, attempting to appear nonchalant as if I belonged in this building that is not mine. The ride remains silent, with only a few pecks exchanged between the couple. The elevator reaches the 17th floor, and they step out. I follow suit, pretending to rummage through my coat pockets as if searching for my keys. The man swiftly unlocks the door, guiding the woman inside as she giggles playfully. The door slams shut behind them, leaving me standing outside with a sense of curiosity. I cautiously approach the door they entered, and I linger there for a moment, hoping to catch a snippet of their conversation or any sound that might offer a glimpse into their world. But I can't hear anything, so I turn away and make a quick exit.

Back home, I am enveloped by the comforting warmth of my home and the eager welcome of my cats. They twine around my legs, purring and nuzzling. I set about preparing their dinner, noting the persistent blinking of the voicemail light on my phone. With a sigh, I hit play and scoop food into their bowls.

"Satara, it's me. Answer your phone. You should be home from work by now. Just wanted to check in with you. How are you doing? Call me... bye."

I let out a deep, wearied sigh, tearing the plastic off the top of the lasagna with quick, frustrated movements before throwing it in the oven. Then, I grab my phone and dial Lilah's number, each ring elongating the anticipation like a taut string ready to snap. "Hello," she answers.

"Hello."

"How are you Satara?"

"I'm okay. Just got home from work."

"I just wanted to check on you after last night. You seemed upset as we were leaving."

"I'm fine, Lilah. Really."

"Are you and Dean okay?" She asks, her voice dripping with performative concern. Bitch.

I close my eyes, grinding my teeth. "Me and Dean are great. He's flying to the Hamptons tomorrow morning to see his mother." The silence stretches, heavy and loaded.

"Oh."

Genuine surprise colors her voice. She was expecting him to tell her. The image of them together sets a fire raging under my skin, the anger roiling to the surface like boiling water.

"Yes, so I'll be alone for a bit. You should drop by tomorrow evening."

"I'll bring the wine."

"Marvelous," I respond, flatly.

After five more minutes of insipid small talk, we hang up, and I head for the shower, timing it perfectly so that the lasagna is ready just as I step out. I pull it from the oven and eat it straight from the pan, hunched over the kitchen counter, fork scraping against metal. I keep eating until I feel sick, the self-loathing mixing with the food in a nauseating cocktail. I shove the leftovers into the fridge for tomorrow's lunch. I would've never done that if Dean were alive. He always demanded perfection—a size two, the pinch of his fingers on my sides whenever I dared to indulge, whispering in my ear, *Whoa there, tiger. Let's not go up a dress size.*

Asshole.

Even though it's only a little past six pm, I climb into bed, the ache of the day pulling me under. I touch myself, fingers conjuring the image of Chris in his royal blue suit. Eventually, I fall into a fitful sleep, dreams tangled with fragments of Chris, Dean, and the unraveling threads of my own sanity.

* * *

The next morning before work, I find myself seated across from Dr. Maggie, a regal-looking woman with silver hair that spills over her and mesmerizing blue eyes that seem to peer directly into my mind. Over the years, I've seen my fair share of therapists, but with Dr. Maggie, I've finally found the right fit. I've been seeing her for almost eight months now. She exudes intelligence without a hint of condescension, and when I share my strange thoughts and peculiar quirks, I can sense that they don't faze her. Her face remains impassive and composed, her legs crossed, and her chin resting in her hand, supported by her bony elbow on the arm of her chair. She rarely takes notes during our sessions; she just simply listens. I'm sure she must think I'm crazy, but what matters most to me is that she doesn't show it.

I still vividly remember the look on my previous therapist's face—a man whose name I couldn't be bothered to recall—when I told him how I constantly masturbated to the thought of my married coworker and how I drove to his house one night and spent over an hour hiding in his bushes. I saw the horror etched on his face. I decided to never see him again after that. The shame was too overwhelming. Dr. Maggie, though, she's different. In her presence, there's no crippling shame, no sense that I'm a monster in human skin. I can share my darkest thoughts and deepest desires without fearing judgment. And for someone like me, that means everything.

"How are you doing?" Dr. Maggie asks, her maroon turtleneck and matching lipstick perfectly suited for the impending autumn season. A delicate gold necklace adorned with a wedding ring hangs around her neck. She lost her husband to cancer years ago.

"I'm okay," I say. "But I'm still following people."

"Tell me more about that."

"I saw this couple yesterday sitting on a bench. I call them 'The Bench Couple,'" My gaze shifts down to the floor. "They looked so happy. I followed them into an apartment building, all the way to the front door. They didn't even notice."

Maggie uncrosses her legs slowly, leaning forward just enough to signal seriousness. "We've discussed this behavior before, Satara. You know it isn't healthy."

I bite my lip until I taste metal. "I know. But it feels like it fills something."

"You cannot follow people. It's dangerous and intrusive," her gaze is steady and unblinking. "I understand that you long for a loving and happy relationship, but following strangers is not the solution. You are only torturing yourself."

"Maybe I want to be tortured."

She tilts her head slightly, her blue eyes searching for something. "How is Dean, by the way?"

"He's fine."

That's the thing with Dr. Maggie. She gets too close to the truth. She's fishing for more, for the details that paint me as unhinged yet redeemable. She can probably sense what I don't tell—my lack of empathy, my lack of regret for things that a person would normally regret. Inside, I am the master of detachment, happy and feeling nothing, a serene tempest of apathy and desire. And somehow, in this chaotic symmetry, I find a twisted kind of happiness in my emptiness, a place where feeling nothing feels like everything.

An hour later, I'm at work. Chris arrives late again, visibly stressed. He's wearing a white button-up shirt, a yellow tie the color of piss, and grey slacks that cling to his frame in all the wrong ways. I preferred his attire yesterday; the royal blue suit that made him look like he had walked out of a daydream. There was an edge to him today, a tension I hadn't seen before. Was it work-related stress or something simmering beneath the surface at home? A dark, selfish part of me hopes that it's the latter. Chris's eyes scan the room briefly, barely acknowledging my presence before he disappears into his office. The idea of his perfect life fraying at the seams gives me a twisted sense of hope, a cruel undercurrent of desire that makes me feel alive in the most contradictory way. I make a mental note: find a moment to check on Chris.

The moment comes during lunch hour, the office hushed and emptied out, a ghost town of abandoned desks and half-drunk coffee cups. I walk by Chris's open office, my hand resting casually on my hip as I lean against the doorframe. I'm glad I wore my pink dress today—the one that hugs all the curves in just the right places and the highest heels that make my legs look a mile long. My long dark hair cascades in meticulously styled curls that took way too much effort but were worth it. I feel good, truly good, for the first time in years. "Hi."

Chris looks up from a splay of papers on his desk, his brow furrowed in concentration. "Satara. Can I help you?" he asks flatly, barely glancing in my direction. I take that as an invitation to walk deeper into his office, so I do.

"I was just seeing how you were doing. You seemed a little stressed coming into work today."

He blinks, confusion momentarily softening the rigid lines of his face. "Why are you asking me how I'm doing? This is work, Satara. I'm not going to talk to you about my feelings," he laughs, a hollow sound. "I'm fine."

My heart sinks. He barely even looks at me. It's not as if I'm ugly. My smooth tan skin, a gift from my Native American mother and Black father who died before I even met him, glows under the fluorescent lights. I've got a nice figure, though sometimes I feel a bit too round. But I'm certainly not overweight, I'm somewhere between size two and four—depending on how many sweets I indulged in the week before—and I'm extremely well-endowed in the chest area. Yet,

Chris never looks at me like I'm a woman. He looks at me like I'm some wretched, ugly creature. I don't get it.

"Oh," I say, trying to maintain my composure. "I was just trying to be nice." My eyes flit to his desk and land on a framed photo of him, Lizzie, and their daughter. They're all dressed in white, standing in a field somewhere, beaming happiness. Chris looks handsome in his white T-shirt that fits snug around his arms. Lizzie looks... okay. My throat tightens.

"Thanks for checking in. I'm fine. Have a good lunch, Satara." He turns back to his papers. Anger bubbles up from somewhere deep, an undercurrent of volcanic heat. How dare he brush me off like I'm insignificant? I turn around, my movements stiff with barely contained fury. As I walk out, I feel the sting of rejection like a brand, marking me in ways that lipstick and high heels can't conceal.

The walk back to my desk feels like a march of shame. I straighten my back, forcing myself to hold onto the remnants of my dignity. The pink dress clings to me like a second skin, now a mocking reminder of my failed attempt to be noticed, to be desired. A few minutes later, I watch as Chris leaves the office presumably for lunch, not bothering to look in my direction.

I walk back into his office and shut the door behind me. The space smells like him—a mix of expensive cologne and the faintest hint of minty aftershave. I sit in his leather seat, and without thinking much more about it, I lift my dress, and I start to touch myself. I close my eyes and breathe in deeply. I see the framed family photo sitting innocently on his desk, mocking me. Lizzie, her smile a sanitized version of joy, their daughter caught in mid-giggle, Chris looking every bit the proud husband and father. It ruined my mood.

I snatch the photo off his desk, the frame feeling cold and solid in my hands. I step back out into the hallway, the weight of the stolen photo a strange comfort against my side. Sitting back down at the front desk, I glance around, half expecting someone to call me out, to expose my petty act of rebellion. I wonder, fleetingly, what I'll do with the photo. Maybe I'll keep it hidden, a souvenir of my audacity. Maybe I'll rip it apart in a fit of cathartic rage, tearing their perfect smiles to shreds. Or maybe I'll return it one day; slip it back onto his desk without a word, leaving Chris to puzzle over its brief disappearance.

For now, though, it feels like a victory, however minor, however fleeting. A sliver of control in a world where I often feel powerless. The office hums on, oblivious, and I sit at my desk with a quiet smile, the stolen photo a secret promise that I haven't been entirely diminished.

SUGAR

Lilah Patrick shows up at six pm sharp, ever punctual, with a bottle of expensive wine cradled in her delicate hands. She looks beautiful, as usual, with her red hair cascading in wild, frizzy waves and her pale, perfect skin that always makes me burn with envy. Lilah has that kind of glassy complexion that seems lit from within, almost too perfect to be real. Her deep-set green eyes flicker with a hint of mischief, framed by lashes that seem to flutter even when she's perfectly still. Her body, thin to the point of frailness, moves with an easy grace.

I often wonder how Dean was drawn to her, with her ethereal fragility and meticulous self-care rituals that border on obsessive. I thought of myself as more attractive, more vibrant—a splash of color with my tan skin and raven hair against her muted tones. I don't count her red hair; everyone knew it wasn't her natural color.

"Hi beauty," she says, her voice smooth and dulcet, almost as if carved from silk. We kiss each other on each cheek. The light illuminates her face, highlighting every flawless angle. It's infuriating how she manages to look so effortlessly poised. She glances around, her gaze lingering on the freshly baked cookies cooling on the counter. "You've been busy."

"Just trying a new recipe." I say it breezily, but there's an edge to my tone that I can't quite mask. I watch her appraise the cookies with her usual scrutiny, her expression revealing nothing.

Lilah was never one for indulgence. Whenever I would call her, she'd be in the middle of some intense workout—jazzercise or calisthenics, always something to keep her body lean and taut. She thrived on the burn, the discipline, the control. Lilah reluctantly takes a cookie—she never wanted to seem rude. "*Mmm.* These are really good," she says, taking the tiniest bird bite before setting it back down. "Would you like some wine?" she asks, holding up the bottle. I nod, grabbing two glasses from the cupboard. I watch as she pours us each a glass, her movements precise, almost mechanical.

We sit, the cookies between us like an offering, the wine glinting ruby-red in our glasses. The conversation drifts, her voice punctuating the silences. But my mind wanders, tracing the paths of our differences—her pristine, almost saint-like devotion to perfection is a hard contrast to my fervent and chaotic personality. It's always been a tenuous balance, our friendship; a dance between admiration and envy, between acceptance and resentment. It doesn't take long for her to bring him up, her lips already stained a deep red from the wine, curling into a knowing smile.

"So, how long is Dean gone in the Hamptons?" Her voice is dripping with a casual sort of curiosity that feels anything but.

I take a measured sip of my own wine, letting the bitter warmth of it settle on my tongue as I shrug. "He didn't tell me. Just said he needed to go away for a bit."

Her expression falters for a moment, and I catch a flicker of hurt in her eyes. Inside, I beam with a petty sense of satisfaction. "*Go away for a bit?* What does that even mean? Aren't you the least bit worried he'll be getting into trouble there?" she presses, leaning in slightly.

I shift in my seat, the words tumbling out louder than intended. "What, like have an affair?" I let out a short laugh. "He wouldn't do anything like that. It's *Dean* for goodness' sake."

She forces a smile, her teeth stark against the red stain of the wine on her lips. "Right," her voice adopted that high, sing-song tone she uses when she's trying to mask something. "Well, you never know."

I stare at her, this woman who has somehow wormed her way into my life. My best friend, the woman who welcomed us to the neighborhood six years ago with a plate of homemade brownies (they were disgusting) and that same beauty queen smile. She had come over that afternoon when we moved in; we hadn't even started unpacking yet. She radiated warmth as she introduced herself and mentioned she was a schoolteacher, and she lived just around the corner with her son. Her pretentious air had immediately set me on edge, and I'd given her a hard time, firing back with, "No husband?"

Her smile had faltered then, the look of prissiness draining from her face. "I'm a widow," she said, her voice clipped.

"Oh dear, I'm sorry."

Now, as I look at her across the table, I can't help but feel a twisted kinship. I'm going through my own loss. Even though Dean was a bastard, part of me still loved him. I oftentimes think about digging him up just to see him again.

I sip my wine, the room feels smaller, the tension palpable. Lilah watches me with those deep-set green eyes, waiting for something, perhaps a confession or an outburst. But all she gets is silence, unspoken words coiling between us, as toxic and intoxicating as the wine in our glasses.

"Well, you're a better woman than me," she says with a snort. "I'd be asking him to call every day and every night."

I smile, a tight-lipped, knowing kind of smile. I can practically taste her worry hanging in the air. She's worried that Dean is out there, gallivanting around with other women, betraying the fragile trust she and him built. I chew on the irony, savor its dark flavor. I almost laugh out loud at the thought but catch myself, placing my glass down carefully on the table as though the crystal could shatter under the weight of my secret.

"Well, I've got a lot of faith in Dean," my voice is steady but light. "He's got his flaws, but infidelity isn't one of them."

She nods, her fingers drumming on the table. "Right, of course. I just worry, you know? You never know what men get up to when they're away."

If only she knew that the biggest worry wasn't where Dean might go or what he might do, but where he is right now; buried in our backyard, slowly decaying to just bone. I think about telling her, just to see the shock ripple through her perfect façade; to watch that mask of concern transform into sheer horror. But I hold back, the thrill of the secret too delicious to spill. Maybe one day I'll tell her. But I'd have to kill her too if I did, and I don't like to kill women. Instead, I take another sip of my wine, the rich liquid a comforting burn down my throat.

"Men and their mysteries," I say, a wistful smile playing on my lips. "Sometimes you just have to trust, even when it's the hardest thing to do."

She looks at me like I've just uttered some profound truth, her eyes wide and almost reverent. And for a moment, I feel a strange sort of power rush through me, the intoxicating realization that I hold all the cards, that she sees me as this beacon of strength and composure when in reality, I'm standing on the edge of a precipice.

"Yes," she murmurs, more to herself than to me. "Perhaps you're right." She goes back to sipping her wine, her eyes losing focus as she drifts into her own thoughts. And I remain quiet, the ghost of a smile lingering on my face.

1958

The first day I laid eyes on Michael I knew he was mine. His dark eyes seemed to peck at my soul like a crow on a carcass. He had a rugged charm, an air of mystery that drew me in despite his rough exterior. He was an older man, seven years my senior at twenty-two. I, on the other hand, was just a precocious fifteen-year-old girl, craving attention from boys like a plant thirsting for water. And when Michael's gaze landed on me, I felt a surge of thrill run through my veins. Standing on the sidewalk gripping my history book to my chest, waiting for my mother to pick me up from school, I felt like a moth drawn to a flame.

I saw him pull in. We locked eyes for a second and I could tell he wanted to say something. As he leaned against his pickup truck, his dark hair tousled in the wind, I couldn't help but feel a spark of curiosity ignite within me. Michael's gaze felt like a weight, tracing my figure as if he could read the secrets etched into my skin. His dark eyes lingered on my knees, always marred with bruises from countless childhood escapades, and then trailed up to my curvy hips hugged by the brown corduroy shorts I chose to wear that day. I could feel his scrutiny like a physical touch, sending a shiver down my spine as his attention wrapped around me like a snake, both terrifying and intoxicating.

A cacophony disrupted the charged atmosphere as Michael's brother, Leo, stormed onto the scene, his presence seemed to reverberate in the air like a symphony of chaos. Michael's voice cut through the noise, offering me a ride. Leo shot his brother a look. "Really Michael? There's no room for her."

Leo's protestation fell on deaf ears as Michael dismissed him with a casual wave of his hand, his smile crooked and stained with the remnants of cigarette smoke. There was a dangerous edge to him, a roughness that danced with a hint of something deeper, something elusive and captivating. As I squeezed into the cramped space between the two brothers, the truck roared to life, carrying me into a world that felt both thrilling and treacherous. Michael turned to me, his dark eyes searching mine. "You're something special," he whispered, and I felt a shiver run down my spine. In that moment I knew that this was just the beginning of a romance unlike anything I had ever experienced. On the journey home, a tentative ease settled between us as Michael probed me with questions. As I stole glances at him, I couldn't help but admire the rugged stubble that adorned his jawline. I imagined the sensation of his rough hands, calloused and weathered from the toil of hard labor, tracing a path of electrifying heat along my thigh. With bated breath, I willed Michael's hand to stray from the safety of the steering wheel and onto my thigh.

From then on, Michael picked me up and dropped me off at school every day, and Leo abruptly disappeared opting to get rides from his friends. Left alone together, I found myself crushed into the narrow world of Michael. Flirts masqueraded as innocent rides to school with stolen glances and pauses filled with meanings more profound than the silence they inhabited.

After a couple weeks of getting rides to and from school, Michael finally pivoted the dance of our silent exchanges into something tangible. In the hurried morning rush, he leaned into me. At least, I thought he had. His face nearing mine, I got swept up in the moment and leaned in too, only to crash into the cruel wall of rejection. Michael pulled back, staring at me as if I had two heads. My heart dropped. Panicked, I gathered my bag, clumsily excusing myself with a shaky, "I have to go," and then ran away from my embarrassment towards the school entrance.

The school day gnawed at me like a relentless beast. Whenever I could, I hid in the girls' bathroom, letting the cold tile walls absorb my tears, convinced that it was my own foolish imagination. When the final school bell rang, I found no anticipation in my step. My heart pulsed with the dread of not seeing his truck. But when I crossed the school's threshold, he was there. Against all odds, seated in that pickup truck, he was there.

Opening the creaking door, I saw his face painted with lines of torment. We were statues in a cluttered parking lot—sitting in silence. I found myself reaching towards him, my hand tentatively hovering above his leg, my eyes on him, waiting for permission to touch. "You're really young, Satara," His voice was teetering on the edge of a precipice. "I don't know if you're ready for this."

"I am," I said. He took sight of me, his gaze meticulously devouring my body, mapping the landscape of my face, neck, chest; my entirety. And then it happened—the flip of a switch, a soul-revealing moment. The revelation flashed in his eyes, his surrender to the profound connection that had pooled between us. In the very next moment, Michael steered his truck inelegantly into the barren parking lot of an abandoned building.

After fashioning a palate we could comfortably lie on he pulled me to the bed of the truck, impatient fingers grabbing at the fabric that separated our bodies. I let it happen, even though I thought we would just cuddle, talk, kiss for a bit. There was a torturous pleasure in the way his mouth found mine. The electricity of his touch ignited an overwhelming sensation within me, the raw contact amplifying the sensations coursing through my veins. Yet, it was all too much. His hungry hands wandering my body without restraint. It was fierce and urgent.

The whirling contradiction of desire and confusion plagued me, and I could do nothing but surrender to the inevitability of it all. He pushed into me quickly, with not an ounce of gentleness. I yelped in pain, but he didn't stop. My hands instinctively went against his chest trying to push him off, trying to stop the pain but at the same time, giving into Michael's primal desires. I gasped, the air heavy, the taste of rusty iron in my mouth. I was pinned under him, the barbs of intimacy puncturing the tenuous fabric of my innocence. My skin burned, blistered under his touch, punctuated with furious thrusts as if he was trying to pound our souls into one rough stone. His eyes were shut tight, as if willing himself into a world where feelings are kept at bay.

Bound by his tunnel vision, he became unaware, or perhaps, conveniently oblivious to the tears running down my cheeks. My silent pleas, my resistance was lost in his determined rhythm—a dance that he has choreographed with a startling disregard for the partner, disregarded in his fervent pursuit of pleasure. All the while I wish he would open his eyes, for once glance my way, notice the destruction he was causing. But he remained blind to my plea as he navigated the contours of my body, his sweat dripping off his brow and onto my face.

Look at me, I wanted to shout, but the words faltered in my throat, held hostage by the enormity of what was happening. And I was left wishing, waiting in the quiet storm, hoping to be seen. The intensity of it stretched on, an unending road, and all I yearned for is a glimpse of empathy in his closed eyes; the warmth of his gaze acknowledging the hot tears traveling down my flushed cheeks. But his finish was as impersonal as the sex, staining my body with his sweat and semen, leaving me visibly tarnished.

He must have known I was a virgin, because he handed me a towel muttering, "Here, sit on this so blood doesn't get on my seat."

I turned to him, holding more tears at bay as I apprehensively examined my potential ruin. "Thank you."

He swiftly pulled his jeans on, his urgency surprising on some level. pulling my own clothing over my tender skin, struggling to keep the howl of my thoughts from slipping out.

"I have stuff on my shirt," I stated, voicing my shame, hoping to perhaps shatter his indifference. It didn't.

He maneuvered out of the parking lot. Our ride drew on, under the shroud of oppressive silence, the air between us thick with my unshed tears and his unperturbed calm. He dropped me off, planting a kiss on my forehead. With a weak smile I whispered goodbye and headed towards my home, listening to his truck loudly peel out onto the road. Shower streams washed over me, the hot water felt good against my skin that felt like it was marred and bruised from the rough sex. There was evidence of my recent ordeal, the unwanted blood— yes, I *was* bleeding—my thoughts a whirlpool, trying to make sense of what happened earlier, the confusing mix of repulsion and yearning. Despite everything, a part of me still craved Michael, desperately hoping he wouldn't perceive me crying as being an over-emotional, immature little girl.

A few hours later Mother walked into my room. "There's a boy on the phone."

Her words yanked me from my sleep. "There is?"

"He doesn't sound fifteen."

Her doubtful note about his age didn't hinder me from bounding down the stairs and cheerfully snatching the phone off the counter, nerves bouncing like a live wire. "Hello?"

"I just wanted to check in on you, you looked pretty upset when I dropped you off."

"I wasn't upset I just…"

"Satara, you know I really like you, don't you?"

"I know."

"And I'm sorry about earlier. I know it was abrupt, but I just couldn't help myself. You had on that white shirt that clings to your breasts and…" his voice faltered.

"It's ok. I liked it."

"I'm glad," he said. I could hear his smile. "Would you do it again?"

With a knot my stomach, I blurted out the words he wanted to hear, "Yes, I would do anything with you."

There was a long silence. "Then it's best to keep this a secret, ok? I just don't want anyone to come between us. If your mother asks I'm just your classmate's brother who gives you rides to and from school."

"Ok."

"I have to go. I'll see you tomorrow."

I hung up and ignored my mother's penetrating gaze following me as I ascended back up to my room.

We spent three years off and on together. Michael would propel into my life when it suited him, showering me with affection, care and sweet nothings. Then, with the subtleness of a storm, he'd flip and become a spewing volcano of unexpected cruelty.

On my sixteenth, Michael decided to celebrate it with a homemade cake, balloons, and a surprise that one could only expect in romantic films—all left on my doorstep at midnight. Like the proverbial Wicked Witch, Mother found him creating this Cinderella moment and turned furious. Drawing from her very maternal reservoir of wrath, she demanded him to leave, and they argued for ten minutes straight before Michael finally let up and stalked back to his truck and peeled off. I watched it all go down through my bedroom window, screaming bloody murder. Mother let me keep the cake, never wanting to waste food, but she threw the presents away and popped the balloons with a kitchen knife.

Mother stood as a firewall between Michael and me, but I found my way to him every time. At seventeen, Mother finally conceded defeat in her battle to keep me away from him. Weekends became our slice of heaven— I'd spend them at his newly rented apartment, making meals together, indulging in bouts of films and board games, feeling the intermittent sparks of his insatiable lust. The teenager in me found affirmation in Michael's constant wanting, yet, even at that tender age, I had a growing sense of unease about his sexual appetite. His demands for sex were a dark cloud that loomed over our love. On nights I couldn't muster the will, Michael would pitch an indecent fit, hissing threats about older women who could serve his desires more willingly. He had custom-built a roadmap of triggers, and boy, did he know how to steer me down that road. His threats—the murmurs of finding an older, more experienced woman and the fear of him leaving me—each were well-aimed darts, each carrying the sting of guilt. I'd relent and give him sex because I wanted him to love me.

Just somewhere shy of my eighteenth birthday, a casual conversation with Michael leapt off a cliff and crash-landed into a minefield. He decided he wanted to pack his bags and move away to Chicago and expected me to come with him. Courage or stupidity, I put my foot down, saying I wanted to get my high school diploma before I could move away with him. He became furious, spinning wildly into a series of livid outbursts— yelling, hurling objects and insinuations that my love for him was not real. The tension in the apartment could've felled a wall, it was too much, too thick; it was an exit sign, screaming in red that I needed to pack up and leave.

I had to call Mother. As I expected, I was met with an I-told-you-so. Through salty streams coursing down my face, I managed to choke out an SOS. The sound of my voice being drowned out by his yelling punctuated by rhythmic thuds—my belongings being thrown together in an unceremonious heap by the door. Like a dependable failsafe, Mother came, silently setting about packing up my discarded life. Michael had locked himself in the bedroom, probably a schemed attempt to avoid confronting my volcanic mother. "You're done, Satara. You're not seeing him again, or so help me God," Her words sliced through me. Her rage-filled order to leave mingled with my chaotic symphony of desperate sobs. "Let's go," she escalated her tone, matching it with the direness of the situation.

I was frozen on the spot, my weeping eyes latched onto the bedroom door. The sounds coming from my mouth were barely discernible—a pitiful cry of *"Michael..."* A plea that I didn't even understand.

"Let's go Satara, *now!*" Mother's command pierced the cluttered puzzle in my head. I blinked through my tears, took shivering steps towards the door, walked past my mother and ran straight out to her car.

Days passed, and I hadn't heard a word from Michael. The depression was like milk left out in the sun, curdling and sour, reaching an acrid peak. Leo had dropped out of school the year before so I couldn't ask him about his brother. Even if I did ask him, I doubt he would tell me anything. His dislike towards me was about as subtle as a gunshot.

Coming home felt like entering a mausoleum. I'd make a beeline to my room, entombing myself in blankets. From the other side of the door, Mother's knocks would eat into the quiet. I'd take her offerings of food and comfort snacks. Her tolerance, robust as it was, began to wear at the seamed edges after three weeks, telling me to get up and stop crying over him. I retaliated, ferocious, screaming my refusal like a curse.

I will never get over him!

"You will, sweetie. It feels like an apocalypse now, but I promise you, the pain will pass."

A month later, late at night the phone incessantly rang, Mother had gone to bingo, so I answered. I heard his voice on the other end, and I felt the earth tilt beneath my feet.

"Hi sweetheart."

My heart ricocheted against my ribcage. My knees gave away, directing me gently to the cold kitchen tiles where I folded myself into a ball. "Hi Michael."

"I'm sorry. For everything."

Any words I had once known escaped me. Swallowed by the silence between us.

"I'm in Chicago now. After our fight, it just felt right to leave. Staying there after everything was hard."

The knot in my throat swelled like a storm-enforced wave, threatening to hurl me into an abyss. Clenching my jaw, I tried to keep the mounting tears under control. "Does being in Chicago mean we're not a couple anymore?"

The silence loomed large, cloaked in torment along the wire stretching between us.

"I want you to come visit me. It's nice here. I'm in Northern Chicago," his words ripped the control I had over my tears, my grip on the phone tightening. "You'd love it here. I'll give you my address so you can write to me before you come. I still love you, Satara."

A silent sob slipped past my lips, followed closely by damp relief. "I love you too."

Floating on cloud nine, my heart thrummed with the thought that our love story might continue. But I quickly realized that he had just told me another ornately decorated fabrication. His face—once as familiar as my own reflection—became an elusive ghost, one I never saw again until two years later.

SUGAR

1963

The wave of murderous intentions came late at night, swelling up inside me like a tide that couldn't be turned back. The thought of Michael being happy without me made my blood boil, each heartbeat echoing with the fierce sting of betrayal. He hadn't called. He hadn't written. He had well and truly moved on, and I couldn't let that happen.

Not now, not ever.

I was twenty years old, drifting through a haze of odd jobs at diners and clothing boutiques in Los Angeles, scraping together just enough to keep my head above water. But I had managed to save up some money, more out of habit than intention. The moment I saw how full my little piggybank had gotten, the moment the realization hit me, I knew exactly what I'd use the money for: a plane ticket to Chicago.

It was a random Monday in January, the kind of day that slipped through the cracks of memory, but not for me. This random Monday was special, and I'll remember it forever. Oblivious to how biting the cold would be in Chicago during that time of year, I boarded a plane with a heart full of rage and a mind locked on revenge, and no winter coat.

It was okay—I wouldn't be staying very long.

The flight felt like a suspended eternity, each minute dragging and amplifying my resolve. My thoughts swirled and churned, each one darker than the last. I ordered a cheap motel room near his neighborhood, a grimy little place, a fitting backdrop for what I intended to do. I brought a singular switchblade knife—simple, unassuming, but enough. I wasn't exactly sure how I'd go about it, but I was too blind with revenge to care about the details. The knife felt heavy in my hand as I walked the cold streets, my breath visible in front of me like wisps of smoke, fading into the air. I thought about Michael's laugh, how it used to fill the room, how it would never do that again.

The city was a blur of lights and shadows, of people moving through their own narratives, blissfully unaware of the fury I carried within me. I reached his house, the sight of it a cruel reminder of what I'd lost. I hovered near the door, the cool metal of the knife pressing into my palm, grounding me in my purpose. I took a deep breath, the night air sharp and unforgiving, and pressed on. I wasn't a murderer—I was just a woman wronged. The distinction blurred in my mind, the edges of morality softening under the weight of my obsession. In the end, the plan was simple. I would see him, confront him, and make him understand that happiness without me was a betrayal that I could not stand.

He had done well for himself, the house wasn't big, but it was a good size. It was big enough for a little family, something I had wanted with him. I should've been living in this house with him, filling it with laughter and our shared dreams, not someone else. My hands shook, my heart pounded with a rhythm of betrayal and anger that reverberated through my entire being. I found the doorbell, the cold metal doing little to dampen the heat swirling inside me. He answered almost immediately, the door flying open with a force that matched the storm brewing within me. There he was, my beautiful Michael. He looked even more like a man than he did two years ago, time sculpting him with merciless precision. The look on his face was pure shock and confusion.

"Satara…what the fuck are you doing at my house?" His voice was a mix of bewilderment and exasperation, a needle pricking an already overinflated balloon.

I stared at him, my tongue tied in knots, the words fighting to escape but caught in the web of my fury.

"Do I need to call the police?"

"Don't be ridiculous, Michael." My voice barely masked the venom behind it.

"What are you—"

"You abandoned me," I said flatly, the syllables falling heavy and unforgiving in the quiet night.

He stared at me, shook his head, a dismissive laugh escaping his lips, mocking and cruel. "Are you still not over that? Satara, I'm happy. I'm in love. I'm sorry but you need to move on. It's old news."

"You fucker," I said darkly, my voice trembled, the raw wound of his betrayal bleeding anew. "You preyed on me at fifteen years old. You were a full-grown adult *man*. You raped me, manipulated me, led me on. And you expect me to just *move on?*" Each word was a jagged piece of my shattered heart, flung at him with all the force I can muster.

I will never move on!

He stared at me, the color draining from his face, his voice a whisper. "I didn't rape you. You said you liked it."

At that moment, the fury consumed me, the beast inside breaking free. I pulled the blade from behind my back, watching his eyes widen in terror as he stumbled backwards. But I was faster, driven by an unholy mixture of rage and heartbreak. I pushed the knife right into the middle of his stomach, feeling the resistance give way under the pressure.

His gasp was a guttural, agonized sound, his hands instinctively clutching at the wound as he collapsed to his knees. Blood bloomed around the blade, the dark red staining his shirt, spreading like an accusation. His eyes locked onto mine, filled with pain and disbelief, as if he never truly thought I was capable of this. I stepped back, the knife slipping out of his wound and from my grasp, clattering to the floor. The silence that followed was heavy, oppressive, broken only by his ragged breaths and the distant, indifferent hum of the city. I watched him, my mind oddly clear, the storm inside finally quieting as he crumpled to the floor.

"Ironic, isn't it?" I whispered, leaning over him, my voice soft but deadly. "You manipulated me, broke me, and now look at you— broken, bleeding, finally feeling a fraction of the pain you left me with."

His eyes fluttered, struggling to stay open, his lips moving but no sound came. I straightened up, feeling a strange, cold satisfaction wash over me. The house, the life that should have been mine, all of it now tainted with his blood, with the truth of what he did to me.

I looked around the house, and it's dark, all the lights out. Michael must've been on his way out. And then I decided to do something risky. I walked around. The sunken living room was nice—wooden planked walls, a big soft green couch, a brick fireplace. I opened the cabinets in the kitchen—rows of neatly stacked dishes and glassware, a pantry stocked with organic snacks and seasonings, all labeled in perfect handwriting. It wasn't Michael's handwriting—I remembered his chicken scratch well; it was clearly a woman's. I bit down on my tongue until I tasted metal, staring at that handwriting for what seemed like eternity.

I moved upstairs through the dim hallway, my fingers brushing against the salmon-colored walls. I found a medium-sized room that was empty, holding just a few boxes, seemingly used as a storage room. I kept going, reaching the master bedroom. The decor was quite tasteful and understated, calm, serene colors. Browns and greens. I wondered if his new lover picked out all this decor. I tried to find a photo of her, or photos of them together, but I could find nothing.

I moved to the closet and saw clothes—lots of them. Almost too many. I grabbed the satin robe hanging on the outside of the door and undressed, slipping it on and tousling my hair. I looked in the mirror, modeling it. This could've been me. This could've been my life. This beautiful, safe, suburban life. I looked at myself in that pink robe, standing in the middle of someone else's dream, feeling the weight of what could have been versus what was. For a moment, I tried to hold onto that illusion, the idea that I could just slip into this life as easily as I slipped into this robe. But then reality came rushing back, and I knew I should leave before she returned. I took one last look around, imprinting the calm of the space into my memory.

I headed back down the stairs, each step a soft, hesitant echo in the silence. Halfway down, I froze. I saw him lying there, right by the doorway. Reality crashed over me then. I did it.

I killed Michael.

My heart pounded in my ears as I descended all the way down the steps, each one heavier than the last. I stood over Michael, feeling detached, as if I was watching myself from somewhere far away. His face was slack, his features softened as if he were just sleeping. But the blood, a vivid red spreading everywhere, told me otherwise. He was not just sleeping. I kneeled, hearing the world dissolve into the background, and picked up my knife. I took one last long look at Michael, trying to memorize the peace that death had brought to his face, even if it was fleeting and unwanted. Then I turned and headed out of the house, my footsteps careful and deliberate. I slinked away into the night.

I headed back to the motel, the walk feeling like a marathon in slow motion. I took a shower, letting the water wash away the remnants of Michael, the evidence of my act. I slept, and it was the most peaceful sleep I ever had, dreamless and deep, like a soul finally unburdened. The next day, I walked thirty minutes to a diner. It was a dingy spot teeming with truckers and the scent of greasy food. I ignored their looks, the perverted thoughts practically written on their foreheads. If only they knew I killed a man less than twenty-four hours ago, and that the knife I used was still hidden on me. I sat at a booth in the back, the vinyl seat screeching loudly as I got comfortable. A waitress with the thickest Chicago accent I ever heard sauntered over.

"What'll it be sweetheart?" she asked, her voice a gruff melody of disinterest.

"Coffee with two sugars and a croissant," I said, my voice steady, betraying nothing. She eyed me strangely for a moment but shrugged and walked away, returning suspiciously quick with a steaming coffee and a croissant, golden and crisp. I picked it up and took a bite.

That is when I noticed a man staring at me. Almost all the men there were staring at me, but his stare was different. He seemed…amused. I surveyed his face—sharp features that seemed almost out of place among the tired, weathered faces of the old men in the diner. He was younger, with sandy blonde hair slicked back, each strand catching the light. The white material of his work attire stood out, pristine and smooth. He wore a white short-sleeved, button-up shirt, a small pocket on the left breast with a nametag patched on: *Tom*. When he saw me staring at him, he walked over, each step deliberate and confident. There was an amusement etched into his features, like he caught the punchline of a joke no one else was in on. What could be so funny? He slid into my booth across from me with an easy, practiced smile. "Hello, little lady, you from around here?"

His voice caught me off guard—higher than I'd imagined, almost grating, like a radio tuned just slightly off. I stared at him. Should I tell the truth? Should I lie? I had killed someone last night; I shouldn't have been speaking to anyone. Or maybe I should have, to blend in, to act normal, so no one suspected a thing. I was not sure. This was all new to me.

But as I locked eyes with Tom, his brown eyes scanning mine with a hungry curiosity, I thought… maybe I could have a little fun.

"No," I replied, my voice steady.

His smile widened, the amusement deepening. It hit me then that this was his default mode, a mask of smug confidence permanently affixed to his face. He looked like a man who believed he was always one step ahead, like he was in on a secret that the rest of us didn't know. Did he know my secret?

"I already knew you weren't from here. Otherwise, you'd know it's dangerous for pretty ladies like you to come waltzing in here all casual-like," he said, leaning in.

I blinked, holding his gaze. "I'm fine."

"Are you sure? 'Cause you looked pretty upset coming in," he pressed.

"I'm not upset, just hungry."
I tore off a piece of my croissant and popped it into my mouth, chewing slowly to buy myself a moment to think.

"You need a ride somewhere? I can drop you off. I got my work truck today," he offered, and there was a flicker in his eyes—something between genuine concern and a glint of opportunistic curiosity. I considered the offer, the edges of the room blurring slightly as I weighed my options. As I looked back into his eyes, I recognized that look and I knew he wanted me.

"Sure," I brushed the crumbs from my fingers. "A ride would be great."

Pretty soon, I was climbing into the truck of a handsome stranger that I met at a truck stop Diner. It would've been terrifying for most women, but for me, it was nothing. I looked over at Tom the Delivery Man, smiling goofily.

Tom the Delivery Man wouldn't hurt me.

But if I was wrong, I had my knife tucked snugly in the inside pocket of my jacket. As we pulled out of the parking lot, he started with the basic script. "So, where ya from?"

I didn't respond.

"Okay, well how about your name?" he tried, still hopeful. I blinked and turned to face him. His persistence was almost endearing in its simplicity. "Oh, come on, woman, you gotta give me something!"

He was right, I suppose. I had to give him something.

"My name is Susan."

He narrowed his eyes. "You don't look like a Susan."

"What's that supposed to mean?"

"Well, you look too... exotic to be named Susan," I let his ignorance hang in the air, refusing to bite. The silence spoke more than any words could. He nodded and laughed. "I'll play along. Well, Susan, what are you in town for?"

I swallowed the knot in my throat, the urge to spill the truth almost maddening. But that would be stupid. "Visiting someone. A friend."

"Well, where the hell is your friend then? They abandon you?"

"No, I... she had no room at her house, so I got a motel room."

"Well, where's your motel? I'll drop you off."

"You already passed it."

He glanced at me, incredulous. "Well, why the hell didn't you say something, girl?"

I shrugged, my eyes fixed on his profile, studying the way his jaw moved when he spoke. I wondered if I'll have sex with him or kill him tonight. Maybe both. It depended on whether he was good or not. If he tried something without my permission, I had no issues killing him, no matter how handsome he was. "I guess I didn't want to go back there yet."

His gaze kept darting back to the road, then to me, then to the road again. He couldn't seem to settle. "Where do ya wanna go, little lady?"

"Your house?" I proposed, my voice soft but with an edge that cut through his bravado. He blinked, thrown off balance. "You're married, aren't you?" I pushed, feeling the power shift in the cramped space between us.

"No, no, I'm not. I'm only twenty-two. I don't wanna get married until I'm at least twenty-five. That's a good age to get married, right? Twenty-five. My parents want me to get married now, though. I said nope, I want to enjoy some time alone before I shack up with someone."

"So, let's go to your house," I insisted, leaning back a little, watching the cracks form in his composure. I saw his confidence waning, replaced by something raw and uncertain. I made him nervous, and I loved that. The way he babbled incessantly, the way he swallowed hard as if trying to keep his composure. He made a U-turn and headed for the highway.

We drove to downtown Chicago, the city's pulse thrumming around us, neon lights melting into shadows. He parked on the street outside a modest apartment building, nothing luxurious but nicer than the place I called home. I watched as he fumbled with the keys, the weight of the silence pressing between us. He laughed, glancing over. "Sorry," he said, finally swinging the door open. "I wish I had known I was going to have a lady over. I would've cleaned up a bit," he offered sheepishly.

I walked in, surveying the apartment. It was a palette of browns and beiges. The black leather couch was pressed against a brick wall, a solid anchor in the room. I sat down; the fabric was rough.

He stood there, watching me, and for a moment, we were bound by silence. "You want a glass of water or something?"

"Do you have wine?"

He laughed, the sound bouncing off the bare walls. "No, but I could go get some."

"Okay," I said, my voice smooth. "Can I take a shower? The shower in my motel room is terrible."

His eyebrows arched up in surprise. "Oh, sure. Of course, you can. How about this? I get you all set up for a shower, and while you're doing that I'll run down the street and grab some wine."

"Sounds like a plan."

He nodded, gesturing for me to follow. We walked down a narrow hall and quickly reached a small, simple bathroom. Nothing special, just functional. He fiddled with the knobs in the shower and looked back at me with a boyish smile. "Sorry, hold on."

"So, your shower is terrible too," I teased, leaning against the doorway.

He laughed again. "It's a hell of a lot better than a motel room shower, I bet," his voice was a mix of pride and apology. "All set," he said, stepping back to make room for me.

"Thank you."

I shrugged off my jacket, letting it fall to the floor, and started undressing right there before Tom even left the room. His eyes widened, frozen to the spot as I pulled off my shirt, my breasts exposed to the cool bathroom air. "Go get the wine," I said, my voice a soft command.

He snapped back to reality, shaking his head. "Oh, of course. Sorry, I'll...I'll be right back."

He stumbled down the hall, the door swung shut, and then clicked with haste. The apartment was mine now, filled with nothing but the sound of my breath and the distant hum of the city. I let the steam envelop me as I stepped into the shower, the hot water running over my skin. It was a baptism of sorts, a moment of renewal, and as the water cascaded down, I couldn't help but smile.

Tom the Delivery Man was out there, buying wine, probably wondering what kind of storm just swept into his life. The thrill of the unknown danced at the edge of my consciousness. After my shower, I wandered back into the apartment. The place felt different now, more mine to explore, to dissect. Curiosity gnawed at the edges of my thoughts. I needed to know if Tom the Delivery Man was truly as harmless as he seemed. I drifted into his bedroom, stark and functional with just a large bed dominating the space. The minimalist setup left little to hide, but I knew better than to underestimate the potential secrets tucked away in the mundane. Bending down, I peered under the bed and saw it was used for storage. I dragged out a brown shoebox. Sitting cross-legged on the floor, I lifted the lid to reveal a collage of memories.

Family photos, frayed at the edges, spilled over. Young Tom Delivery Man, a child in the innocent grip of time. There were other photos—awkward school portraits, a candid of him chasing a dog through a field. Evidence of a past lived with a naive kind of joy. Stuffed beneath the photos were letters, a bundle of them, tied neatly with twine. They were marked from New York, addressed from someone named Mary. My breath caught. Tom the Delivery Man already had someone. Or maybe these letters were relics of a past connection, an old flame. I pulled out one letter, the paper brittle, threatening to disintegrate in my fingers. Mary's handwriting was tiny and neat. At the bottom, a lipstick print sealed the sentiments, a signature in red. Intrigued, I began to read:

My Dearest Tom,

New York is a harsh mistress, colder than the winters back home. Each morning, I peel myself from the comfort of our memories, stepping into a city that never pauses to breathe. I often think of us, of the nights we spent by the river, your laughter echoing against the stars. Life here is different—noisy, relentless—but in every chaotic corner, I search for a trace of you. Sometimes, I see your face in the crowd, hear your voice in the din. It's maddening, this longing. But I hold on to the hope that we'll find our way back to each other. Take care of yourself, my love. The world is vast and indifferent, but within it, there's a space carved just for us.

Always, Mary

The lipstick kiss marked the end, a poignant touch to words saturated with yearning and love. I closed the letter carefully, placing it back among the others. Questions swirled through my mind. Who was Mary? What happened between them? And what kind of man did this make Tom? I placed the letter back into the shoebox and pushed it back underneath the bed. He should have been home soon, it had been a bit. I rushed back to the living room, picked up a magazine, and opened it up, but as soon as I did, the door clicked open abruptly. Tom stepped in, holding two bottles of wine and wearing a sheepish grin.

"I got the wine. Shower good?"

I stood for some reason. My god, did Tom the Delivery Man make me nervous? "Yes. Your shower is much better than the one at the motel," I said, offering him a smile to mask the whirl of thoughts behind my eyes. He set the bottles on the counter, rustling for glasses.

"You want red or white?"

"Red," I said, watching him move about.

He uncorked the wine with a satisfying pop, and we settled in the living room, the dim light casting gentle shadows across his beige world. He put on a record—some slow rockabilly that softened the edges of the evening. The music filled the room, weaving a tapestry of notes and murmurings that somehow made the silence between us comfortable.

I took a sip of the wine, the warmth spreading slowly, mingling with the curiosity that hadn't dimmed since my discovery. Tom the Delivery Man sat beside me, his own glass in hand. There was something about the way he watched me, his eyes never straying from mine. Maybe it was the wine, or the intimate cadence of the music, but the barriers between us thinned.

"So, delivery man by day," I teased, swirling the wine in my glass. "What's the rest of the story?"

He chuckled, leaning back into the couch. "It ain't glamorous, but it's honest work. Keeps me moving, seeing different places. I like that part."

"You ever come across anything interesting on your routes?"

His eyes lit up, a playful glint. "Once, a little girl gave me a drawing she made. Said she wanted to give it to the nice delivery man. That was a good day."

"That's sweet," I mused, taking another sip of wine. "Do you ever wonder about the lives behind the doors you deliver to?"

"Sometimes. I think about the people, the stories, what they're going through. It's kind of like getting a glimpse into a thousand different lives."

Our conversation flowed, and all the while, our eyes stayed locked, a connection fortified by every word and lingering gaze. Eventually, the wine had nestled comfortably into our veins, the bottle half-empty, the room curling around us like a warm embrace. I felt the question bubbling up, the one I had been dying to ask. "Have you ever been in love?"

Tom's eyes flickered, the remnants of his easy smile fading into something more serious; rawer. He took a moment, as though sifting through memories before he spoke. "Yeah," he said, the word heavy. "It was... intense. Beautiful, and then, well, complicated," I nodded, encouraging him silently to continue. He set his glass down, running a hand through his hair. "Her name was Mary. We grew up together, we were childhood friends. From the beginning it was like we were meant to find each other. She was my first for everything. I thought for sure we'd get married, we even talked about opening a little candy shop together here in Chicago one day. It was a silly little dream, though. Life got in the way, and she moved to New York, and long distance... it's tough, y'know?"

"Yeah, I know," I murmured, feeling the pull of my own concealed past, my own long-distance love with Michael. How it ended.

"We tried, for a long time. Letters, phone calls, visits. But eventually, it felt like we were holding on to something that was slipping away no matter how tightly we gripped it." His voice was tinged with regret, a quiet sorrow that hovered in the air between us.

"Do you still think about her?"

His silence spoke volumes. "Every day," he confessed. "There's always a part of me that wonders what could've been. But she moved on, and I had to, too. Don't mean I don't still care."

The vulnerability in his admission stirred something deep within me. I reached out, placing a hand on his knee, offering a semblance of comfort. "Thank you for sharing that with me."

He covered my hand with his own. "Thanks for listening," The music played on; each note a gentle reminder of the delicate beauty in laying bare one's heart. "Hey, let's lighten up the mood a bit. Enough mushy talk," Tom the Delivery Man said, bounding towards his room. He came back in less than ten seconds holding a tiny Ziplock bag, grinning like a kid showing off a secret toy. "You ever take LSD?"

I looked at him, surprised. He didn't seem like the type to use drugs. I shook my head.

Tom plopped down next to me, so close I could smell the wine on his breath. "It's a fun time. Gets you outta your head."

I stared at the bag in his hand. There were at least five tiny white tabs inside, so unassuming it was almost laughable. I shrugged, a mix of curiosity and recklessness bubbling up. "Oh, what the hell."

Tom's smile widened. "Stick out your tongue."

I stared at him for a moment, the request so intimate it made me pause. I felt a slow, sliding warm feeling in my stomach traveling all the way down to my groin. "Go on ahead, girl. Stick it out."

So, I did, staring straight into his eyes, feeling a strange electric charge in the air. At some point, he'd opened the bag and had already pulled out a tab. I hadn't even noticed; I was too busy getting lost in the deep brown of his irises. With the precision of a surgeon, he slowly and deliberately placed the tab right on the tip of my tongue. The room seemed to hold its breath, vibrating with a sense of expectation, with something I couldn't quite name. I closed my mouth, the taste of paper faint on my tongue.

"Now what?" I whispered.

His eyes glittered, catching the dim light as he placed a tab on his own tongue. "Now we wait," he said, and his words sank into the silence, wrapping around us like a spell.

In that moment, looking into Tom the Delivery Man's eyes, I decided that he was a good man. He didn't deserve to die. Impulsively, I leaned in and kissed him. His eyes widened in surprise, but he quickly responded, threading his fingers into my hair. The kiss was electric, charged with an intensity that felt out of place but somehow right. We moved to the bedroom, our clothes trailing behind us in a forgotten heap. The sex was passionate and intimate, the kind that only lovers who have known each other for years can have, though we were strangers in so many ways.

The acid kicked in just as I had my first orgasm, and I could feel, taste, smell colors. When I closed my eyes all I could see were red blue orange and yellow. When I opened my eyes, I looked up at Tom the Delivery Man and his face looked like what I imagined God would look like. He had a bright smile on his face as he moved in and out of me, and only then did I realize that both of us were laughing hysterically.

For a brief, stolen slice of time, the world narrowed to just us. His hands, warm and sure, found places on my body that had long been untouched by tenderness. Afterward, he rolled to his side and stared at me, his finger tracing lazy patterns across my belly.

"So, are you going to tell me about you at all? Or are you just going to keep being mysterious? Me and you both know damn well your name ain't Susan."

I laid there, staring up at the ceiling, feeling a familiar knot tightening in my throat. "I'm sorry," I said after a while. "I can't."

The disappointment etched on his face was heartbreaking, but he masked it with a laugh. "No big deal. I just...I just thought you liked me."

I sat up. "Trust me, you don't want me to like you."

Silence blanketed the room, heavy and suffocating. It stretched between us, an unbridgeable chasm, until he finally sat up, his movements slow and deliberate. "I should take you back to your motel. It's getting late."

Blinking back tears, I began to dress. The floor felt like it was moving underneath my feet. I looked down and I was on a boat in the middle of the ocean. I put my hands out and tried to steady myself. "Whoa…" I mumbled.

"Careful now, sit down and do that."

I sat down on the bed to put my clothes on. I looked up at Tom. I tasted the color blue on my tongue.

I wanted to tell him everything. I wanted to spill my secrets, to let him in. But I couldn't, it was not a good idea. He couldn't know who I was or where I was from. He couldn't know the darkness that shadowed every step I took. And it hurt. We walked to his truck in a somber silence, the sun sinking low on the horizon, casting long, melancholy shadows.

The drive to the motel was quiet, the only sound was the hum of the engine. When Tom parked, he looked over at me, his eyes seeking something I couldn't give. His gaze dropped to my lips, and I was startled when he gently placed a finger on them, tracing them slowly. The contact sent a jolt of electricity up my spine. "You're going to go places, I know it," he whispered, his voice a low, hopeful murmur.

Tom was an unexpected and pleasant surprise in a trip filled with dark intentions. I came to kill my ex-boyfriend and found someone with whom I could imagine a soft, beautiful life with. But it wasn't possible. For so many reasons. Life, as it often is, is not fair.

I stepped out of the truck and watched as he drove away, his silhouette fading into the encroaching night. I watched until his taillights were but tiny dots in the distance, swallowed by the darkened streets of Chicago. The world felt heavier in his absence, the enormity of my choices pressing down on me, stark and unrelenting. Turning to face the motel, I exhaled slowly, trying to let go of the ache in my chest. Tom the Delivery Man gifted me a glimpse of another possibility. And though it's a path I couldn't walk, it was a memory I'll carry, a testament to the fractured beauty of what could have been.

SUGAR

PRESENT DAY

As the book club gathering approached, I tucked away the framed photo of Chris I cut out from the family photo I stole off his desk. I take a half a tab of acid. Just enough to smooth out my rigid edges.

I was the host this week, which I usually am. I liked hosting; I liked gathering these women into my home and studying them, their polished exteriors hiding their own secrets. I am busy tidying up when the phone rings, its shrill sound slicing through the calm veneer of my meticulously arranged space. I pick it up.

"Hello?"

"Hey, Satara."

The sound of Lizzie's voice on the other end stops me in my tracks. "Hello, Lizzie."

"I had some issues with my babysitter today and Chris is busy working this weekend. Do you mind if I bring my little one this afternoon?"

I swallow the lump in my throat, forcing a delightful, "Of course."

As I hang up without a goodbye, a sense of resignation settles over me like a suffocating blanket, the weight of my own solitude pressing down with unbearable force. I wipe down the counters one last time, smoothing out invisible imperfections, ironing my nerves into submission. The doorbell would ring soon, and with it, my role would resume. Perfectly in place, perfectly in sync. As always.

Later, Cheryl Lewis breezes into my home with a bottle of pink wine in hand, her sunny disposition radiating warmth and charm. She was a black woman, tall with high sharp cheekbones and almond eyes. She's married to a wealthy man who she met on a solo trip to Paris a few years ago, something she loved to brag about. After only a few weeks of knowing Cheryl, he packed his bags up and moved to America just for her, leaving his entire life in Paris behind. Now she was set for life with a beautiful family—two kids, a six-bedroom home in a nice neighborhood, and on top of that, had the looks of a supermodel.

"Satara, you look marvelous. Did you do something different today?" she asks me, pulling me in for a hug. Her black bob brushes against my face. She's wearing a teal green pantsuit and dangling gold earrings. I wonder if her husband got those for her. They looked quite expensive.

"Nothing in particular," I smile. "I just haven't worn this dress in a while." I almost curtsy in my long floral dress that hugged my figure in all the right places.

She looks at me up and down, her eyes lingering on my figure. "Well, you look fabulous. And I love your makeup today."

"Oh, thank you darling, not as fabulous as you look."

I like Cheryl, but there is an arrogance to her that rubbed me the wrong way. She just gave birth two months ago and every week I watched as Cheryl basked in the admiration of the other women, her wide eyes and toothy smile seeking validation in their compliments. Despite my reluctance to play into her need for praise, I begrudgingly offered a half-hearted acknowledgment of her post-baby physique, knowing all too well the game she was playing. Her response, a smile devoid of gratitude, only served to deepen my sense of alienation in the presence of these women.

Next to arrive is Lizzie, a vision of beauty. Her long brunette hair is piled on top of her head in a high sporty ponytail showing off her gold hoop earrings. She's wearing a white cotton tennis dress, the collar neatly starched, shining white bright tennis shoes. Are they new shoes? Or did she take good care of them to keep them this pristine? It's an unimportant question that I ponder for far too long. Her daughter Sophia is in tow with her long sand-colored hair fashioned into two neat little pigtails and pink polka-dotted dress. As Sophia proudly displays her missing tooth and declares her age with a childlike innocence screaming "I'm five!" while holding up a tiny hand, I find myself studying the little girl. The resemblance to her mother is uncanny. The absence of any trace of Chris in her features offers a strange sense of relief that I can't quite explain.

Not even a minute later, Cynthia Bailey sweeps into my house wearing a yellow flowy dress, the belt around her waist cinched so tight it seemed to defy the laws of physics. Despite her departure from W&W, where she had reigned as the queen of style and sophistication, I couldn't help but feel a twinge of jealousy at her effortless beauty. With her dark hair and long dark eyelashes and curves that she was so graciously blessed with due to her Hispanic lineage, Cynthia exuded a magnetism that left me feeling inadequate in her shadow. The admiration from the men at the office only served to deepen my sense of inferiority to her.

Cynthia had gotten lucky with a beautiful man who also came from money, Jeff Bailey. Cynthia meeting and marrying Jeff Bailey were the stuff of fairy tales, a whirlwind romance that swept her off her feet and into a world of opulence and extravagance. Jeff owned

Chef's steakhouse, a high-end five-star restaurant with locations in Los Angeles and Miami. "You look amazing Satara," Cynthia says.

"That is exactly what I said! Doesn't she look marvelous?" Cheryl quips.

"She's absolutely glowing. That husband of yours must be keeping you happy," Cynthia says with a wink. I don't say anything, I just smile.

The last to arrive is Dawn Hartman, and we all fall silent as she walks in, a giant purple bruise marring her delicate features, I felt the surge of discomfort that hung in the air. Her carefully applied makeup did little to conceal the evidence of her husband's violence. Everyone knows her husband hits her, and she didn't do well at hiding it. Despite being a battered woman, Dawn looks impeccable, her blonde locks neatly curled Farrah Faucett style, and her cornflower blue dress immaculately ironed. She is a prim and proper woman, her movements very graceful and precise.

Every week, it seemed like she might come unraveled. Although I never wished anything bad to happen to her, I couldn't help but feel a sense of satisfaction that her marriage was as terrible as mine was. The feigned concern from the other women grated on my nerves, their well-meaning gestures ringing hollow in the face of Dawn's silent suffering. I could see the pity etched into the fine lines of their faces, the quiet glances exchanged over the rims of wine glasses, as if their empathy could somehow sanitize the brutality of Dawn's reality. While the other women would undoubtedly offer their support and sympathy in hushed tones after the meeting, I found myself utterly incapable of mustering the same facade of concern.

The thought of coddling Dawn or offering empty platitudes left a bitter taste in my mouth. If I were in her shoes I would take matters into my own hands. The notion of standing idly by while a man laid a hand on me filled me with a cold resolve, a silent vow to take control of my own destiny, no matter the cost.

I stay quiet as everyone discusses the book, trying not to give away that I've only read two pages total. Instead, I sip on the wine that Cheryl bought. Its sickly-sweet flavor dances on my tongue, getting me just tipsy enough that when I see Sophia placing a half-eaten wet chocolate chip cookie on the arm of my expensive light pink sofa, leaving behind a greasy, wet patch, I don't bat an eye. The wine and the acid blur the edges of my irritation, smoothing the sharp lines of indignation into a dull ache. My ears perk up, and I turn my attention to Lizzie when she brings up Chris. She's complaining that they rarely have alone time anymore and that he's always working.

"Oh yeah, he's been up to his eyes in paperwork lately. I can tell he's been really stressed," I blurt out, the words tumbling out of me like a confession.

Lizzie meets my gaze. "I'm really worried his job is affecting our personal life. I told him that boss of yours needs to give him a vacation. He's one of the hardest workers at W&W, and we haven't had a real vacation in years."

"You should go to the Bahamas. Paul and I went last year, and we stayed at this beautiful resort," Cheryl interjects, her grin bright and sparkling.

"Bahamas sounds nice, Chris would really like that," Lizzie says.

"Can I come too?" Sophia chimes in, her hand shooting up in the air with a childish exuberance that fills the room with laughter.

"No, honey, Bahamas is for grown-ups," Lizzie teases.

"Chris doesn't like the beach," I interject, the room falling silent as all eyes turn to me. I take a sip of my wine, the sweet liquid burning down my throat as I reveal the knowledge I hold about Chris, knowledge that even his own wife didn't even seem to know. "I overheard him talking to some of the other men at work a couple of months ago. He said he didn't like the beach. I would plan a trip to the snow or a nature-type getaway instead. He'd really love that," I offer, my own voice surprising me with its certainty. The room remains silent, the weight of my words lingering between us like an invisible barrier.

Lizzie smiles. "I guess you're right. I do recall him saying he doesn't like the beach."

The awkwardness is palpable in the room. I can tell she's lying. They've been married almost ten years, and she doesn't know her husband doesn't like the beach.

How pathetic.

"Sorry, I don't want you to waste your time planning something he doesn't like," I offer, a feeble attempt to ease the tension that hangs heavy in the air.

"I appreciate the help, Satara." Lizzie's words are laced with a hint of irritation.

I shrug off their silent scrutiny, unapologetic in my knowledge of Chris's likes and dislikes. Lizzie's forced laughter and awkward acknowledgment of his aversion to the beach only fueled my sense of superiority, a smug satisfaction at being privy to a fact about Chris that Lizzie wasn't.

I excuse myself to pour another glass of wine to soothe the unease that lingers in the room. I swirl the wine in my glass, watching the pale liquid catch the light. The room buzzes with a low hum of voices, punctuated by occasional bursts of laughter. Instead, I focus on the sensation of the sugary wine slipping past my lips, the quiet buzz it brought, dulling the sharp sting of reality. He should be with me.

As the book club meeting tapers off, the room still swimming with the dregs of conversation and the scent of spent wine, I tap Cynthia on her shoulder. "Can I speak to you for a second?"

I make my rounds, hugging everyone goodbye, except for Lizzie. Hugging her would be like embracing a cactus, futile and painful. I see the anger simmering beneath her polite facade, spurred by what I said earlier. She can shove it. It's not my fault I knew her husband better than she ever could.

Cynthia lingers by the door, performing the artifice of departure. She waits for the last woman to leave, then quietly shuts the door, her expression pivoting from casual to concerned. "What's going on, Satara?"

I swallow hard, feeling the weight of what I'm about to unload. If I were to trust any woman, it would be Cynthia, and I need to tell someone. Since we were ex-coworkers, I felt a sense of closeness to her that I didn't feel with the other women. As I stew in my hatred for Lilah—who didn't just sleep with my husband but bulldozed through the ruins of my trust—Cynthia is my last real friend. I drain the rest of my wine, hoping it will fortify me, then set the glass down with a soft clink. "So, me and Dean are having issues."

Cynthia's eyes widen, her hand flying to her chest. "Issues? What kind? Don't tell me you're getting hit like Dawn."

I shake my head. "No, not like Dawn. It's—different. Complicated," Cynthia leans in. I take a deep breath, the admission hanging in the air between us, fragile and electric. "I think Dean is having an affair."

She gasps, a sharp intake of breath that echoes the surprise mirrored in her wide eyes. "Oh dear. With whom?" Her curiosity is immediate; probing. "One of the women in the club?"

I shake my head, battling the instinct to hold back. Cynthia and Lilah know each other in the way acquaintances do—surface-level, polite smiles at parties, nods across the room. When I hosted gatherings, they would chat, mingle, do the typical fake social choreography that surface-level acquaintances often did. "Lilah Patrick," I say, the name cutting through the space between us.

Cynthia's eyes widen. She leans forward, her mouth a perfect O of surprise. "You're kidding," she says, a hand to her forehead, shaking her head in solidarity. "I'm so sorry, Satara. I know you two are close."

"Close," I repeat, the word sour in my mouth. "You never really know someone, do you?"

"No, you don't."

"Well, I'm going to leave him," My voice wavers, betraying a bitterness I hadn't intended to reveal. "This is hard to admit but... we haven't even had sex in months," My eyes drop to the floor. "I've been miserable with him for a long time now."

Cynthia places a hand over her heart, her face softening. "I am so sorry, Satara. You're in a terrible situation," she sighs. "I'd leave that asshole immediately if I were you."

"I'm planning on it. He's on the East Coast right now visiting his mother. I plan on speaking to him when he comes home. Asking for a divorce."

"You should leave now, while he's gone, it's the perfect opportunity."

I shake my head. She doesn't know about the grave truths buried, both metaphorically and literally, in my backyard. "I'm getting the house," I say firmly. "He's the one who's leaving."

Cynthia blinks. "How are you going to pay for the mortgage on your own?"

"I have some savings in the bank that will hold me over until I get money from the divorce. It's not a lot, but it'll last me for a bit," my voice is steady. "Until I remarry."

Cynthia's face contorts, as if wrestling with some inner confession. Her eyes dart, collating thoughts weaved between caution and revelation. "You should go to the Love Witch," she finally says, almost too softly.

"The Love Witch?"

Cynthia looks down, then fixes her gaze back on me. "I never told you how I met Jeff."

I sift through memories, through fragments of stories partially told. "All I know is that you went to his restaurant and caught his eye."

"That's true, but…" her voice falters, and I feel my patience fraying.

"Cynthia," I press, my voice taut, demanding. "Spit it out."

"I put a spell on him to make him fall in love with me."

I stare at her, the declaration hanging in the air, a strange blend of disbelief and curiosity coursing through me. "You... did what?"

"Well, not me, technically. The Love Witch did," she admits, her voice grating against the silence. "I paid her to do it."

"Why didn't you ever tell me?"

"Well, I thought you didn't need her! I figured you were happily married to Dean. But now, I think she could really help you."

Despite the outlandish nature of it all, a flicker of desperate hope kindles within me. When you're standing on the precipice, you'll grab even the most unbelievable of lifelines. I stare at Cynthia, my mind still reeling from her words. "Does everyone know about this Love Witch?"

Cynthia's eyes flicker with a mischievous gleam. She leans in. "Cheryl used her," she whispers.

"No."

Cynthia's eyes widen and she nods slowly. I scramble through my memories, puzzle pieces slotting into place with disturbing efficiency. It suddenly becomes clear—all the women orbiting my life with their perfect men, impeccable lives, it was all because of a Love Witch's handiwork. I swallow hard, desperation creeping into my veins like ivy.

I need this. I need her.

"Where can I find her?"

My neediness is naked; raw. Cynthia pulls back, slinging her purse over her shoulder with a sort of dramatic flair that implies she's been waiting for me to ask. She wraps me in a hug, her arms offering a fleeting sanctuary, a promise. "I have her info written down in my address book at home, I'll get it to you soon," she murmurs into my ear. Stepping back, she looks at me, her eyes shining with an odd blend of hope and assurance. "Things will be okay for you, Satara. Soon you'll have everything you want."

SUGAR

* * *

Dr. Maggie and I have been doing this dance where she asks me a question and I dodge it. I should tell her about the affair, lay it all out. But if I do, that might sow seeds of suspicion when Dean eventually turns up missing or dead. Unlike Cynthia, Dr. Maggie might spill to the authorities. Maggie knows every scrape and scar. She knows almost everything, except the small, dark fact that I'm a murderer.

Correction: I've gotten revenge on a few people. That's all. *Murderer* sounds too serious for what I've done.

"How are you and Dean doing?"

I dig my satin black heels into the worn-out brown carpet, grounding myself in the fiction. "He's gone."

Maggie tilts her head. "What do you mean *gone?*"

"Visiting his mother."

"How have you felt since he's been gone?" Her tone is gentle, probing under my defenses.

I take a deep breath. "Free."

Maggie nods. "Free from what?"

I blink, shaking my head as if to dislodge the truth lodged in my throat. "From him. From his lack of disinterest. His control."

"Why did you marry Dean?"

The question slices the air between us, sharp and immediate. I sift through layers of self-deception, the mirage of love I clung to. "I was in love with him, infatuated. *Obsessed.* But as the years passed, I kept lying to myself, telling myself that it could still work, and that I was happy. The truth was, I was just willing to endure the unhappiness."

Maggie's mouth forms a thin, contemplative line. "You feel the need to endure it because you have low self-esteem, due to your past. It all traces back to that traumatic relationship at fifteen with an older man. And I'm using the term 'relationship' lightly." Her gaze is unflinching, dissecting me. Her words prick the thin skin of my defenses, unraveling truths I've woven tightly. The room seems to close in, every secret pressing against the walls, waiting for the moment they can no longer be contained.

"I don't want to talk about Michael again," I mutter, my voice a sullen echo in the small, stifling room. "You bring him up too often."

Dr. Maggie's gaze doesn't waver. "Well, it's a very important part of who you are. That period of your life shapes why you are the way you are, Satara. I know you like to run away from that, but you cannot hide from the truth."

"You know he died, right?" the words cut through the air. "He was murdered."

Maggie's eyes flicker, just a spark of acknowledgment. "I remember you saying that."

"So, it hurts to talk about him. That's why I avoid it. Not because I want to run away from anything."

The thought of Michael swirls in my mind, a maelstrom of mixed emotions—anger that simmers under the skin, fear that lingers like a shadow, and a twisted knot of happiness. It felt good killing him, a savage catharsis. But now, I miss him in an unsettling, gnawing way. Just like I miss Dean.

Maggie's silence stretches, an open invitation for honesty, the kind that dissects you. I lean back, the chair's fabric rough against my skin, and breathe deeply. "Why don't you and Dean both come in for a session?" Dr. Maggie's voice is calm. It isn't really a suggestion—it lands like a demand, and that reality unravels the edges of my composure.

"You're not a marriage counselor."

Maggie shrugs. "I was married for thirty years. It would've been thirty-six years next month."

I shift in my seat, crossing my legs, my mustard yellow tweed dress itching like the persistence of memory. "I'll have to ask him when he gets back."

"Good."

Maggie's response is clipped, a brief punctuation to the conversation, but it carries the weight of expectation. The tension pulls at my seams, but I sit back, trying to maintain the illusion of calm, even as the threads threaten to fray.

"Are you still taking LSD daily?"

I nod. "Of course. You know I rely on it to get me through the day."

"Maybe you can try to get through the day without it? Try for just one day."

I snort. I can't even imagine it. I haven't been dead sober since I was twenty. I don't know how people go through life without at least one substance in their system. "I've tried that before, remember?"

"Right and you said—"

"I felt like throwing myself in front of a moving car."

"Why do you rely on it so much?"

I shrug. "I don't take a lot. Just a tiny dose every day. People call it microdosing. It's normal. If I don't take it daily, I will stick my head in the oven like Sylvia Plath."

She doesn't press the issue after that.

I decide to follow Dr. Maggie at the end of the day. Her demeanor after I mentioned Dean was gone was questionable, and then her thinly veiled demand to bring him in for a joint session—it all feels wrong, the air laced with something off-kilter. I can't tell if she suspects anything, but it's best not to leave it to chance. So, I follow her, hoping to glean some sliver of insight or a telltale sign.

She's oblivious to my shadow trailing her as she slips into her car. I maintain a careful distance, my black sunhat pulled low, sunglasses shielding my eyes from prying glances. She drives with a purpose, ending up at a deli, where she grabs a sandwich with the casual grace of someone who's fallen into a routine.

Watching her from my car, she sits outside on the patio of the deli. I'm almost surprised by the size of the bites she takes, a small, delicate woman devouring half her sandwich like it's the last meal on Earth. She wraps up the other half, her fingers smudged with mustard, cleanly wiped on a napkin. I follow her as she drives down the street to the bank, stopping briefly to pick up today's paper from a stand. For a heart-stopping moment, she glances in my direction, her eyes scanning the space where I sit hidden in my car. My heart races, but my hat and sunglasses offer a disguise. I duck down a bit, holding my breath until her focus shifts away.

Eventually, she finishes her business at the bank. I assume she'll be heading home, and my assumption proves correct. I tail her to a very nice house in a highly coveted neighborhood in Orange County. Fortunately, she doesn't know what my car looks like, so I blend into the background. I park across the street, just out of sight of her windows, watching as Dr. Maggie hurries to her front door. You'd think an older woman living alone would keep her blinds shut for safety, but she doesn't. She must feel invincible, cocooned by the safe neighborhood, never suspecting one of her patients might follow her home. I watch as she moves about her house, from the kitchen to the living room, and then finally up the stairs where I can't see her anymore. I sit back, the shadows deepening around me, the slow churn of curiosity morphing into something colder, more calculating. Now I know where she lives, and that information feels like power, a latent weapon waiting to be wielded.

1966

The next couple of years were wild; a whirlwind of chaotic highs riding the back of searing lows. After killing Michael and discovering acid, I floated on a constant high, my life becoming a fever dream. I found a dealer, a scraggly man named Lester who lived in the same dilapidated building as me. He sold me acid for a good price because he thought I was pretty. His street name was Lizard—a more fitting name, given his slimy appearance and twitchy demeanor. He stood a mere five-foot-four, with greasy, stringy hair clinging to his pale, sallow face, and eyes as jittery as a mouse on meth. Which, I was pretty sure he was tweaking on most of the time.

One scorching afternoon, I made my way to Lizard's place, just a couple of doors down from mine. His door was almost permanently closed, a barrier to the rot and squalor that spilled into the hallway. I banged on it until he let me in, the smell hitting me first—a rotten mélange of old takeout, stale smoke, and the grime of a hundred bad decisions. Inside, his apartment was a devastating testament to neglect. Piles of trash cascaded like disgusting avalanches from corners. Clothes, both dirty and torn beyond recognition, made small mountains on the floor. The only clear spot was a corner of his threadbare couch, which I claimed as my own while lighting a cigarette, its smoke mingling with the heavy, stagnant air. "Do you ever clean?" I muttered.

"Well excuse me, miss prissy," Lizard shot back, his voice a scratchy blend of annoyance and amusement.

"Do you have the shit or not, Lizard? I need to get out of this place before I catch something."

Lizard gave me a leering grin and pulled out a small Ziplock bag from under a heap of magazines. "It'll be free if you screw me," he said, inching closer. His hands were on me, fingers rough and insistent, tugging at the hem of my skirt.

"Not in your wildest dreams." I swiped his hand off my skirt.

"Come on baby," he said. Pretty soon he was leaning over me, trying to climb on top of me. I could smell his disgusting breath on my face. It smelled exactly what it would smell like if you were trapped in a garbage chute on a hot day.

He had hit on me plenty of times, but he had never gone this far. His hand slipped between my legs and without a second thought, I pulled my leg up and kneed him hard in the nose. Colors exploded in a vivid burst as he reeled back, blood spilling in technicolor streams. His expression turned feral.

"Fucking bitch!" he yelled, lunging at me.

Instinct took over. I reached into my frilly white knee-high sock, where a switchblade was nestled. Living near what is now known as Skid Row demanded constant vigilance and protection, it also came in handy for moments like this. Desperation fueled my swing, aiming for his chest, but his short stature caught the blade across his face instead. He stopped. We both stopped. Blood streamed down his clammy skin, a vibrant, surreal painting. It was beautiful.

"Stuck up bitch! Don't ever come to me for shit again!" he yelled as I ran back to my apartment.

A few days later, Lizard was found dead in his apartment from a drug overdose. It's like the universe knew, and intervened before I could.

With Lizard gone, I had to find a new source. I ended up meeting an older woman named Fae; she had big hair and wore feather boas and a ton of makeup. I met her one night in a disco club in West Hollywood. I saw her talking to a bunch of teenagers in the alleyway and that's how I knew she sold drugs. I walked up to her confidently and introduced myself and told her I was going to be her favorite returning customer. Her acid was good; potent. But she gave no discounts for a pretty face like Lizard did. It became expensive. Pretty quickly, desperation pushed me to sell my car, exchanging my main mode of transportation for funds for acid. I found myself catching the bus or hitchhiking. I tried to avoid the latter at all costs.

My job at Louie's, a swanky restaurant bar located in West Hollywood, began dictating my life. Despite my request for no night shifts ever, one day my bitch manager scheduled me from nine p.m. to 2 a.m.—the dead hours when buses didn't run. With a sinking feeling, I headed out to the bustling street, sticking out my thumb. Soon enough, a hippie with a grey mane of a beard pulled up, his gravelly voice calling out, "Where ya headed?"

"West Hollywood. You going that way, sir?"

He sized me up through red-tinted sunglasses. I clutched my switchblade hidden in my pocket.

"No, but I can for you. Hop on in."

Without hesitation, I climbed into his truck, the overwhelming scent of pot greeting me.

"Thanks," I said, trying to sound casual. But something felt off. As we drove, he veered away from the familiar route. My unease grew. "Hey, you're going the wrong way sir, "I said, trying to keep

83

my voice steady. He said nothing, just kept driving until he pulled onto the shoulder of a busy highway.

He turned to me, eyes gleaming with an unsettling hunger. "You either give me ass, or you're getting out right here, in four lanes of traffic. What'll it be sweetheart?"

I should have been afraid, but instead anger bubbled up. I glanced out the window—the left side, a frantic stream of traffic, and to the right, a dark, brushy marsh. I had options, none of them particularly good. I stared him down, my eyes locking onto his faded pink shirt with its mocking yellow smiley face declaring *Spread Happiness*.

"Okay," His eyes widened in surprise. "I'll have sex with you," I say, louder. "Let's go into the woods."

"We're doing it in the car," he insisted.

"With all these cars zooming by? What if someone sees us?"

He paused, licking his lips, "Then I'll drive further out, find a spot where we can have some privacy."

The way he said *privacy* grated on my nerves, all low and seductive like we were lovers. In fact, his entire existence irritated me—the weed-stinking van, his audacity, and the sheer inconvenience of his threats making me late for work. I pulled down his pants and lowered my head. His penis was short and fat so when I started to bite it off, it wasn't as easy as I imagined it would be, his gut kept getting in the way.

His screams filled the van as my teeth tore through the flesh, which was both soft and rough at the same time. I hadn't bitten a man's penis off before, so I wasn't sure how long it would take for him to bleed out and die, but I continued and pulled and tugged with my teeth as he bucked underneath me, screaming at the top of his lungs. After what seemed like an eternity the penis was off and blood began to spray vibrant and beautiful, the colors bathing me in his life force. He clutched his groin, the sound of his choking and crying filling the confined space. I sat there, counting down the minutes it took for him to die, and rolled my eyes at each agonizing second.

When he finally went silent, I felt no remorse, just a weary acceptance. I wasn't sure if he was dead or just unconscious, but I wasn't going to wait around to find out. Wiping away as much blood as I could with a towel I found in the backseat, I knew I wouldn't be making it to work tonight. Covered in blood, I bolted into the marsh, the darkness swallowing me whole.

By the time I stumbled onto a gas station, an hour had passed. An overweight middle-aged woman pumping gas widened her eyes at the sight of me. "Dear god, are you okay, miss? Do you need help?"

"Yes," I gasped, my throat dry, my feet aching from the long walk. She ushered me into her car. Her young son was sitting wide-eyed in the backseat. "Can you take me home?"

"Don't you want to go to the hospital? You're bleeding."

I shook my head. "I'm okay. Promise."

"Did you get stabbed?"

I didn't answer. Not once did she suspect the blood could be someone else's. She saw me and concluded that I couldn't do harm, only harm could be done to me. I might have been angry about that on any other day, but tonight, it worked in my favor. She dropped me off a few blocks away from my place, claiming she needed to get home right away. I just knew she didn't want to venture into my neighborhood with her young son, which was understandable. I thanked her and trudged home, a brisk fifteen-minute walk that seemed to drag on forever.

Once inside, I called Louie's. My manager Carol's nasally voice grated on my already frayed nerves. "Hello, thank you for calling Louie's. How may I help you?"

"This is Satara."

"Satara? Where are you? You're supposed to be on right now."

"I said no night shifts."

"What—"

"I fucking quit." Hanging up, I stripped off my bloodstained clothes and collapsed into bed, the weight of the night pressing me unconscious.

I didn't kill for a long time after that.

1968

Before my job at W&W, a chapter of my life unfolded in the shadows of desire and anonymity. It was a time when I shed the constraints of societal expectations and embraced a persona shrouded in mystery. I was a phone sex operator.

The halls of Whisper, one of the largest phone sex companies in the US, echoed with the hushed tones of confessions and promises, a symphony of seduction that drew me into its embrace. During my onboarding, I was presented with two model options for my persona, both bearing the stamp of whiteness that dominated the industry's narrow perceptions of desirability. My request for a woman of color was met with a dismissive wave.

"White women are popular; they sell the most. Choose one," my manager Svetlana says to me, her long red nails tapping loudly on the photos of the half-naked ladies spread across the table. In a moment of resignation, I chose the model with brown hair, blue eyes, and ample curves, christening myself as Sugar. Sweet. Hard to resist.

As I delved into the intricacies of phone sex, I discovered a hidden talent for weaving tales of lust and longing, my voice a seductive melody that lured callers into a world of their ultimate fantasies. The art of altering my voice, transforming it into a high, child-like pitch that stirred primal instincts in my clients, became second nature. Immersing myself in a world of taboos and kinks, I became a student of desire, studying the nuances of pleasure and pain with a fervor that bordered on obsession. The dimly lit aisles of video stores became my classroom, the young boys behind the registers unwitting participants in my quest for knowledge and exploration. Their furtive glances and awkward questions only fueled my sense of empowerment.

"No, I'm not married. It's for me," I would declare with a sly smile, relishing the flush of embarrassment that colored their cheeks.

The money came easy, each minute on the line was another quarter I earned. Mastering the art of keeping men on the line for as long as possible became my forte, a skill honed through fulfilling their ultimate fantasies. Some men crossed boundaries of decency, their words a reflection of their darkest desires and disgusting fantasies, a mirror that revealed the depths of their depravity and desperation.

The revolving door of women who passed through Whisper's halls became a silent testament to the harsh realities of the industry. I watched as their lives intersected with mine, brief moments of connection and understanding in a world defined by anonymity. As the calls of regulars filled my days, their fetishes and personal lives etched into the recesses of my mind, I navigated the murky waters of human desire. Ramone, the recovering drug addict with a penchant for giantess fantasies; Jim, the middle-aged man who loved brother-sister role-play; Simon, the nineteen year old boy who just wanted to get his rocks off to my moaning——each a chapter in the ever-evolving saga of Sugar.

But it was Waylon who became my Achilles Heel; my everything. From the moment our voices intertwined, I knew that he would be the one to unravel the carefully constructed facade of Sugar, to peel back the layers of illusion and reveal the woman beneath the mask. He was Waylon Caruso, the pastor from North Carolina trapped in a loveless marriage; and I was Sugar, the struggling model just trying to earn extra money by doing phone sex. I found myself drawn into his world. I was a confidante, a lover, a beacon of light in the darkness of his pathetic loveless existence. And as he showered me with affection and attention, I found myself succumbing to his fantasy, a willing participant in a game that would ultimately lead to my downfall.

For a year, I found myself entangled in a love affair with Waylon. In the confines of my apartment, my connection with Waylon unfolded like a twisted tapestry. His voice, with that southern drawl, stirred something deep within me, he became a lifeline in the darkness of my own insecurities and vulnerabilities, a beacon of light. The attention he showered me with was a drug, a rush of serotonin that flooded my veins with a heady mix of desire and desperation. The words of affection, the gifts and tokens of adoration that piled up in my tiny apartment; I was smitten.

I'm short on rent baby.

How much?

A minute later, I'd hear him rifling through his things for his checkbook and the next week I would receive a check in the mail from Waylon Caruso from Fayetteville, North Carolina. Despite the lies and deceptions that defined our interactions, I found myself drawn to the illusion of connection that he offered. But soon the guilt of my deception weighed heavy on my conscience, I found myself torn between his attention and the weight of my own lies.

How has your wife not found out yet?

She's dumb and I'm careful.

Month ten of our love affair arrived, and with it, the sentence I dreaded most finally slipped from his lips:

We should do this in person.

My body tensed, fighting off a rising panic as silence stretched between us. After a few agonizing minutes, he abruptly declared, "Forget it," and hung up. A month passed in a void of communication, leaving me in a pit of despair so profound, it felt like the end of everything. Every shift at work became a struggle, my thoughts consumed by him to the point where I mistakenly called clients by his name. I drowned my sorrows in alcohol and a tab of acid every night, collapsing into bed, my mind haunted by his presence, his face a mystery I longed to unravel.

He once likened himself to James Dean's older brother, so at night I found myself touching myself and thinking about James Dean and pretending that he and Waylon were one and the same person. Unable to risk calling him in case his wife answered, I endured the torment of silence until, at last, a month later his voice pierced the void, bringing tears of relief and joy. Confessing my love and longing, I implored him to leave his wife for me, only to receive a crushing blow in return.

I don't see that happening anytime soon, Sugar.

His words shook me to the core, leaving me trembling with the weight of reality. Questioning his feelings, I was met with assurances clouded by complications and obligations; his son leaving for college and needing to save money, his wife finally growing suspicious of him—these things resulted in the dwindling of money and gifts he once showered me with constantly. Unable to keep away from him, our conversations resumed as normal, the dwindling gifts of money no longer a concern compared to the precious sound of his voice. I didn't care about the money anymore; I just wanted him. On Valentine's Day, a token of affection arrived, a teddy bear clutching a crimson heart and a card bearing his initials.

To my favorite girl. I'm so grateful to have found you. Love you always, W.

In the hazy March of the year 1969, his voice crackled through the phone line, a promise of excitement and possibility weaving its way into my consciousness. The mere mention of him coming to California sent a tremor of anticipation down my spine, a mix of fear and longing swirling within me like a storm. Despite my reservations, his persistence wore down my defenses, and before I knew it, tentative plans were made. One night, I confessed the truth that had long lingered between us like a shadow.

I'm not the woman in the photos.

I know, sweetie. I've known for a long time.

His response soothed my frayed nerves, a reassurance that cut through the layers of doubt and insecurity that had plagued me for so long. I asked him if it bothered him, my heart pounding in my chest as I awaited his answer. And when he said he didn't care; that he still found me beautiful and loved me despite what I looked like, a wave of relief washed over me. I stared into the mirror, my reflection a stranger staring back at me, and I wondered if his words would ring true when he finally laid eyes on me.

In the days that followed, I threw myself into a frenzy of self-improvement, working out tirelessly, restricting my diet to only vegetables, and dyeing my dark hair a brassy blonde in a desperate bid to transform myself into someone worthy of his love. Each day was a battle against my own insecurities, a war waged in the quiet solitude of my apartment as I practiced my smiles and perfected my poses in front of the mirror.

And then, the day arrived in early April, a day that felt both interminably long and fleeting in its passage. His call in the early morning sent a jolt of anticipation through me, the reality of his presence in Los Angeles a surreal dream come true. Dressed in a skin-tight cocktail dress that left little to the imagination, my feet ached in protest as I made my way to his hotel, the click of my stiletto heels echoing in the empty streets. As I stepped into the hotel lobby, a sense of unreality washed over me, the world around me blurring at the edges as his gaze met mine. Despite never having seen him before, I knew it was him standing there, hands in his pockets, clad in a black blazer, a white collared shirt with a bolo tie, and a black cowboy hat. The recognition in his eyes mirrored the strange familiarity that tugged at my senses.

"Sugar?"

I mustered a thin smile in response, though beneath the facade of pleasantries, a wave of dread washed over me.

This man before me was not the one I had known through months of intimate phone calls; he was a stranger wearing the mask of familiarity that left me feeling hollow and exposed. Despite my misgivings, I embraced him, taking in the scent of aftershave and cinnamon that clung to his skin. It was neither unpleasant nor enticing, a neutral blend of earthy and sweet that left me feeling oddly disconnected. His scrutiny as he looked me over spoke volumes, I could see it in his eyes.

"You're disappointed."

"No, no, I just..." he faltered, his words trailing off as he struggled to find the right response.

"Just what?"

"I just didn't think you'd be Indian."

And I didn't think you'd be a fat piece of shit, but here we are.

"I'm Native American and Black," I corrected, my voice tinged with a mix of defiance and resignation.

"Right, right," he chuckled awkwardly.

"I'm sorry I'm not white."

"Don't be ridiculous, Sugar. You're beautiful."

As we made our way to dinner, I couldn't shake the sense of disappointment that lingered like a shadow over the evening. Our conversation veered towards safe topics, the warmth of connection we had once shared reduced to polite small talk and superficial pleasantries.

"Do you want me to keep calling you Sugar?" He inquired.

"If you want." My voice was tinged with irritation that I didn't bother to hide.

"What do _you_ want?" his gaze bore into mine, a challenge lurking beneath the surface as he awaited my response.

I couldn't tear my gaze away from him, my eyes tracing the contours of his face with a mix of fascination and disappointment. The man before me was a far cry from the image he had painted over our countless conversations. His rounder frame and shorter stature stood in stark contrast to the tall, lean figure he had described.

When he took off his cowboy hat I glanced up at his curly brown hair streaked with hints of grey. His beard matched his hair, thick and brown also with hints of grey, and even some red. Fair complexion with rosy cheeks, a crooked bulbous nose, and honey brown eyes completed the portrait before me, a mismatched collection of features that bore little resemblance to the idealized version he had presented to me. No sensible person would ever say he looked like James Dean's older brother. But dear Pastor Waylon Caruso was not a sensible person.

As the waiter approached with the check, I made my decision. "I want you to take me to your room."

The words hung in the air, a final surrender. The scene unfolded before me like a twisted tableau, a grotesque pantomime of desperation played out in the confines of the hotel room. His hands, rough and urgent, tore at my dress with a primal fervor, his teeth grazing against my skin as he stripped away my clothing. I reciprocated in kind, a mechanical response born of obligation rather than passion, my movements tinged with a sense of detachment. As he loomed over me, his gut pressing against my skin, I averted my gaze, unwilling to confront the harsh reality of our encounter.

The minutes that followed were a blur of frenzied motions and muted moans. I endured seven minutes of mechanical thrusts and feigned pleasure, culminating in a climax that brought neither satisfaction nor relief. Pushing him off me, I stumbled towards the bathroom, the taste of bile rising in my throat. The sound of my retching echoed through the bathroom. Emerging from the bathroom a few minutes later, I found him already dressed, a bottle of water extended towards me in a feeble gesture of concern.

"Thanks," I muttered, taking it from him.

Sitting at the foot of the bed, he watched in silence as I began to dress. Rose petals littered the bed, a sad and pathetic attempt at romance that only served to highlight the hollowness of the night. My eyes settled on the chilled bottle of wine and the array of condoms strewn across the dresser. As I gathered my belongings and prepared to leave, I couldn't help but feel a sense of profound sadness at the sight of what we had become: two strangers bound together by a shared desperation for connection, yet ultimately doomed to remain isolated in our own private hells.

"I shouldn't have done this, I'm sorry Sugar."

My response was tinged with bitterness, a reminder of the irreparable damage we had wrought upon each other. "Well, you can't unfuck me."

"I know," he murmured, his voice heavy with defeat, a pastor undone by his own desires and shortcomings.

I buckled my heel in silence, the weight of disappointment settling upon us like a shroud in the aftermath of our failed encounter.

I watched him, his defeated posture, his gaze fixed on the floor, he spoke in a voice tinged with resignation, a shadow of the man who had once professed his love for me. "You wanted to meet me. This was *your* idea."

"What do you want me to say? I thought I was in love with you." His admission cut through the silence. He thought he was in love with me. But not anymore. The realization washed over me like a wave of cold water, a bitter truth that left me feeling like a failure. I had managed to disappoint a man to the point where he questioned the very foundations of his feelings. If nothing else, that should be my superpower. In that moment I had concluded that I would always be someone men wanted, but never wanted to keep.

Ten minutes later, he hailed a taxi for me, giving me a weak hug and muttered a promise of a future call. As the taxi pulled away, a sense of finality settled upon me, a recognition that I would never hear from him again. Two weeks passed, the memory of my disappointing night with Waylon lingering like a ghost in the recesses of my mind. Late at night, I found myself consumed by thoughts of him, the feelings we had shared before reality shattered our fantasy. The magic we had once believed in was irreparably broken, yet a desperate part of me still longed to recapture it, to feel his love and validation once more.

It was a craving that consumed me, a drug that I could not resist. Memorizing his wife's schedule became a twisted obsession, a means to reach him when she was away. When he finally answered my call, only to hang up without a word, a spark of rage ignited within me. I called again and again, the phone ringing endlessly until it went to voicemail. And in that moment of fury and desperation, I brought the phone to my lips, my voice dripping with venom as I issued my ultimatum:

Answer the fucking phone or I'm going to tell your wife everything.

The power I held over him was intoxicating, a heady rush of control and manipulation that left me feeling invincible. One night as I lay in bed, the glow of my victory still lingering, I called him again, relishing the knowledge that I knew his wife was home at that time. This time, she picked up the phone, her voice sharp and commanding. "Who is this calling so late?"

I hung up without a word, a smirk playing on my lips as I scribbled his number out of my address book, a sense of satisfaction washing over me at the chaos I had unleashed upon his life. The next morning, Svetlana summoned me to her office which confirmed what I had already suspected. The gravity of her gaze and the sternness of her tone left no room for doubt—I was being fired. Svetlana's accusations cut deep, her words a condemnation of my actions. I had broken the rules, crossed boundaries that were beyond inappropriate. As she asked for my defense, I remained silent. I stood and walked out, the weight of her judgment heavy on my shoulders. I hadn't even given it a thought that Waylon would rat me out like he did; I was too drunk off my own power to even think of such a thing.

With my last paycheck from Whisper dwindling, I survived on a diet of snack cakes, eggs, and vegetables for a month; a meager existence that mirrored the emptiness I felt inside. It wasn't until I landed a job at Weinman & Weinman that a glimmer of hope flickered within me, a chance at redemption in the face of my past mistakes. Despite the passage of time, Waylon's absence lingered like a ghost in my life. I continued to call his number and hang up without a word. One day when he finally had enough and called me late at night and demanded I cease all contact, not even bothering to get a response before hanging up, I felt a pang of regret mingled with relief.

The urge to confess to his wife simmered beneath the surface, a temptation that threatened to consume me. Yet, before I could act on it, the dial tone and automated voice announcing the disconnection of their number served as a final, definitive end to our twisted tale.

SUGAR

1970

Except of course, that wasn't really the end.

The end came later, and it started with me driving cross country to Fayetteville, North Carolina to Calvary Christian Church—Waylon's church. I planned my trip meticulously, like a maestro orchestrating a symphony. I drove through the night, the hum of the engine a steady companion to my thoughts, pulling at the thread of my sanity. I stopped only twice, curling up on the backroads of small towns, the car a makeshift cocoon as I slept.

In those stolen hours of sleep, dreams were replaced by the cold precision of my mission. I kept human contact to a minimum, intentionally slipping through the cracks of the waking world. I've long since learned that the fewer people who see you, the slimmer the chance you'll be pinned to the crime.

I wasn't here. I never was.

Ghosting through the geography of nowhere, I erased my presence with every mile.

I wish I had known this when I killed Michael, but back then, I was young and dumb, emotionally raw. Mistakes were made— sloppy, glaring missteps that gnawed at my peace. Still, despite my naivety, I wasn't caught. Not even a suspect. Michael's death hung like a foggy memory; untraceable. Perhaps I'd done something right.

As I entered North Carolina, the sky a spreading bruise of dawn, the looming silhouette of Calvary Christian Church came into view. I was close now, close to the end I'd crafted, the finality I craved. The anticipation coiled inside me; a snake ready to strike. I parked a safe distance from the church, the car blending into the early morning shadows. This was it, the confrontation that would reconcile my past with my present, a deadly dance choreographed in silence. This time, there would be no mistakes. No loose ends. No getting rides from random delivery men and falling into bed with them.

The end was now, calculated, and inevitable.

My wig was a deep auburn with loose curls that barely brushed my shoulders, and my sunglasses were sleek and dark enough to shield my identity, though I was aware they made me look like I was trying too hard. I didn't care. Assurance in a strange, uncharted territory was all the more critical when you're on a mission.

Waylon Caruso was not just anyone. He was beloved in a way that suggested folks here would drop whatever they were doing to render assistance or justice if he was murdered.

As I strutted to the front of the church, A woman walked out as I was walking in. Her eyes scanned me from wig to heels, her suspicion was palpable as the summer heat. "Excuse me," I said, my voice smooth as honey.

She turned to face me, eyebrows arching in faint curiosity. "Yes?" she replied, the word stretched taut between her thin, tight-lipped smile

"I'm looking for Pastor Waylon. Is he in his study?" I adopted a southern accent that matched hers.

"He's busy, gettin' ready for service in a few hours. May I ask what it's about?"

I let a small, sharp smile cut my face. "Is that any of your business?"

Her jaw tightened—the chill in her eyes crystallized. "I would say so. I'm his wife."

Surprise skittered across my thoughts like a startled bird. Of course, Waylon's wife was here—what a blind spot.

As my gaze flitted over her, I noted the rigidity in her posture, the way her eyes dared me to trespass. Tall and slim, her figure would've been enviable if not marred by her constant expression of distaste, like someone fed her lemons one day and she hadn't recovered since. I just knew that her vagina was as dry as the Sahara Desert. Her blonde hair was pulled into a tight bun, severe and unimaginative. Someone should tell her a gentler style might soften her perpetual scowl, but not me. I was about to gouge a hole through her world, and critiquing her hair seemed redundant.

"Oh, hello, Mrs. Caruso. Nice to meet you." I extended my hand, knowing full well it would be left hanging. No disappointment when she doesn't take it. And here I thought Southern people were nice.

"Do you go to our church? I don't recognize you."

I shook my head. "I recently moved to town, and I'm very interested in joining your congregation." The lie tasted acrid but convincing enough. She still stared at me unconvincingly, and I felt the weight of her suspicion.

"Okay. So why do you need to speak to Waylon?"

I shuffled, rifling through the catalog of excuses, but I had never been religious, so it felt like shooting in the dark. Until it came to me, almost too obvious. "Prayer request," I spat out, the words abrupt and jagged in their urgency. "I wanted to meet the pastor and make a prayer request. I've been having a tough time lately, and I need all the help I could get from the congregation…and Jesus." I plastered on the most earnest smile I could muster.

Her stare cut into me for one more agonizing beat, then finally, her guard dropped. "I see. Well, I'm Donna. Nice to meet you," she said, her condescension mellowing to a tepid hospitality.

"Leslie Roberts. Nice to meet you."

"I'll walk you to his office," she offered flatly, moving past me with a briskness. She pushed open the door, and we stepped into the church. Our heels clicked in tandem against the ground as we walked.

"You're too kind, Mrs. Caruso," I said brightly, the saccharine inflection straining against my nerves.

She cast a glance over her shoulder, the shadow of suspicion never quite leaving her eyes. We continued down the hallway, Donna's steps quickened as though she could leave behind the unease I had cast over her. We approached an office door, and I steeled myself, every nerve ending on high alert. Donna stopped, turning to face me one last time. "He's inside. I hope you find what you're looking for."

"Thank you, Mrs. Caruso."

As she reached for the door handle, I couldn't help but wonder if the uncertainty in her eyes was for me or if perhaps it was a reflection of her own wavering faith in her husband being alone with a younger, prettier woman. Donna opened the door, and there he was—Waylon, sitting at his desk, the halo of a dim desk lamp casting a somber glow over his rounded figure. My heart hitched, and I was immediately transported back to that night we met. He looked even bigger now than he did a year ago, cheeks puffed like overripe fruit, and his overgrown beard thickened his face. His head was bowed, eyes devouring the worn pages of his Bible, and I can see the bald spot that he normally concealed with a cowboy hat, now glaringly exposed under the light.

"Waylon, you got a visitor." Donna's voice was a cool breeze across the room before she departed swiftly.

Waylon's eyes lifted slowly, creeping from scripture to stranger, and there was no flicker of recognition in his gaze. "Why, hello, nice to meet you," he said, standing up and extending his hand as though I'm any other worshipper walking through his door. The handshake was firm and short. Disappointment slithered through my veins, cold and spiteful. He didn't remember me. I truly meant nothing to him. The weight of that realization settled over me like an unwanted cloak, oppressive and suffocating.

"Leslie. Leslie Roberts."

"What brings you here today, Leslie?" his eyes betrayed nothing—not guilt, not curiosity, not fear.

"I recently moved to town and heard a lot about you. I was hoping for a prayer request."

He nodded, settling back into his chair, his body sunk into the familiarity of his role. "Of course. What can I help you pray for?"

I hesitated, the words forming like poison on my lips. "Guidance. Strength," I began, each syllable a dagger I wish I could plunge into him. "And forgiveness," I added, letting my gaze burn into his. For a fleeting second, I thought I saw a shadow cross his face—perhaps a memory stretching out from the abyss of his conscience to grasp at the edges of his mind. But it was gone as quickly as it appeared, and he resumed his pastoral demeanor.

"We can always seek those from our Lord. What do you need forgiveness for?" His voice cut through the thick air; his eyes tried to seek mine even though I was shielded by dark sunglasses.

"I've done a lot of bad things."

He smiled thinly, a practiced gesture that didn't reach his eyes. "Well, the best thing you can do is repent," he said.

I let out a short laugh. "What about you? Have you ever done anything bad, Pastor Waylon?"

He shook his head and smiled with amusement. "I'm human just like you. Sometimes I mess up."

I took my coat off and leaned back in my chair. "Yeah? Like what?"

He looked at me, a faint trace of amusement still playing on his lips. "You know, we're not here to talk about me. Let's pray," he said, trying to steer the conversation back into safe territory.

"Have you ever fucked another woman who wasn't your wife?"

The words were a knife, slicing the air between us. His face drained of color, eyes widening in stark panic as he steadied himself on his desk. "Sugar," his voice was quiet, shaky, drenched in fear. "I... I didn't recognize you."

"Yeah, no shit. I'm wearing a disguise," I responded flatly, dropping the southern accent.

He pushed his chair back, ready to bolt. From beneath my dress, I pulled out the knife I had hidden in a holster. "Sit the fuck down," I commanded, pointing it towards him.

Reluctantly, he sat, pulling his chair back into place. Sweat beaded on his brow, glistening under the dim light. "Did...did you say anything to my wife?" His voice trembled with desperation.

I shook my head. "No, but I will if you scream or try to run. Not only will I kill you, but I'll also kill her."

"What—what do you want?" His voice cracked, and for a moment, I see the terror of a man who's realized his sins had caught up to him.

I looked at him, disgust curling in my stomach. "Repent."

He stilled; eyes fluttered closed as he tried to summon the script he's lived by. "Dear heavenly f—"

"Stop!" The command was sharp and immediate.

His eyes flew open. "You told me to repent."

"Repent to *me*, you idiot. I'm the one holding you at knife point. I am your God right now."

He stared at me, his eyes filling with tears. The power thrummed through me. He was at my mercy, and his god couldn't save him now. "I'm sorry," he whispered, the words ragged and trembling. "I'm sorry I broke your heart, I'm sorry I got you fired... I'm sorry for... for everything. Forgive me." Tears spilled from his eyes, unabashed and messy.

I couldn't help but smile. "You know, Donna's a bitch, but she still deserves better than you," I said. "Get on your knees and beg me for forgiveness."

His face contorted in confusion.

"Now!" I demanded, standing up, my presence towering over him. He scrambled out of his seat, knees hitting the floor gracelessly.

He looked up at me, his eyes shiny with desperation, and started pleading—a pathetic, bumbling mess. "I'm sorry, please forgive me. I'm sorry, I really am," he cried, his voice cracking as he devolved into blubbering apologies.

"I forgive you," I whispered, looking down at him, the power held tight in my grasp. He stared up at me, a mix of confusion and relief washing over his tear-streaked face.

His sobs halted abruptly. "Really?" He asked, hope blossoming in his eyes.

"Yes," I said. "Stand up, Waylon."

He scrambled to his feet and with one swift motion, I swiped the blade across his neck. Blood cascaded out, painting the room in broad strokes of technicolor. Reds, oranges, yellows, blues, all over the room. I stared in awe. He clutched at his throat; his eyes wide as he gurgled in agony. He fell to his knees again, then collapsed sideways onto the floor. His gurgles dragged on for what felt like an eternity before they ceased, leaving only silence. His lifeless eyes stared blankly, emptied of the man who once dwelled within.

I smiled, pulling a scarf from around my neck to clean the blade meticulously, and then I tucked it back under my dress, and wrapped the scarf back around my neck. The scarf-turned-cleaning-cloth hid some telltale splatters on my dress. I grabbed my coat from the chair and threw it on, covering any other incriminating evidence on me. As I stepped outside, Donna was conversing with another blonde woman who radiated the same judgmental air.

"Oh, that was quick. How did it go?" she asked me.

"Swimmingly," I replied, heading for the parking lot. Then I paused, turning back. "Oh, and by the way, he told me to tell you not to bother him until service starts. He's got a lot to do."

Donna raised her eyebrows. "Oh, alright then," she said. "And will you be coming back for service?"

I nodded. "Yes, just a bit peckish. I'll be back."

"We'll see you then, Leslie," Donna said with a wave, her friend mimicking the gesture.

I returned a wave and a smile and walked deliberately to my car, my steps measured, no rush betraying my escape. I drove away, the building and Waylon's fading presence shrank in my rearview mirror. As I headed back to California, the tension unwound bit by bit, the grip of the encounter loosening, leaving only the satisfaction of closure and the open road ahead. I wasn't here. I never was.

PRESENT DAY

My glass of whiskey serves two purposes— to numb the creeping pangs and gently blur out the reality that I'm currently living, the other is liquid courage to find a man to take home tonight. The truth is I've grown tired of solitude, tired of the absence of a gaze that worships me from head to toe. The aching void of unfulfilled desire gnaws at my soul. I long to be ravaged, to be claimed by a hunger that shouts, *you are wanted*. Even when Dean was alive, he couldn't give me that satisfaction.

I watch a couple across the bar, wrapped in one another's embrace, staring into each other's eyes. The man only lets go of the woman to take a drink of his whiskey. The woman is nursing some sort of red, fruity cocktail. I can tell she isn't a big drinker just from the way her nose scrunches up whenever she takes a sip.

Robert Klein, with his devastatingly conventional charm cleverly manicured into the persona of a typical finance tycoon, is a delicacy to some. Claire Morrison, a literary agent, that lucky woman, seems to have no awareness of how good she had it. Two weeks of tailing them had me learning the rhythms of their lives. Their cozy Sunday brunches. Their exotic getaways. His nightly gym routine. Her frequent trips to the local library, burying herself in books.

I knew they were coming here when I overheard their conversation at a café, snippets of their plans slicing through the room to land in my lap like a secret gift. It was an accident, really. But once I caught the rhythm of their lives, it was easy to stitch together the details: their names, where they worked, the banal specifics that made them real. Gone were the days when they were just The Bench Couple. I found an odd happiness in knowing their names, as if calling them anything other than The Bench Couple shrouded them in reality, made them flesh and bone rather than abstractions of romance and routine.

"Another drink?" His voice drags me back from my thoughts; the boy behind the bar pours more whiskey in my glass, uninvited but not unwelcome. He's handsome—a mop of chestnut hair fighting with his brow, blue eyes flickering. He's so tragically lovely, my heart thrums an erratic tempo.

"Cheers," I say, before shooting him an unexpected question. "What's your name?"

His eyebrow dances on the edge of confusion. He points at himself. "Me?"

I offer a nod. "Yes."

"Matthew Walsh." He unfurls the words like a sail catching the wind.

"How old are you, Matthew Walsh?"

A smile plays on his lips. "I'm a boy of twenty-three summers."

Incredibly young. the words circle my thoughts, hungry vultures waiting to swoop. I battle disappointment with a non-committal hum, "Oh, got it."

He contorts his features, confusion giving birth to a delicate frown, though the corners of his mouth cling to a smile. "Let me know if you need anything else."

I clamp my eyes tightly shut as I think *he could be fun. Imagine how those beautiful blue eyes will look as he mounts you.* Followed quickly by the thought of *stop being foolish, Satara. You need a man, not a boy.*

And then as if the universe were finally on my side, a glorious mirage takes flesh next to me. A man of sculpted beauty unfolding in impressive height, kissed golden by the sun, his raven-black locks gelled back. Time has kissed him with graceful lines adorning his forehead and around his hypnotic gaze suggesting a comforting maturity.

Suddenly a wave of courage fuels me. "Can I buy you a drink?" I ask him as soon as he takes a seat next to me.

This titan of a man narrows his gaze, assessing my worth in the market of time. Relief washes over me as his gaze softens and he shifts, angling himself towards me. "Wait. You want to buy *me* a drink?"

This is him. A formulated question chokes on my sudden realization. An attempt to blink back the tears fails as he questions my state.

"Are you ok?"

"Yes, sorry, just had a rough week." I manage to conjure a serene smile while balancing my teetering display of emotions.

The right corner of his mouth curls into an amused grin. "Looks like I'm the one who needs to buy you a drink." His hand gesture summons Matthew, and a serving of whiskey fills my almost-full glass again.

"What's your name?"

"Name's Jasper. Yours?"

I tattoo his name onto my memory. Jasper. This is the man I need to familiarize myself with. "Satara."

"Are you Native American?"

His question finds me robbed of words. "Yes, I'm half. How could you tell?"

"Part Native, part Mexican, myself. I can recognize my own kind," His eyes are lagoons of honeyed caramel, intense and inviting. "You have nice lips, Satara."

I pick up my glass of whiskey, lips parting to inhale the soothing elixir as I scramble for an apt response, but all words decide to play hide and seek. It's a unique feeling, a state of speechless admiration that leaves you yearning for more. My gaze settles on Jasper, an unspoken question hanging in the air between us. "Feel like escaping?"

A short taxi drive later, we're at my house. I hastily throw an apology at Jasper for the felines that have already curled around him on the couch. "No need to apologize, I adore cats." His hand lazily caresses the crown of Avocado, who purrs approvingly on his lap. I struggle to contain my glee. Nice. Attractive...and has an affinity for cats. I couldn't have asked for anything better.

"That purring ball of cuddles is Avocado, the good one. Whiskers the orange cat is the bad one," I say with a smile.

As we nestle in glasses of wine serving as knighted companions, his life unfurls before me. His involvement in a non-profit catering to homeless youth and children in foster care is heartwarming. "I have a portfolio of luxury estates spanning both ends of the country although the non-profit remains my pet project."

"Are you into fitness?" The words escape before I could reign them in.

A roar of laughter breaks free of his chest, ringing through my home. "Sadly, no. That's my cardinal sin. Can't resist a well-baked cake and despise a gym."

There it was— my checklist manifested in human form. I couldn't hold back my smile. Emotion takes over and my hands trip over themselves as they desperately start to peel off his clothes. My lips break into a satisfied grin as he's as hard as I thought he might be, until his sudden wince halts my eager exploration. Protests fall from his lips as he goggles down at his state. "I'm sorry."

"What's wrong? Please don't tell me you have a venereal disease."

"No, I don't have a venereal disease."

"So, what's the matter?"

His posture stiffens, the fringes of a half-said apology hanging in the air. "I'm fresh out of a twelve-year marriage."

"Oh."

"And I am eager to move forward. It's been almost four months. I feel like I should be ready."

"Oh. Did you two have kids?"

He shakes his head. "No. We tried but it just never happened," he looks down at the ground, unable to think of what to say. Finally, he grabs my hand and more electricity jolts through me. His searing gaze softens my worries. "The attraction I feel for you is undeniable, but it's been only my ex-wife for so long…and it feels wrong to think about being with another woman."

"So… you don't want to have sex with me?"

His laugh is soundless, his eyes crinkling with amusement. "You're straightforward. Refreshing."

I responded with a shrug. "You'll never get anywhere by beating around the bush."

He brushes a stray lock of hair from my face, his touch electric. "How about slow and steady? A nice dinner tomorrow night."

"You're asking me out on a date?"

"Yes."

I sigh, pressing the edge of my lower lip against my teeth. "Okay."

His smile is relief in human form. "Okay."

Our lips lock together for a few more intoxicating minutes before he reluctantly pulls away from me to put on his jacket saying that he needs to go. "Wait," I stop him. "What's your last name?"

Amusement flickers in his gaze, his lips dancing with laughter. "You want to know my last name?"

"Please."

"Sanchez."

My heart catapults itself to my throat as the name Satara Sanchez echoes in my ears. It's like it was always meant to be my name. I clench my fist in giddy anticipation. Initially, I was only looking for sex, something primal and uncomplicated; the kind of encounter that leaves you breathless and, for a fleeting moment, whole. But then came Jasper, with his steady gaze and deliberate touch, and he made me reconsider everything.

Jasper is husband material. He is perfect, in a way that almost scared me. But my heart betrays me with its obsessions, and it's Chris who occupies the spaces in between my thoughts. I've always imagined Chris at the end of the aisle; the one I see when I close my eyes and picture a future with. I was going to need to make a significant assessment after tonight, weigh the solidity of Jasper against the unpredictably of Chris. It felt like standing at the edge of some seismic shift, the ground beneath me about to tremble and split, forcing me to choose which side to cling to. And yet, there's a thrill in this brink, an excitement that's both intoxicating and terrifying.

* * *

I find myself in the break room, making a pot of coffee. The rhythmic drip of the machine is oddly comforting, a steady pulse that drowns out the static in my head. I'm caught in the hypnotic dance of the coffee stream when I hear his voice behind me——rough and stern, a jagged interruption slicing through the monotony. There is a gravelly edge to his words, a firmness that sends a shiver down my spine and pulls me out of my reverie. When I finally spin to face him, my pulse quickens, the beat matching the drip-drip-drip of the coffee. I swallow hard, the taste of anticipation sharp on my tongue.

"Hi, Chris. What's going on?"

"Are you hard of hearing? I said I need to talk to you."

The anger wasn't outright, but it was bubbling under the surface, ready to rise from the depths at the slightest provocation. I mark the tightened jaw, the defiantly lifted head as he towers over me. I'm not sure why he wants to speak to me and that terrifies me. I try to hide it with nonchalance.

"Sure."

I follow Chris into the cooler air outside. I fish out a cigarette from my pocket and the orange tip glows as I work at my composure. Inexplicably drawn closer, I catch a whiff of his cologne. He slides his hands into his pockets, his jaws still taut, and I return his silence with a slow exhalation of smoke.

"Why is my wife under the impression that we're having an affair?"

Fighting the tremble in my hands, I pull in another lungful of smoke from my cigarette. "I have no idea."

A grunt of irritation escapes him, his fingers nervously combing through his hair. I watch in awe. His frustration with me makes my heart palpitate. There's a twisted satisfaction in pulling out anything other than indifference from him. "Clearly you must've said something to make her think so."

"I just mentioned you didn't like the beach. Her overactive imagination is not my problem." My voice quivers despite my best effort to conceal my emotions. His gaze burrows into me, intense as ever, the dark circles underneath his eyes revealing sleepless nights spent arguing with Lizzie.

"She's convinced. Accuses me of being distant. I told her it's absolute bullshit to even think for a moment that I'd cheat, especially with you," his words fill the air like a noxious gas, heavy and cruel. I desperately try swallowing the knot building in my throat, fighting off the tide of tears that threatens to drown me right there on the sidewalk. Slow realization dawns on Chris as he shuts his eyes tight, a hand running over his face, "I didn't mean it like that…I meant-"

"You don't have to explain."

His attention is pulled to the burning end of my cigarette, studying the ashes as they slowly crumble to the ground. I take another puff, fighting to keep my composure as a lone tear threatens to fall. He breaks the silence. "Satara, I've seen the looks, I've noticed your odd behavior around me. I've heard the rumors."

"What fucking rumors?" I threw back defensively.

"I know about your little crush on me. Which is fine—"

"You don't know a damn thing."

"I need you to reassure Lizzie that nothing is happening between us. That this little crush you have on me is one-sided. Can you do that for me?"

The ground at my feet suddenly becomes interesting as I stare at it intently, trying to keep my emotions in check.

"Can you do that for me, please?"

Fighting the urge to put my lit cigarette out on my own arm, I toss my stub to the ground, wiping the rebellious tears that had managed to escape. Just as I'm about to respond, he manages to turn the knife once more in my already wounded heart, "Nothing will *ever* happen between us, you understand that?"

I freeze. The words hit me like a car. I know this is the reality, but the rejection is still tough to take. I don't say anything, I just meet his gaze and smile wide.

SUGAR

Back home, the blinking voicemail light on my phone snaps me back to reality. A recorded message from Jasper brings a rush of mixed feelings.

"Hey Satara. I'm so sorry but I need to cancel our date tonight. Work stuff. Looking forward to catching up soon. Last night was quite the—" I stop the voicemail halfway. The blinking light signifying another message beckons and I press play.

"Hi Satara, it's Cynthia. We girls have been chatting and we...we feel that a parting of ways would be for the best. You seem to not connect with the books we've been reading, and a few of us feel that there's some unnecessary drama creeping in. We just want to keep things simple and light in the club. I hope we can still be…" again, I stop the message. I open my cabinets and my fridge, my mind seeking comfort in a glass of wine. The empty fridge and cabinets mock me, and I curse my luck. Tonight, of all nights I'm all out.

With a quick shrug I slide back into my coat, letting the familiar weight settle around my shoulders before ducking out into the night. There's this homely bodega open late downtown, wedged between a rundown apartment building and an antique store. I drive there with purpose, the cool glow of the alcohol section is a beacon in the darkness that I follow, a moth to the flame. My hands are sure as they select a bottle of unassuming red wine and a brutally honest bottle of vodka; one to numb, the other to feel. I trudge over to the snacks next. Autopilot takes hold as my coat pockets fill with an array of sugary sweets, a colorful assortment of chocolates, taffy candies, and Hostess snacks. An oversized bag of chips completes my standard grieving kit, the rare touch of something savory as I was a sweet over savory girl all the way.

I dump my late-night selection at the counter before the man stationed there, his thick mustache twitching with suppressed amusement. I recognize him as the owner's brother, the dayshift being the territory of his sibling. Night is his, and he wears it well. A quick glance is all it takes to note the bat in the counter, a silent statement, a firm promise of retribution, although it probably wasn't needed. We are in Orange County, after all. The only danger here was the smog, and me. I guess you can never be too careful.

"Wild night?" He asks, one eyebrow rising in mortal curiosity.

"It's for me and my husband," I mutter in response, a ready lie slipping off my tongue. My cigarette flares to life as I light up, silently observing him take in the contents of my late-night haul. There's a look in his eyes, baffled and somewhat concerned, as if I'm stepping off the precipice of normalcy and into the realm of crazies.

Stumbling back into my home, I can feel the rooms echoing the hollowness I feel inside. The vodka bottle kissing my lips makes a slight hissing noise as I unscrew the cap. It's harsh, it burns. I choke, gasping a bit, but continue to let it drown my sorrows. A twisted, lazy banquet begins; I feast on a variety of sugar-coated delicacies stuffed inside my pockets, a banquet of self-pity and gluttony. I take a piece of candy and eat it with a tab of acid. Each bite, each gulp is a war cry to my insides, a declaration to grow numb and let go.

The muffled purrs of Whiskers and Avocado resonate in the pit of my stomach as I take off all my clothes and lie on the floor and cling onto them, enveloped by the comforting feel of my companions. The floodgates of my tears rage as I grab the half-empty bottle of wine. Gulping down in haste and letting its velvety taste mingle with the pungent bitterness of Vodka, a drinker's delight sets in. For a minute I contemplate my gradual plunge into alcoholism, but I quickly decide to push it to the back of my mind. It feels good to hurt myself.

Each breath, each muscle contracting feels like a burden. A mental and physical strain agonizing the fragments of my heart. And all I seek is love. A primal instinct takes over as I crawl, guided by pulsating emotional suffering, only to reach the kitchen and let out a bitter mix of my liquor feast in the sink. I pick up my phone, steadying myself as I dial Cynthia's number. I hold the phone to my ear, the room spinning slightly as I lean against the fridge for support. Cynthia picks up immediately, her voice crisp against the murky fog in my head. "Hello?"

"You're kicking me out of the fucking book club?" I slur, my words tumbling out with an edge sharper than intended.

"Satara… you're drunk." Her voice is a blend of exhaustion and concern.

"So, what?" I mutter, struggling to keep the resentment out of my tone. "I'm a grown woman. I am allowed to get drunk if I please."

A heavy sigh travels down the line. "It wasn't my idea to kick you out."

"My husband is gone," I spit out, venom lacing every word. "He cheated on me, and now I'm being kicked out of the club. Do you *want* me to jump out a fucking window?" My voice fractures, teetering on the brink of sobs.

"Satara, I'm sorry—"

"It was Lizzie's idea, wasn't it? That bitch is jealous of me. She thinks I'm fucking her husband."

Silence. Cynthia is quiet, too quiet, and it tells me everything I need to know. "Give me the name of the Love Witch. Right now," I demand.

"Satara, I don't think you're in the right mind to—"

"Just give me her information *now*, Cynthia. God you are so insufferable." My head falls back and connects with the refrigerator door with a loud thud.

"Do you want me to come over?"

"I'm going to tell everyone you put a spell on Jeff Bailey to get him to fall in love with you."

"You wouldn't," she whispers.

"I will shout it from the goddamn rooftops."

"You're drunk. You don't mean it."

I smile lazily, savoring the power shift. "Maybe. I guess you'll never know."

A pause, the kind that stretches thin and fragile between us, barely able to hold the weight of what's being considered. "Her name is Millicent Garcelle," I grab a pen and piece of paper and scribble down the address she gives me. "Bring cash and don't be rude, or she won't help you. You need at least a hundred dollars."

"Bye, Cynthia."

"Wait—"

"What?"

"Can you tell me who you're going to put the spell on?"

"I don't think so. You'll know soon enough." My voice is icy, detached.

"Okay, but please don't—"

I hang up the phone, leaving her words to dissipate into the void. The room is silent again, save for the hum of the fridge, and I'm left alone with the echo of my decisions and a pounding headache.

* * *

Millicent Garcelle is nothing if not a vision when she swings open the door, her imposing figure swathed in a black organza dress, the ethereal subtlety of the fabric climaxing in a satiny rustle as she moves. A black woman no more than thirty with high cheekbones and raven hair that cascades down in a torrent of exquisite midnight-black, and her eyes are the focal point of her face with their stunning shade of green, accentuated by a deep purple eyeshadow. Millicent is a velvet-wrapped riddle, and I am captivated by her mysteriousness. If anyone can brew a remedy for my solitary anguish, it is her.

"Hello, darling. Come in." Her husky British accent swirls around me. Time and space seem to hold its breath in Millicent Garcelle's downtown apartment. She filled the apartment with luxurious furniture, satins and velvets and gold, each piece intricate and beautiful. Almost too beautiful as if it were a TV set. "Sit, let me make you some coffee," she demands, her words gliding over her crimson lips. As she walks away, the sheer, dark fabric of her gown blurs into her inky black hair. "I would normally make tea around this time, but I know how you Americans are with your coffee."

I settle into the plushness of a velvety, crimson-colored sofa and pounce on the silence. "So, what's a Love Witch and how can you help me?"

She responds with a chuckle, rich and smooth, her eyes shimmer with amusement as she glances at me over her shoulder, "You're an impatient little bird, I see."

I pull out my wad of cash and hold it up to her, the crisp bills trembling slightly in my grip. "I brought money. One hundred dollars, right?" I steady my voice. "I need you to make someone fall in love with me."

Millicent looks at me, one perfectly arched eyebrow lifting in mild amusement. "Put the money on the table, sweetheart." Her movements are fluid as she prepares the coffee.

"I've never given much thought about witches. Although I've always believed in psychics," I blurt out nervously.

Millicent lets out a melodious laugh. "Psychics are phony, sweetheart," she says, placing the kettle on the stove with a loud *thunk*. "The women who claim to be psychics—the ones who aren't faking it for money—are just powerful witches, but they call themselves psychics instead," I watch her as she moves with purpose around the kitchen. "You'd be surprised at how people treat you when you say you're a witch. The word 'psychic' elicits a less abrasive response," as she pours the boiling water into a French press, the aromatic steam rises, filling the air with a comforting warmth. She turns to me, a wry smile playing at the corners of her crimson lips. "Who's the lucky bloke you're trying to ensnare?"

"His name is Chris."

She moves to the table, taking a seat across from me, the dark organza of her dress pooling around her like ink. "Love is a complicated thing," she says, her voice softer now, almost contemplative. "It's not just about making someone fall for you. It's about the connection, the bond that forms between souls. I can cast the spell, but the rest is up to you."

I nod. "I just need a chance," I whisper, the words carrying the weight of my yearning.

She studies me for a moment, then she reaches across the table, her hand brushing against mine. "Alright, sweetie," she says softly. "Let's see what we can do."

A tendril of hope curls its way around my heart. "Thank you."

"You need a piece of him," she states matter-of-factly.

"A piece of him?"

"His DNA," she clarifies, bringing the coffee cup to her lips. "Sweat, blood, semen—"

"Hair?"

Millicent nods once, her green eyes locking with mine. "Hair works as well."

A smile spreads across my face, the edges of my relief blooming wide. "Not a problem." I bring my cup up to my lips and take a sip, feeling the warmth seep into me, grounding me, tethering me to this moment. Millicent watches me, a small smirk playing on her crimson lips.

* * *

I'm busy cleaning when the doorbell rings, the sound blurring into the noise of the loud vacuum. "Coming!" I yell, hurrying to the door. I fix my hair and smooth my dress and primp my hair before opening it. I see Lilah standing there, and my smile fades. "Lilah. What a surprise. Please, come in."

"Hi darling. Sorry I didn't call before I dropped by. I just…" her voice trails off as she looks around the house. "You redecorated." The pitch of her voice goes up two octaves.

I laugh and shrug. "Oh, you know, it's nothing, just needed a little refresh."

"It's very…pink," she observes, her eyes roaming over the light pink floral curtains, the giant pink shag rug, and the pink fluffy accent pillows on the pink sofa that we already owned. Dean knew it was my favorite color and surprised me with it the day after we moved in.

Oh honey, it's perfect!

Consider it a gesture of love. No more pink though. The couch is enough.

"Isn't Dean going to hate this?"

I give her a once over. She's wearing a white flowy dress that is way too springy for a fall evening. She tries too hard. Not that I can judge, because I try hard as well, but it's infuriating that Lilah is so effortless about it. She's like a mirage, all soft edges and sunlight. She's infuriatingly poised, each movement a ballet of casual grace that leaves me feeling like a marionette in comparison. Her eyes dart around, taking stock of the pink assault, and I can't tell if the slight twitch of her lips is amusement or disdain. Maybe both. Lilah's ever the duality, shimmering on the edge of empathy and condescension. She tries too hard, yes, but her version of trying hard looks like a lifestyle, while mine feels like an act. There's a part of me that hates her for it—even before I knew about her and Dean—for the ease with which she occupies space, for the way her presence highlights my insecurities like a spotlight on a blemish. But there's another part that's envious, that wishes I could slip as effortlessly into my own skin.

"Oh, I spoke to him about it before he left. He said he didn't mind."

"Wow. He's such a nice man for letting you do that."

The air between us tightens like a rubber band stretched to its limit, taut and ready to snap. I can practically hear the unspoken thoughts ricocheting around her skull; her eyes flickering with the same unsettling mix of envy and pity that always sets my teeth on edge. "I agree, such a lovely man," I reply, "Care for some wine?" I turn quickly on my heels and glide into the kitchen without waiting for her response.

"It's okay, sweetie, I'm not staying long." She follows me anyways.

I grab a glass and pour myself an ample serving of wine.

"How's Dean doing?"

I take an indulgent gulp before answering. "I haven't heard from him," I say casually.

"It's been almost three weeks, Satara." Her face folds into an exaggerated frown that I hope leaves permanent lines.

"I'll give his mother a call tomorrow." I swirl the wine in my glass, pretending her presence isn't gnawing at my patience.

Lilah's silent for a minute, her gaze dropping to her hands, as if she's searching for the right words in the creases of her palms. When she finally looks up, her eyes are sharp, cutting through the pretense like a blade. "Look, Satara—"

"Yes?" My lips curve into a half-smile as I prepare for whatever performance she's about to deliver.

"I saw you bring home a man a few nights ago," she says steadily. "A man who wasn't Dean."

"And how did you see that when you live around the corner?"

She shakes her head, flustered. "I was just out—"

"You were stalking me."

Her eyes widen, her shock almost laughable. "Satara, I swear, I was just out on a jog and passed your house. I saw you two," her voice cracks. "You can't turn this on me and make me seem like I'm the bad guy."

I glare at her, the truth seeping through my clenched teeth. "If you had stayed, you'd know he left only fifteen minutes later. Nothing happened. We just kissed once, that's all."

"I just think it's all a bit strange," she says, her gaze flitting around the room. "You're redecorating, you don't seem to care about Dean's whereabouts, you're bringing home random men…" her voice trails off, tears welling up in her eyes. "Where is Dean?"

"I need you to leave my house," I whisper. Lilah stares at me, her eyes searching mine, tears threatening to spill. "Go!" She skitters off quickly, her heels slamming hard on the linoleum, the final door slam echoing through the empty house. My heart thumps hard in my chest. I finish my wine in one gulp, the glass hitting the counter with a sharp clink.

Fuck.

PRESENT DAY

Without protocol, without a warning tap against the dense, dark-wooden door, it flings open to reveal Millicent, silhouetted by the gentle glow of a thousand flickering candles. "Did you get it?"

I nod. Retracing my steps cautiously, I played out the day's events to her. I told her how as the secretary, I had a front row seat to everyone's life, a backstage pass into their calendars. On Chris's sheet, between upcoming meetings and uninteresting reminders, lingered the words *haircut today*.

I followed him to an obscure barbershop downtown, a place that time and trend had forgotten. Nestled between brick-and-mortar conglomerates, it held on. Waiting. Just as I did, outside under the aging awning. Chris wasn't unbearably vain, so his quick touch-up meant only a few follicles would be available. But that was all I needed. Mustering every ounce of bravery, I strolled into the barbershop. The difference of my presence clashed with the muscle-clad duo working there. Intimidating in their size and their camaraderie, they filled up the room with testosterone, booming laughter, and bristling energy that receded quickly when I walked in.

But there was no time for shame. I pitched my request directly. "Can I have some of the hair clippings on your floor?" The men's brows twitched up in unison, a humorless mirror. "It's for a school project."

"You don't look like you go to no school," one of the men quipped.

"Go ahead," the other man relented. He waved his friend's protest away. "It's just hair. We're gonna clean it up anyway."

I flashed a smile at the men as I gingerly picked up the strands of Chris's hair; dark and lightly wavy. A tide of thoughts and emotions roiling within me—crazy, surreal even. The world as I knew it was standing right on the precipice of change.

"Come in, ignore my friend," Satara beckons.

I step into the low-lit room and my gaze immediately meets a man sprawled on the couch, half-naked in white underwear. The sinews of his muscles are peeking out from the fabric, his body a canvas of human perfection. It was as if he'd stepped right out of a Grecian statue, edgy, handsome, and enticing despite his obvious state.

"Your boyfriend?"

She let out a husky laugh, something that was part amusement and part satisfaction. "Oh no, darling. Don't be ridiculous," she says, her humor rippling through the room. "He only wishes," casually, she walks over to the man and swats him lightly on the abs with a throw pillow. "Get up, it's time to go," she orders.

His eyes fly open, and he looks up at Millicent with a childlike innocence that didn't fit his statuesque figure. "My love, must I go?" His voice is as touchingly helpless as his expression.

Millicent glares down at him, hands perched authoritatively on her hips. "Yes. I have company and you need to leave." She tosses his shirt at him, and he catches it, his face twisted into a pout. He slides his shirt on, not bothering to button it up. He lazily pulls on his pants.

"When can I come back over?" he pleads, and I can't help but be astounded by the situation unfolding before me—this man, a physical specimen, reduced to putty by Millicent's commanding presence.

"When I say you can," she pulls him in for a kiss. His response is desperate as his fingers fumble to hold onto her. "Bye Grady." She pushes him away and then hurriedly guides him towards the door.

His retreat is reluctant, his eyes never leaving her face. "I'll call you soon," he promises, before slipping out the door without as much as a glance in my direction.

Millicent turns back towards me, her smile tight-lipped, "He's such a bother. But great in bed."

Her candor leaves me bewildered as I sink down onto the couch. "Can you make men fall in love with you too?"

"Of course. Now give me the hair."

I comply, pulling out the bag of hair from my purse. She takes it, inspecting it with an expert eye.

"A witch needs to practice her abilities somehow," she says matter-of factly. "So, I have many devotees." A hint of a smirk plays on her lips. If anything, her prowess is terrifyingly fascinating and equally exhilarating. She looks up at me, her green eyes boring through me. "Are you sure you want this Chris person to fall for you?"

I only think about it for a beat. "Yes."

She nods slowly. "Then let's get started."

Millicent languidly holds up the strand of hair. She whispers spells under her breath. I observe her, transfixed and horrified in equal measure. She is sitting cross-legged on the richly woven Persian rug that covered her living room floor. "Nexus to destiny," she breathes, weaving the hair into an intricate knot. "Entwined paths, bound hearts."

I watch the scene transpire with a growing knot in my belly. Millicent withdraws a blade then, the silver flashing wickedly in the dim light. My breath hitches seeing the sharp edge, already knowing where this is leading. She grabs my hand and places the blade on my palm. The fire in Millicent's eyes hold me captive, and I could do nothing but nod, consenting. The blade pricked. A whiff of antiseptic steel, a rush of red. I clench my fist around the hurt as Millicent hastily catches the falling ruby droplets into a tiny silver bowl. Then the chanting came to life again, shaking the room, vibrating deep within my bones. The energy around us accumulated and crackled in time to Millicent's rhythm. It is powerful, it is subtle, and then it was gone.

The aftermath is no less dramatic. An overwhelming tide of emotions swirl between us. Millicent drops the strand of Chris's hair into the bowl, signifying an end to the ritual. I could do nothing but watch, my palm throbbing in rhythm with my heart. My words seem to come out in a shuddering whisper. "Did it work?"

Millicent, her eyes ablaze with an unnatural light, nods slowly, intentionally, as if every movement she makes is part of a grand, secretive ritual. "It certainly worked," she confirms. Her words seem to hang in the air, the reality of it all seeping into my consciousness.

My eyes draw from her to the illuminated incense in deep thought. I blink. Once. Twice. Trying to ground myself in the moment, to grasp the sheer absoluteness of it. "So, it's… immediate?"

Millicent nods yet again. Her confirmation confident, almost matter of fact. "The moment he lays eyes on you, he becomes yours and yours alone."

My heart throbs jubilantly, its every beat echoing the chorus of victory. It is more than elation that I feel, it was ascension. An unrestrained smile splits across my face. A lightness, a joy, which was hard to fathom only moments ago now fills me to the brim.

Chris Stiles is mine. A dancing, tumbling figure in the panorama of my heart, an anchor I have sought for so long, metamorphosed into a tangible being in my life.

* * *

Today, I've decided to make peach cobbler. The peaches and cinnamon mingle together, creating an amazing aroma that fills every corner of my home. Peach cobbler was Dean's favorite. I would make it for him on his birthday every year. Even the smell of it brings him back, the memory threading through the air like an old, persistent ghost. I curse under my breath. I can't have anything that reminds me of him. I pull the cobbler out of the oven, its golden crust hissing slightly, and throw it directly into the trash.

I start cleaning up the mess, flour dusting the counter like a veil of regret. In the midst of rinsing cinnamon from a measuring cup, I find myself thinking about what Chris's favorite dessert might be, what I'd have to master making once we live together and get married. The doorbell rings, yanking me from my reverie. My breath catches in my throat as I peek out the kitchen window above the sink and spot the black and white police cruiser parked outside my home. I freeze, listening to the doorbell ring again, its chime now an insistent demand rather than a polite inquiry.

I glance down at myself. My apron is covered in flour. How embarrassing. I can't be seen like this. I pull it off quickly, flour cascading around me like snowflakes, and fix my hair with hurried fingers. I smooth out my dress, trying to compose myself, willing my heart to slow its rapid pounding.

"Coming!" I say brightly. I catch a glimpse of myself in the hallway mirror—hair tousled but not disastrously so, face flushed but not unattractively. I look decent; presentable. I'm wearing a tight pastel blue turtleneck and jean capris and black flats. Not too try-hard, but still put together. I take a deep breath and head to the door, each step measured, each breath deliberate. As I grip the doorknob, I paste on a smile. I open the door, greeting the officers with practiced ease, my smile never wavering from my face. "Good afternoon, officers. Can

I help you with something?" My voice doesn't betray the cacophony in my chest, the way each heartbeat feels like a drum signaling some impending doom. The mask holds, and for now, that's enough.

"Good afternoon, Mrs. Stratton," the female officer says. She looks strong and mean, her eyes steely and devoid of amusement. "We're following up on a call about a potential missing person."

Lilah. That bitch.

"And… who is the missing person?"

"Dr. Dean Stratton, your husband," the male officer replies flatly. He's attractive, tall with a square jaw, the kind of attractive where he knows it. He's also the type of man who's easy to manipulate. One smile, a flip of the hair, and he's putty in your hands.

I steady my eyes on him, knowing he's my best bet in gaining sympathy. "Oh, I'm sorry for the misunderstanding, but my husband is not missing," I say with a laugh, shaking my head incredulously.

"He hasn't been to work in three weeks, and we asked your neighbors. Nobody has seen him," he continues, unphased for the moment. "But his vehicle is parked out front."

"Did you try calling his mother? Because that's where he is."

The officers exchange glances. "We haven't started making phone calls yet, ma'am. We thought we'd come to you first…since you're his wife," the female officer says with a patronizing air.

"But you just said you went to his workplace and asked our neighbors. So, you *didn't* come to me first. If you did, you'd know he's perfectly *safe* in the Hamptons, visiting his mother for a bit," I say quickly.

"Mrs. Stratton—"

"I can call his mother right now if you'd like. You can speak to him yourself." My voice is firm, my smile unwavering.

The officers look at each other again. The male officer nods. "Sure. May we come in?"

"Of course."

They step inside, their eyes scanning the room, taking in the decor. "You and your husband must really love pink," the male officer comments.

"Oh, Dean lets me do whatever I want to the place; he trusts me."

"It smells lovely in here," the female officer says. "What is that, peach cobbler?"

"You have an amazing nose, that's exactly what it is. Would you like some?"

For a split second, I see her hesitation, but then she nods. "I'd love some."

I smile big, glancing at the male officer who shakes his head at his partner. "Mrs. Stratton, where is your phone? We'd like to just hear from Dr. Stratton so we can be on our way."

"Phone and peach cobbler coming right up! Follow me," I chirp, heading towards the kitchen. I hum in delight as I quickly scoop out a helping of peach cobbler from the trash can, depositing it into a bowl before they enter. I hand the bowl to the female officer. "Here you go, officer. I hope you enjoy it," she takes the bowl, her eyes scanning it for a moment before she digs in, the sweetness masking any hint of its trash can origin. "Now, let's get that phone call going," I say, dialing Marlo Stratton's number. I put the phone to my ear, steadying my voice as someone picks up on the other end.

"Hello?" Marlo Stratton's voice is tinged with curiosity.

"Hello, Marlo, it's Satara," I inject a false note of cheerfulness into my voice.

"Oh, hello Satara. How are you?"

I glance over at the cops, both with stern, scrutinizing looks on their faces as they watch me intently. I force a smile again, hoping it reaches my eyes. "I'm fantastic, Marlo. I just needed to speak to Dean. There's been a misunderstanding. Can you put him on the phone, please?" I say it casually as if we're discussing the weather.

"I'm sorry? Dean isn't here."

I furrow my brow. "What do you mean he's not *there?*" I let a note of desperate confusion creep in.

"He's not here, Satara. Is something going on?"

I put on my best performance, covering my mouth with a shaking hand. "Oh dear," I whisper darkly, my voice trembling just enough to sell it. The cops noticed my change in demeanor and inch closer. "Dean told me three weeks ago that he was flying there to see you." I make my words slow and deliberate.

"Satara, he hasn't come here. I haven't seen or heard from him. What are you talking about?"

I let my eyes fill with mock tears, glistening but not spilling, a perfect image of distressed confusion. "I don't know, Marlo. He said he was coming to visit you, to... to clear his head." My voice cracks artistically, enough to pull at heartstrings.

The female officer steps closer. "Mrs. Stratton, is everything okay?"

I look up at her, my eyes wide and pleading. "I thought he was with his mother," My bottom lip trembles. "I had no idea..."

The male officer's eyes narrow, but there's a flicker of sympathy, a sign that he's buying into the act. "Do you want to file a missing person's report?" He asks.

I lower the phone, pressing it against my chest dramatically, and then put it back up to my ear. "Marlo, I'm so sorry. I need to speak with the officers. I'll call you back." I end the call and stare at them, every ounce of sincerity I can muster radiating from me. "I honestly thought he was with her. I... I don't know where he could be." My shoulders slump as if the weight of my fabricated concern is too much to bear.

131

* * *

It started off very subtly. The next day at work, I decide to go all out on my appearance. Perfectly rolled curls in my hair, perfectly applied makeup with bright pink lipstick that popped against my complexion. My outfit is a satin emerald-green long-sleeved collared dress and black tights. I put on my highest heels. I stand out. I feel confident. And I want to see if Chris would notice me, if there was a difference in how he looked at me compared to every other time, which was with complete and utter indifference.

I get to work early, too anxious to wait, too desperate to see if the spell had worked. People filter in, each one giving me a look as if they had never seen me dressed up for work before. Even Sebastian, the office's resident flaming gay and unflappable gossip, is taken aback. His eyes almost fell out of his head when he saw me. "Wow, look at you, Ms. Satara. You look amazing!" Are you going to let me in on your secret on why you've been looking so amazing lately?"

I look at Sebastian and smile. "I'll tell you someday."

Sebastian's face falls, the disappointment palpable. "Why are you holding out on me? Come on, tell," he pouts, leaning across my desk, his head propped in his hands, giving me that exaggerated puppy dog look.

Just as Sebastian's persistent gaze becomes too much to bear, Chris walks in. Crisp white collared shirt and blue slacks, his suit jacket slung over his shoulder as he saunters in. I watch intently as he lifts his head, and without thinking, I swat Sebastian out of the way. Our eyes meet, and that's when I see it. The change in his demeanor, the look of surprise as he stares at me. My heart flutters, and knots tighten in my stomach. I don't even realize I'm standing up at my desk, every nerve ending on high alert. Chris blinks, his eyes still locked on me, as if trying to maintain his composure. "Morning, Chris," My voice barely masks the quake beneath.

He stands there a few feet from my desk, awestruck for a moment. "Good morning, Satara," he says loudly, almost too loudly, his voice cracking the stillness of the office. He squeezes his eyes shut, then looks down, embarrassment painting his features. I watch as he walks away, his steps leaden with shame, each motion seeming to drag on in slow motion.

I grin, sitting back down in my seat, my heart soaring. The spell worked.

* * *

My husband is officially a missing person. I filled out a report the day after the officers came to my home, asking too many questions. Today, I'm swinging by the police department to speak to them again at the request of the officers. If I had it my way, I'd never step foot in a police department.

Pulling up to the station feels like a pig's last trot to the slaughterhouse, the kind of dread that starts deep in your bones and radiates outward until it's all you can feel. As a killer, it's the place you least want to be—surrounded by astute gazes, every detective a Sherlock, every cop a silent observer. But I've honed the art of innocence.

To them, I'm just a secretary with a tendency to bake too much and a flair for immaculate style. I had even decided on my most virginal ensemble: a sweet gingham light blue dress with puffed sleeves that gracefully flared out and stopped just at my knees. Light pink purse and matching shoes complete the look. No one would suspect the pastel-encased venom within. I plaster on my brightest smile and yank the door open with faux eagerness.

I'm met by a man who's decidedly a detective. Brown tweed suit and big sunglasses worn indoors like it's an intricate part of his persona. He's the ambiguous kind of old where he could be anywhere from forty-five to a fabulous looking sixty. Salt and pepper hair, a giant dark mustache, squinty blue eyes. He pulls off his sunglasses for a better view, his gaze trailing over my ensemble with apparent curiosity. "Mrs. Stratton, thank you for coming in," his voice is low and gravely. "I'm Detective Joseph Wells, the lead investigator in your husband's disappearance."

I nod, a rehearsed shudder creeping into my shoulders, eyes glistening with a perfect blend of fear and sorrow. "Thank you for your help detective."

His gesture directs me down a corridor of uniform doors, each promising a different kind of doom. "I can only imagine what you're going through."

I offer a small, fragile smile. "It's been...difficult, but I'm managing," I reply, keeping my tone breathy; fragile. We stop before a nondescript door and Detective Wells opens it, revealing a cramped room cluttered with paperwork, and the stale scent of institutional neglect. I enter, feeling the prick of his eyes on my back, the predator assessing the prey. It's a game of chess, each move calculated, each word a step closer to unveiling or to further concealing. In my sweet gingham dress, I am the epitome of a loving, worried wife.

I sit down, the metal chair cold and unyielding under me, and Detective Wells pulls out a file, flipping it open with the nonchalance of a man who's seen it all. "Let me know what you think of these," he says.

I reach for the file, my fingers steady but my pulse quickening. The first sight of the missing poster flyer makes my heart catch in my throat. My sweet Dean. The photo—a shot, taken at work by a colleague, catches him in his white coat, a formal, almost solemn expression etched on his face. His eyes are steely, the lines around them rendered harsh by unflattering hospital lighting. It doesn't capture the essence of him, the man I once loved.

"This photo," I start, my voice tight with barely controlled outrage, "who chose this? It's completely wrong," I hold up the flyer, my hand trembling just a touch. "This is not my Dean. You should've come to *me!*"

Detective Wells remains unfazed, his face a stoic mask. "Mrs. Stratton, I—"

"Look at this!" I cut him off, stabbing a finger at the statistics listed beside the photo. "You didn't even get his weight correct. He is not 190 pounds! He is 160 at the most. He is *not* fat!" I feel the tears welling up, hot and manipulative, and bury my face in my hands. "Oh dear, you all are fucking incompetent, aren't you?"

"Mrs. Stratton, I apologize. One of his friends came by and provided the information. She said she knew him well and was eager to help. We obtained the photo from his workplace…"

"*She?*" I spit out, the word laced with venom. "Who are you talking about?"

Detective Wells clears his throat, fumbling as he pulls out a notepad from his pocket, pages rustling like dead leaves. "Ms. Lilah Patrick."

Anger boils in my stomach, a roiling, visceral thing threatening to spill over. I try to contain it, but the heat reaches my ears, flushing my face. "Lilah Patrick," I say darkly, her name a curse. "Does not know my husband better than me," venom drips from each word. I push the missing poster flyers across the table toward him, my movements precise, controlled. "Redo these. And I'll provide you with a better photo of *my* husband."

Wells stares at me, his giant mustache twitching with something I can't quite read. "Will do, Mrs. Stratton," he says casually, almost dismissively, brushing off my rage like lint from his sleeve. "In the meantime, would you be able to answer some questions for me? We usually don't file missing persons for a grown man unless they are endangered in some way, but we feel like Dr. Stratton wouldn't just up and leave, abandoning his job. He seemed very dedicated."

I lean back in my seat and cross my arms around my chest. "If you're going to ask the same questions as the officers that came to my house, then I have nothing else to say."

"Mrs. Stratton, you must understand, everything we do has a purpose. We want to find your husband safely and quickly, and the best way to do that is for you to be cooperative," his voice is firm, each word a controlled punch. I say nothing. "When was the last time you saw your husband?" he presses on, unyielding.

"The fourth of September," I reply steadily. "We went out for sushi the night before. That same night at home, he told me he was feeling burnt out and wanted to book a trip to spontaneously visit his mother on the East Coast—the Hamptons. When I came home from work the next day, he was already gone."

"And so, he just left without saying goodbye?"

"We said goodbye to each other the night before," I lean into the next part as I watch for his reaction. "He made love to me all night."

His face flushes, a dark hue spreading from his cheeks to his ears. Detective or not, men are all the same. "Okay," he says, clearing his throat like he's expelling the image from his mind. "Did he say he'd contact you when he got to the Hamptons?"

"He did," I pull out a cigarette, sticking it between my lips. "May I smoke?"

"No, you may not."

I gawk at him. A man telling me no. I pull the cigarette from my mouth. "Fine. It's not as if I'm stressed out or anything."

"Mrs. Stratton—" He stops mid-sentence, his eyes fixed on something behind me. I turn, following his gaze. There's Lilah, led by a cop toward the exit. Our eyes lock through the glass. Her face is a raw mix of worry and contempt, her bottom lip quivering as she bites back words or tears, maybe both.

I stand up abruptly, an electric surge propelling me toward the door. "Mrs. Stratton!" Detective Wells calls after me, but I'm already moving, each step amplifying my intent.

Lilah quickens her pace as she sees me approaching. "*Whoa, whoa,*" a male officer says as I brush past him; but he's a blur, insignificant in my tunnel vision.

I catch up to Lilah at the exit, my hand seizing her shoulder. She spins around, her movement abrupt, sharp, like a cornered animal ready to strike back. "What the fuck are you doing?" My voice is low, lethal.

Her eyes blaze with a flicker of defiance, a hint of fear. She tightens her lips, the quiver barely controlled. I can feel Wells closing in behind me, the tension thickening the air like smog. But in this moment, with Lilah pinned by my gaze, the rest of the world dissipates into mere background noise. "I am trying to help find Dean." Her eyes cut into me like daggers. She snatches her shoulder out of my grip, a swift, defiant move.

"I don't need your help," I snap back, my voice low and acidic. "In fact, I don't *want* your help. Stay the fuck away."

"Why don't you want me to help, Satara? What are you afraid of?" Her eyes glide over me, appraising, challenging.

"Nothing," I say, the word almost a purr. "Definitely not you."

Lilah's gaze flickers behind me, and I follow her line of sight. Detective Wells is watching us, curiosity etched into the lines of his face, his hands shoved into his pockets. The officers have paused too, spectators in our little drama. We are under scrutiny, our every movement dissected.

"I know, Lilah," I say, my voice dropping darkly.

She stares at me, her expression betraying nothing. I'm almost impressed by the mask she wears. "Know *what?*"

I laugh breathlessly, nodding my head with a tinge of madness. "And you *know* that I know," I let the words hang heavy between us.

Lilah frowns, a wrinkle marring her composed facade. "I have no earthly idea what you're talking about, Satara! You're acting strange. I don't understand why you wouldn't want me to help."

"Why *do* you want to help so badly, Lilah?" I ask, my voice rising, challenging. "How close were you and my husband *really?*" I enunciate the last part loudly, making sure Wells and the officers hear it. If she's going to paint me as a villain, I'll be damned if I don't dip her in the same ink.

Lilah shakes her head, taking a step back, glancing around nervously. "I'm going to go," she whispers, turning abruptly before hustling out the door. I turn to face the spectators, the entire police force seemingly hanging on to our every word. I clear my throat, the silence almost unbearable.

"That's my best friend," I say casually.

* * *

Digging up Dean's body wasn't supposed to be part of the plan. He was meant to stay there forever, nestled under the lemon tree, hidden and safe beneath my watchful eye. But Lilah's meddling has ruined that. Now I have to move him. Just in case. Just as I did when I killed him and buried him, I wait until three a.m. The dead hour—early enough that I can be done by sunrise, but late enough that the entire neighborhood is lost in sleep.

With a helmet light strapped to my forehead and a shovel in hand, I get to work, each stroke gouging the earth with a rhythm that's both primal and painstaking. My arms burn, muscles screaming, but I can't stop. My limbs are limp noodles, but there's no turning back now. The shovel hits something solid, and I brace myself. I grab the tarp I'd stashed in the garage weeks ago and lay it out next to the open grave. The helmet light illuminates the body, and I gasp. Even though I've killed before, I've never faced them in this state. Dean looks inhuman, a parody of life, a horror show. His face is a grimace of liquefied features—eyes sunken into hollow pits, cheeks sagging into a death mask. The skin is a sickly shade of gray, stretched taut like decaying parchment over decomposing muscle. His lips have peeled back in a grotesque, eternal smile, teeth grinning yellowed and cracked. His suit, once pristine, is now a tattered shroud, clinging to his rotting frame.

By his arms, I start to pull him out of the hole, my stomach churning with every tug. His skin disintegrates under my touch, turning to mush, flaps of gray dead tissue sloughing off the bone. It clings to my fingers, cold and slimy, like wet, decayed paper. My mind is screaming, every instinct rebelling, but I force myself not to react, smothering my screams of disgust and horror. I pull and pull, each movement a march through hell. His limbs are stiff, a macabre puppet in my grip, every inch a testament to the life I extinguished.

Finally, he's out and on the tarp. I stare back at him as he stares back at me. "Hi my Deany," I whisper.

I then wrap him up, the tangy scent of the lemon tree mingling with the stench of decay. The night is deep and silent, but I can't shake the feeling that the earth itself is holding its breath, watching, waiting. My task isn't done, but for now, Dean rests uneasily under my control, his future as uncertain as the night that embraces me. I drag his body, cocooned in the tarp, and wrestle it into a big black suitcase. It's a dark dance, fitting him in, bending and twisting limbs that resist, reminding me of his stubbornness in life. But the suitcase is big enough, just barely. As I zip it closed, the finality of it is a blade slicing through the fog of my thoughts. I roll it to my car, the suitcase gliding over the rough ground too easily, unnervingly silent. In this moment, I'm almost grateful Dean had an SUV. Even in death, his possessions are convenient.

I drive, the night pressing against the windows, an oppressive darkness that seems to seep into the car itself. My eyes burn from the lack of sleep, each blink a desperate plea for relief. But I'm determined. One hour, maybe more—I lose track of time, the clock becoming a meaningless entity. The landscape blurs, shifting from suburban familiarity to the vast, empty expanse of the desert.

When I finally stop, I step out into a world that's eerily still, the desert wrapped in a shroud of quiet. The moon hangs low, casting a pale, ghostly light that stretches shadows into shapes. The air is cooler here, crisp and biting, carrying the faintest scent of sagebrush and dust. Cacti stand sentinel, their spiny arms reaching out like skeletal fingers. The distant mountains are dark silhouettes, jagged lines against the night sky.

The ground underfoot is hard, unyielding, the occasional crunch of gravel breaking the silence like a whisper. Sparse bushes dot the landscape, their twisted branches casting eerie shadows that dance in the moonlight.

I find a cluster, a place where the earth seems to fold in on itself, creating a shallow hollow. Here, under the indifferent gaze of the stars, I dump the suitcase, its contents a horrific companion to the natural beauty surrounding it. The suitcase lands with a dull thud, settling into the brush like it belongs there. I stand back, the reality of the scene hitting me like a tidal wave. I inhale deeply, the cold air filling my lungs, grounding me. I am alone with my actions, the desert my only witness. The stars blink overhead, indifferent, eternal, and I turn back to the car, each step pulling me away from the darkness I've buried.

SUGAR

* * *

I carefully take the curlers out of my hair, each strand bouncing back in perfect waves, and apply my red lipstick with a steady hand. Red lips, red shoes, black dress. I feel like a femme fatale, which, in truth, I am. I hum, delighted at my reflection, the mirror reflecting someone who had everything under control. It's as if nothing happened last night; no one would suspect I spent hours exhuming and driving my husband's body to the desert. It's as if I got a full eight hours of sleep, when I only got less than four.

Sometimes, I genuinely amaze myself.

Stepping out the door, my heels click satisfyingly on the ground. I stop in my tracks when I see my next-door neighbor, Glenda Hanson, watering her roses out front. Mrs. Hanson, the epitome of fabulousness—an older lady but ageless, rocking her short haircut with the poise of Liza Minnelli.

Normally she smiles and waves at me; but today, she just stares, her expression unreadable, eyes narrowed. I watch her set the watering can down and retreat inside, not a hint of her usual warmth. Strange. I'll have to speak to her another time. Right now, I'm late for book club. I climb into my car, the engine purring to life, and drive to Cynthia's house. Cynthia's house is an architectural marvel in a very upper-class neighborhood in Orange County. The kind of place that stands as a monument to success and modernity. Big and imposing, yet sleek and chic. Its exterior is a blend of glass and stone, reflecting the sky in a way that makes the house seem to float. Floor-to-ceiling windows offer glimpses of immaculate interiors—tasteful, minimalistic decor that screams subtle opulence.

Manicured lawns flank the long driveway, and the garden itself is a sculpted masterpiece, the sort of landscaping that requires a small army of gardeners to maintain. As I pull up, I can almost smell the fresh paint and polished marble. Cynthia's house is the kind of place where every detail is a statement, where each piece of furniture is curated, every plant meticulously chosen.

I step out of the car, my heels clicking against the pristine driveway. I knock, straightening my dress. Today, I'm just another woman at a book club, not a woman who got rid of her dead husband's body in the desert last night. Cynthia opens the door, her face a canvas of shock and confusion. "Satara. What are you doing here?"

I flash a bright, unwavering smile. "I'm here for the book club, silly."

Cynthia stares at me, flabbergasted. "But you're kicked out," she insists, her voice rising slightly, raw edges of panic slicing through her composed veneer.

"No, I'm not," I reply, my smile widening. I tilt my head, giving her an almost playful look. "That is not a pretty face you're making."

Cynthia's mouth gapes open, her mind clearly racing to find something to say. She stutters, but before any coherent words form, I cut her off, leaning in slightly.

"Remember, I know your little secret," I say through my smile.

She stills, a flurry of emotions battling across her face. Anger, then the resignation of defeat. She steps back, pulling the door open wider. "Satara, please come in," she says flatly, her voice drained of its usual warmth.

"Thanks, doll," I blow her a kiss as I step inside. My heels click purposefully on her pristine marble floors, echoing through the expansive, modern foyer. The entryway is a testament to her impeccable taste—clean lines, sleek surfaces, an impressive chandelier that catches the light just so, creating a dance of glimmers on the walls. Modern art pieces are strategically placed, each one a conversation starter on its own. Her home isn't my taste. My house is perfect for me; it feels like a warm hug with the bright pastel colors and antique China hung on the walls. Although Cynthia's home is beautiful, it feels lifeless.

We move deeper into the home to a second sunken living room where Cynthia held the club when she hosted. I enter the room, and immediately, the air thickens with tension. Every eye turns to me, shock painted across their faces. "Hi, ladies." I keep my voice light and airy. My gaze flits to Lizzie, whose brows furrow with displeasure, her arms crossed tightly over her chest.

"Look who decided to surprise us," Cynthia says, her voice strained as she follows me into the room. Lizzie and Cheryl are on one sofa, while Dawn and Cynthia take the other. I nestle myself beside Dawn, directly across from Lizzie.

"I'm going to address the elephant in the room," I announce, feigning sadness masterfully. "My husband, Dean, is unfortunately missing," I place a hand over my heart. "I couldn't handle being alone during this time. I needed to see you ladies."

A heavy silence follows, the room holding its breath.

"Oh, I heard. I'm so sorry, Satara," Dawn says genuinely, her eyes soft with sympathy. "It's really awful what you're going through."

I smile thinly and turn to Dawn, my gaze lingering. Poor Dawn. Poor naive, useless Dawn. Sweet as pie, but she reminds me of a baby bird with broken wings, vulnerable and fragile. At least the bruise on her face has finally disappeared. "Thank you, Dawn. That means a lot."

"We're so sorry. We hope he turns up fine," Cheryl echoes.

"Yes we do," Cynthia chimes in, her tone flat and lifeless.

"Shall we get back to discussing the book?" Lizzie interjects, lifting her copy of *Go Ask Alice,* which ironically was about a young girl who takes LSD and descends into a life of debauchery. My smile sharpens just a fraction, but I quickly wipe it from my face.

* * *

I walk around the office, methodically handing out missing person posters for Dean, a painted mask of worry and helplessness over my usual confidence. "If you haven't heard, my husband is missing," I say with each handoff, watching the uncomfortable looks that paint themselves on people's faces. Pitied stares, mumbled apologies thrumming in the air like a dissonant symphony. "Thank you for your concern," I offer. Inside, I marvel at how easy it is to manipulate the narrative, to twist perceptions with just the right tilt of my head, the perfect quiver in my voice.

I intentionally pass Chris's open office, letting my heels announce my presence in sharp, staccato clicks. His head snaps up, eyes locking onto me. "Satara!" He calls before I can move out of his view. I smile to myself, a private little victory before turning around to face him. His eyes are a tumult of emotions, a storm of pity mingling with something else, something that makes my pulse quicken.

"Yes, Chris?"

He opens his mouth to say something, his gaze holding mine in an almost desperate search for composure. "I'm so sorry to hear about your husband," he says standing up, his concern genuine. "How are you holding up?"

I raise an eyebrow. "I thought you didn't want to discuss feelings with me. *It's work*, remember?" I tease, enjoying the way his discomfort makes him flounder.

Chris laughs weakly, shaking his head. "I did say that didn't I?"

"You did."

Chris clears his throat. "Well, I apologize for that. You can come to me anytime, Satara. I hope you know that." His eyes delve into mine, and for a second, I'm almost swept away by the intensity.

"Thank you, Chris," I move closer, slowly, deliberately. I watch as he retreats slightly, nearly imperceptible, but I catch it—the way he can't handle my proximity, the way it almost tips him over into dangerous territory. "Keeping this between you and me, Dean was never really good to me," I confide in a hushed whisper, my voice a silken thread easing through the tension.

His face falls into shock. "Really? Well, that's unfortunate."

"I was planning on divorcing him before he disappeared."

"Marriage is hard, isn't it?"

I shrug, drawing even nearer, my hand bracing against his desk. The distance between us shrinks to less than a foot—a tantalizing closeness that feels electric. "Not if it's with the right person."

He smiles weakly, eyes dropping to the ground. "Sometimes I feel like I might've not chosen the right person."

"Oh?" My voice is a gentle prod, my lips curling into a frown to conceal my growing delight.

Chris sighs heavily. "I mean, Lizzie's an amazing mother to Sophia. I wouldn't change that. But…I don't know. Sometimes I feel like she doesn't appreciate me as much as I appreciate her. And she's always complaining about my job. You know she wants me to quit and find another job with less hours, right?"

"That's absurd."

"Right? I'm sorry I can't stay home and cater to her every need. I'm busy making money so we can live. God knows she's not going to do it." His frustration boils over, and he runs a hand through his hair, leaving it deliciously tousled.

I stare at him, my desire flaring into something nearly uncontrollable. To say I'm turned on would be a gross understatement. Watching him badmouth Lizzie, seeing the raw edges of his emotional turmoil; it's intoxicating. I want to devour him.

Chris shakes his head, a heavy exhalation of regret. "I'm sorry, Satara. I shouldn't be dumping all of this on you, especially since you're going through your own thing right now," he mutters, his voice fraying at the edges.

Without thinking, I put my hand out and place it gently on his arm. A jolt of electricity runs through me, sparking a bright, visceral connection between us. "Please don't apologize," I say softly. "Just as you said you're here for me if I need to talk, the same goes for you. Don't be afraid to talk to me."

Chris stares back at me, his gaze flickering down to where my hand rests on his arm. I can see his throat work as he swallows hard, his body tensing. "Thank you."

The intensity in his gaze is almost tangible, and I smile, savoring the delight as his eyes shift to my lips, glossy and inviting in their pink hue. My lipstick, cotton candy flavored, makes my mouth look tantalizingly sweet. I hold his gaze, leaning in just a fraction, enough to breach the boundary without overstepping. The air between us is charged, every breath a potential spark. In this moment, Chris is trapped between his growing attraction and the suffocating layers of his guilt, every fiber of his being pulled taut with the conflicting desires warring inside him.

I let the silence stretch. "I mean it. You can talk to me anytime, Chris," my voice is a soft caress. "We don't have to be alone in this."

For a fleeting moment, I think he might lean in, his body swaying almost imperceptibly towards mine. But then, he stops himself, pulling back with a strained breath, his jaw tightening. "I'll remember that, Satara."

The tension lingers, a heady mix of anticipation and restraint. I step back, reluctantly giving him room to breathe, but the connection between us remains, a taut wire humming just below the surface. As I walk away, I don't look back. I don't need to; I can feel his eyes on me, burning with a mix of longing and frustration.

In my head, I marked each chapter of my life with the men I had loved, as if they were bookmarks in the dog-eared novel of my existence. My early teens were defined by Michael's brooding eyes and his manipulative tendencies, my mid-twenties were the Waylon chapter—filled with nightly phone calls—and as I transitioned into my late twenties and early thirties, that chapter segued seamlessly into Dean. Dean, with his Golden Boy charm that left me with countless insecurities that I was slowly untangling from my psyche. Now, approaching my mid-thirties, a new chapter was dawning, one to be marked by Chris.

This is how I viewed love: not just as the most important thing, but as the singular narrative thread weaving through the tapestry of my life. It was a strange, almost clinical obsession, a need to have my identity mirrored and validated by the man who occupied my thoughts. When I looked at a photo of myself, I could pinpoint exactly which man had been the center of my universe at that moment. Each captured smile, each distant gaze was a timestamp of obsession. Even now, when most of them were dead—unfortunate casualties of my intensity—their impact lingered. Their ghosts lived on in the most mundane details of my life—a favorite perfume, a song on the radio, the way I styled my hair.

My lovers, those lost obsessions, were etched into every aspect of my being, haunting my steps, my choices, my very breath. And now, as I stood on the precipice of a new infatuation, I wondered if Chris could sense it—the legacy of those who came before him. Love, for me, was an endless cycle of rebirth and death; each man a phoenix rising from the ashes of the last, burning brightly before succumbing to the inevitable. And I, ever the devoted keeper of these flames, continued to mark my life with their passage, a perennial witness to both conflagration and smoldering ruin.

* * *

Dean was a lot more popular of a man than I thought. The candlelight vigil was his mother's idea, and she flew in today for it, claiming the guest room with a sense of entitlement. She announced it as if she were doing me a favor, though if I had any say, I would've told her to get a room at a hotel. But of course, there was no way I was going to tell her that. Not only would it seem suspicious, but to argue with Marlo Stratton was to invite disaster; the woman thrived on conflict like a wolf on raw meat.

So, with passive aggressiveness seeping into my veins, I accepted her presence and her help in organizing this spectacle. We were at the park, setting up as people began to trickle in, a mix of Dean's coworkers, old friends, neighbors. A sea of candle flames flickered against the encroaching dusk; the scene almost unbearable in its saccharine sincerity. If only they all knew that Dean was a lying, cheating bastard.

Marlo and I worked side by side, our hands busy. She had that aura of a woman who masked her grief with efficiency, her hands moving with a determined grace. "You know, Satara, Dean's always been the kind to inspire loyalty."

"Apparently," I mutter, barely concealing my resentment towards both the task and her obliviousness. Just then Detective Wells, a looming figure in the crowd, catches my eye, and I knew I had to maintain this facade of the devoted, somber wife. I straighten up, forcing a tear to glisten on my cheek as I place a small bouquet of roses in the center of the vigil setup. I glance at the growing crowd, amazed at the number of Dean's coworkers and old friends who had already arrived. It seems every other person bore a glint of admiration in their eyes, recounting tales of his prowess as a doctor, his kind-hearted nature. The detective's presence ensures that I couldn't falter, couldn't let the mask slip for even a moment.

Inside, though, my heart is a coiled spring, ready to snap. This performance, this charade—each act brought me closer to getting away with it all. I just had to keep playing the part. That's when I see the camera. Its unblinking eye trained on me, ready to capture every move I make. Detective Wells had warned me that news stations would be here but seeing them in the flesh made it all feel too real. What else did I expect? A man as highly regarded as Dean missing—of course, it would make news. I swallow the knot of fear in my throat.

Oh, I am so terrified, but I am also very entertained.

This is almost like a game, the stakes high, the performance thrilling.

I'm rearranging a floral bouquet that Marlo had put together—she'd done a terrible job mixing the flowers, their colors clashing rather than complementing each other—when I catch a flash of red in the corner of my eye. I turn to see Lilah in all black, staring at the blown-up photograph of Dean, her hand clutched to her heart, tears misting her eyes. The sight of her, feigning grief, brings a rush of anger that bubbles up inside me like a volcanic eruption.

I stalk over, my footsteps purposeful, my voice laced with derision. "Of course, you'd show up."

Lilah turns, exasperation etched on her face. "Please, not right now, Satara."

"Why not?" I retort, my voice rising.

She stares at me, her eyes hardening. "What were you implying the other day at the police station? Were you trying to make it seem as if I did something to Dean in front of the detective?"

"I don't know, did you?"

"We both know it wasn't me," Lilah says, leaning in close, her voice dropping to a whisper. "We both know Dean is dead by someone else's hand." Her voice breaks on the last word.

I shake my head, my anger simmering. "You should be grateful I don't kick you out right now you hussy."

"Hussy," she repeats, a sharp laugh escaping her. "I'm not the one who brought another man home when my husband's been missing for only a few weeks."

"Yeah, but you slept with a married man. That makes you worse."

"Sleeping with a married man and sleeping with a man *while* you're married is the exact same. No better, no worse," she says indignantly. "You know what is worse? *Murder."*

"You have no idea what you're talking about, Lilah."

"Don't I?" she says, her head tilting, her gaze unwavering.

The silence stretches between us, a taut wire of hostility. We stare at each other, daggers in our eyes, the tension palpable. I only break my stare when I hear Marlo call out for me. "If you'll excuse me," I say, my voice dripping with irony. "I have to go speak about my missing husband."

I turn away from Lilah. The camera captures my every step, the lens an omnipresent reminder of the performance I must uphold. I move toward the podium, the weight of the evening pressing down on me like a shroud. It's time to play my part, to weave another layer into the intricate game I've set in motion. I look out into the gathering crowd. It's a pulsating mass of faces, flickering candlelight casting ghostly dance shadows, the whole scene a surreal tableau of collective mourning. Just as the weight of the moment starts to suffocate me, I tap Marlo on the shoulder. "You should go first," I whisper to her.

Marlo looks surprised, her eyebrows shooting up in a fleeting moment of hesitation before she nods. She grabs a box of tissues, walking to the podium with a solemn grace. The crowd quiets, their collective breath almost palpable in the evening air. Marlo takes a deep breath, clutching the sides of the podium as if to steady herself. Her eyes scan the sea of faces, each one expectant and somber.

"Thank you all for coming," she begins, her voice quivering. "It means the world to our family to see so many of you here tonight. It speaks volumes about the kind of man my son, Dean, is—it tells me that he has touched many lives, much more than I ever imagined," she pauses, a shaky hand lifting to swipe at her tear-streaked cheeks with a tissue.

Marlo's shoulders tremble, her tears flowing freely now. She breaks into a story about the time Dean was nine and he saved a turtle from being run over, jumping out the car as they shouted for him to come back, but he was determined to save it. After she's finished with the story, she crumples the tissue in her hand, her gaze unwavering as she continues. Marlo looks down for a long moment, gathering her courage, her resolve.

When she looks up again, her eyes are fierce, shining with a mixture of sorrow and determination. "Thank you, each and every one of you, for being here tonight. For standing with us, for believing in Dean, for not giving up hope. Together, we will bring him home."

As Marlo makes her way back to my side, she nods once at me, gesturing it that it's my turn to go up, unable to speak. I walk up to the podium, my mind a dizzy carousel of thoughts. The crowd is a blur of faces, the flickering candles casting an eerie glow that makes everything seem dreamlike, almost unreal.

I take a deep breath, grounding myself as I step up to speak. "Thank you all for being here tonight," I begin, my voice steady but heavy with emotion. "Dean is a man who has touched so many lives. As a doctor, he has healed countless people, brought comfort and hope wherever he goes. As a husband, he was… dependable, a constant presence in my life," my hands grip the edges of the podium, the wood grounding me as I continue. "We've all felt the weight of his absence. Each day without him has been a struggle, a void that can't be filled. But seeing all of you here, it gives me strength."

Just as I'm about to go on, my eyes scan the crowd and land on a familiar face. Jasper. I stare, my heart lurching in my chest as he stands there, his confusion palpable. He looks bewildered, his brows knitting together as if trying to unravel some invisible thread of understanding. My words falter, and in that split second, Jasper turns and walks away, his form weaving through the crowd. My pulse quickens as I see Detective Wells observing the scene, his eyes narrowing before he follows Jasper, his steps purposeful and intent on uncovering whatever truth lies behind his sudden departure.

I swallow hard, my heart pounding so loudly I can barely hear my own voice. I had been ignoring his calls since the night we met, unable to find the words to tell him that I had changed my mind about him. He was no longer the chosen one. If I had known he had stalking tendencies like me, I would have just called him and told him that it was over before it even started. I throw my entire planned speech aside and I force myself to continue, quelling my emotions.

"There's something I need to share, something that's been weighing on me," I choke out. "Dean was not perfect. He had his flaws, just like any of us. I recently discovered he was having an affair with my best friend and neighbor, Lilah Patrick."

Gasps ripple through the crowd, a collective murmur of disbelief and shock. Faces turn, eyes narrowing in on Lilah like a spotlight zeroing in on a guilty party. The camera's lens zooms in, capturing her look of utter astonishment, her cheeks flushing as she raises a hand to cover her face. She stands frozen for a moment before she bolts, pushing through the crowd, her retreat a hasty mess of broken dignity. I take a deep breath, steadying myself as I focus back on the task at hand.

"Despite his betrayal, despite the hurt he caused me due to his infidelity; I still want Dean to come home. Dean, if you can hear me… I know you're ashamed of your actions, and I can't pretend they didn't hurt. But everyone misses you. Your colleagues, your friends, your family... we all miss you," I let my gaze sweep across the faces in the crowd before settling on the camera. "Dean, please come home. We need you. *I* need you. We can work through this together. Just come back to us."

The silence that follows is a heavy, expectant thing, hanging in the air like the closing curtain of a tense play.

* * *

Do you think Dean's actions are the reason he disappeared?

How do you feel about Dean now that you know he's been unfaithful?

Do you think you somehow facilitated the affair between Lilah and your husband?

I shoot my head up. I didn't expect that last question. It's a line of thought I'd never pursued until now. This is why I liked Dr. Maggie. Sometimes my blinding rage and desperation clouded my thinking, and it was a relief to have someone sift through the chaos for me, someone who could cut through the tangled depths of my rage. But now, as her query hangs in the air between us, it feels like a gavel striking down with a cold, clarifying force.

Did I facilitate the affair between Dean and Lilah?

Dr. Maggie looks up from the magazine splayed across her desk, one of those free local rags with Dean's face plastered on the page like someone trying to sell hope. I walked into her office feeling like a child summoned by a stern teacher, a knot tightening in my gut. The story had already slipped past my lips in rehearsed lines, the same lines I'd fed the cops, but with an acid twist here, a sharper sting there. I could never call Lilah a bitch in front of Detective Wells, but within the safe, suffocating walls of Dr. Maggie's office, the word felt like a release valve. "Lilah is a fucking bitch," I spat out, enunciating each consonant with a venomous satisfaction. It felt good, like breaking a glass just for the sound of it shattering.

Dr. Maggie's pen froze, mid-note, and for the first time, I see her eyes widen just a fraction. Was it that serious? I guess when one of your patients' husbands goes missing, you start taking your job very seriously. I still had no idea if she suspected me, if those eyes that were now intently searching my face were measuring for guilt or sorrow. Her silence seemed to amplify the weight of her unasked questions, but only one that truly mattered.

"Are you blaming me for the affair?" I ask, bewildered, my words tinged with an edge that tastes like panic. I know it wasn't her intention to accuse, but I am entrenched in defense mode, my walls erecting themselves in an instant. She watches me, her gaze steady and unyielding, as if she's waiting for me to confront not just her questions, but my own truths. The silence stretches, a chasm filled with my insecurities, my grievances, and that gnawing, unspoken fear—is this my fault?

Dr. Maggie folds her hands and leans in just a little, her voice a murmur of reason slicing through my inner tumult. "It's not about blame," she says softly. "It's about understanding."

Understanding. The word hangs heavy, and I realize that this is the crux of it, the reason I'm here, not just to vent but to unravel the tight coils of my own complicity, whether real or imagined. And perhaps, to finally see through the smoky haze of my rage and grief, a clearer glimpse of the tangled, painful truth.

Almost a year ago, Dean and I, along with a few friends, rented a cabin in Big Bear for six days. It was during the snow season, and Dean was all about skiing. The trip was his brainchild. If I had it my way, it would have been a cozy, romantic getaway for just the two of us. But Dean, being Dean, invited his friends, Kenny and Lee. I only invited Lilah. I didn't need to invite a whole crowd—Lilah and my husband were more than enough.

The first few days were a blur of laughter, endless glasses of wine, and exhilarating ski runs. During our stint there I baked a variety of desserts while Dean's friend Lee, who happened to be a professional chef, took over the cooking. We gorged ourselves on food and alcohol, the room alive with the infectious energy of old friends and new conversations. We played charades and gin rummy, the fireplace crackling and laughter ricocheting off the wooden walls.

On our last night we all got high on acid and played charades. I noticed Lilah and Kenny flirting a bit—something I had anticipated. Kenny was an eligible bachelor and exuded rugged handsomeness. When you put two single beautiful people together, sparks are bound to fly. I pulled her aside, both of us giggling like schoolgirls. "Do you like him?" I whispered; my voice tinged with playful curiosity.

Lilah's face was flushed. She looked extra beautiful that night, with her minimal makeup and a pop of red lipstick, her hair pulled back into a tight ponytail. She held a wineglass between her index and middle fingers, swinging it delicately in the air. I envied how effortlessly graceful she was; if I tried the same thing, I'd probably drop the glass and shatter it, embarrassing myself in the process. But not Lilah—she was as graceful as a deer. She grinned, shaking her head. "Sort of. He's kind of a redneck though. We don't really make a good match," she said, her expression half-teasing.

"What do you mean? Kenny is a stud. And I thought you loved the rugged look. It's not like he wears a cowboy hat. Imagine dating a man who wore a cowboy hat, how crazy would that be for us?" I laughed, and she shuddered dramatically.

"I don't want to imagine it," Lilah said with a smile as she leaned against the wall, her eyes sparkling. We stood chatting in the middle of the dark hallway as if it was the most natural thing in the world. Back then, it was. "I don't know. I'm just... not ready to pursue anything serious right now," she said, her voice softening like she was letting me in on a secret.

"Who said anything about something serious?"

She shot me a knowing glance, and we both cracked up again, the kind of laughter that racked your entire body. We kept laughing hysterically until someone yelled out at us.

"Hey, what are you ladies doing, putting on lipstick? Get in here!" It was either Lee or Kenny, all I knew was that it wasn't my Dean. I couldn't be bothered to differentiate the difference between men's voices that weren't my husband's.

"We better get back in there," I said, linking my arm in hers and leading her back to the living room. I snuggled back up to Dean, settling into his lap and feeling the reassured weight of his arms around my torso. My hand squeezed his thigh, my fingers digging in just enough to feel the meld of muscle and comfort.

"You okay?" He whispered in my ear, his breath warm against my skin.

"Very," I replied, a smile painting my face. I looked back at him, the crinkles around his eyes behind his black-framed glasses giving me butterflies. His light brown hair was delightfully messy tonight, and he wore my favorite sweater, the blue cashmere one I got him for Christmas the year before. "I can't wait for you to ravage me tonight," I whispered slyly into his ear.

Dean's face fell flat, and disappointment settled into my stomach like a stone. His eyes, soft and apologetic, met mine with a rueful smile. "I've had too much to drink, sweetie," he said. I didn't say anything back. I got up, grabbed the rest of the wine bottle we'd been sharing, and stormed out of the room. I stalked back to our bedroom and slammed the door behind me, the sound reverberating in the stillness. Sad and angry, I crawled into bed and pulled the blankets over my head, tears pricking at the corners of my eyes. The least he could've done was say that he'd try. What man wouldn't want to make love to his wife during a cozy cabin getaway? It was upsetting.

A few minutes later, I heard a soft knock, and the door creaked open. "Go away," I said, my voice muffled by the blankets.

"It's Lilah."

I didn't respond, just pulled the blankets off my face and grabbed the wine bottle off the nightstand, taking a long sip before setting it back down. Lilah sighed and crawled into bed with me, wrapping her leg around me in a comforting hug. Her body was small enough that it felt like nothing was on me at all, just a faint, weightless presence.

"My husband doesn't want to have sex with me."

She smoothed my hair out of my face, her touch gentle and soothing. "He does, trust me." Her voice was like warm honey.

I sat up quickly, staring at her. "So why did he turn me down?" I asked, my voice tinged with frustration. "It's as if I'm a goblin to him."

Lilah laughed, a soft, melodic sound. "You just need to make him more intrigued," she suggested. "He's a man, Satara. You need to seduce him. Drive him wild."

I shrugged, a mixture of doubt and curiosity swirling within me. "Got any suggestions on how?"

Lilah smiled, her eyes locking onto mine with a knowing glint. And then, without warning, she leaned in and kissed me. Not just a peck, but a full-on French kiss, her tongue exploring my mouth. I pulled back in shock, my fingers pressed to my lips, the taste of her lingering, a mixture of red wine and strawberries. Lilah stared at me knowingly, and suddenly, it all clicked. Maybe it was the acid and copious amounts of alcohol in my system, but I thought it was a brilliant idea. I smiled and jumped off the bed, running to the door. "Hey honey, would you come in here please?" I yelled, my voice carrying through the cabin.

Lilah giggled, and I giggled along with her as I climbed back onto the bed. We sat up on our knees, the air between us electric. I grabbed Lilah's face and started making out with her, my tongue exploring her mouth. It felt strange; foreign, making out with my best friend, but at the same time, it felt utterly and completely normal. I saw colors. Red, orange, yellow, blue. I stopped kissing her to look at her face. She opened her mouth to laugh but instead let out an inhuman noise, somewhere between a squeak and an inhalation of breath, like she couldn't breathe properly. Her pupils were completely dilated. Mine probably were too. We both grabbed each other's faces and started laughing. "Ow, too hard," I said with a laugh, pulling her hands off my face. She screeched like a dinosaur, and we both fell into a fit of laughter, and then went back to kissing.

I heard Dean's loud footsteps bounding towards the door. He probably thought I was hurt, the urgency in his steps unmistakable. The door flew open. To say Dean was shocked would be an understatement. His mouth hung open as he stood there, eyes wide, taking in the sight of Lilah and me locked in a heated, unexpected embrace. Lilah was getting into it, her hands tangling in my hair, cupping my butt and breasts. Her touch fueled me, made me bolder, and I responded similarly, my hands covering the entirety of her tiny, perfect breasts. For the first time in a long while, I felt truly sexy; empowered by the rawness of the moment. I paused just long enough to beckon Dean into the room. His eyes were wide, still watching, perhaps trying to decipher if this was real. It was hard to tell if he was turned on; Dean was always a puzzle when it came to sex.

"Come join, sweetie," I said with a giggle, feeling electric. Just as Lilah pulled my top off and put my nipple in her mouth, Dean finally closed the door behind him, stepping further into the room. His movements were deliberate, methodical, as he undressed. He pulled off his glasses and tossed them aside, a careless gesture that told me just how turned on he must be.

"I can't believe this is happening," he muttered, his voice a mix of awe and disbelief as he climbed onto the bed. I grabbed him, pulling him into the thick of things, making sure I got a piece of him before Lilah. Our mouths melded together with a newfound urgency, a desperate need to reconnect. I wanted him to feel me, to want me as much as I wanted him. Lilah was already pulling off his underwear, her hands working to get him hard. But he still wasn't, which surprised me. A flicker of doubt threatened to pierce my euphoria.

"Here, let me try," I said, gently pushing him onto his back and taking him into my mouth. Time seemed to both fly and stand still, a paradox of pleasure and tension. I ignored the gnawing jealousy of Lilah making out with Dean and tried not to let it ruin the moment. He seemed to be in a trance, his eyes halfway open as Lilah's tongue explored his mouth, as if he was caught in the surrealism of the moment.

The room was filled with sounds of soft moans, the air thick with the scent of skin and wine. I moved my mouth with intent, trying to coax a response from him, while Lilah's fingers traced patterns on my back, her touch soothing and a spark all at once. I felt the weight of Dean's hand on my head, guiding me, grounding me in the reality of us, of this rare, wild moment. It was chaos and clarity, an unexpected adventure that was rewriting the boundaries of our love, our desire.

I glanced up, catching a glimpse of Dean's eyes—no longer bewildered, but ignited with a hunger that mirrored my own. The shock was wearing off, replaced by something raw and primal. Soon, he got hard enough for me to mount him. The connection was instant, electric. In the mess of tangled sheets and flaring desires, he came in two minutes. Relief washed over me, a torrential wave drowning out the edges of my insecurity. He didn't have sex with Lilah. It felt like an unspoken declaration of love, a deliberate choice. I couldn't help but beam. Lilah slipped out of bed, the remnants of our night clinging to her like an unearthed secret she wasn't sure she wanted. She muttered something about needing a cold shower, her eyes avoiding ours. The room felt emptier without her, like we'd just thrown the universe off balance.

The next morning, the three of us made a pact. A solemn promise that last night would dissolve into nothing, swept under the rug of our collective memory. We'd vowed for nothing to change. I had deluded myself into thinking the threesome had somehow fixed our problems, that the fire and chaos of it had rekindled something long lost. I clung to the idea that maybe, just maybe, the undercurrents of that night would sew us back together, yet the reality was a heavier burden. We had ventured into uncharted territories of desire, thinking maybe it would lead us back to each other.

I could see it in Dean's eyes, a distant flicker of doubt. Maybe we'd unearthed not a cure, but a truth we weren't ready to face. In the end, the memory of that threesome, the heat and the blur of it, lingered bittersweet, a token of a night that might've just pushed us further apart.

"Do you want to talk about that night in Big Bear?" Maggie asks me, her voice soft but insistent, like she's peeling back a scab.

I shake my head. "Not really," I say. "Besides the fact that it was a huge fucking mistake, I have nothing else to say about it."

Maggie's gaze doesn't waver. "Do you think that's when the affair started?"

My chest tightens. "He started to become distant after that trip. It was only shortly after Big Bear that I began to suspect he was cheating." I shift uncomfortably in my seat.

Maggie's blue eyes bore into mine, unflinching. "You can't completely blame yourself for what happened."

"You're right, because the threesome was Lilah's idea. That bitch was probably plotting to steal him away from me the entire time. That's why she wanted to do it," I say, feeling the bitterness coat my tongue.

Maggie leans back, studying me like she's dissecting a complex equation. "You think she had ill intentions that night?"

"*Of course* she did," I say, the words rushing out. "I was so wrapped up in trying to fix whatever was broken between Dean and me, I didn't see it. She played us both."

"And Dean?" Maggie presses, her voice gentle yet probing.

A sigh escapes me. "He wasn't blameless, but he was a weak man. Vulnerable. And she took advantage of that."

Maggie nods, her fingers tapping lightly against her notebook. "That doesn't make it your fault."

I don't say anything, I just close my eyes and think about Dean who I loved so much, who was now dead, stuffed into a suitcase and discarded like trash in the desert. The thought is too much, a weight presses down on my chest, making it hard to breathe, thinking about the finality of it all.

"Are you contemplating whether Dean is alive or not?" Maggie asks suddenly, her voice slicing through my thoughts like a knife. My head shoots up and my heart thumps hard in my chest. I stare at her, her demeanor calm, composed, like she's talking about the weather. How could she know?

"He's alive," I say confidently, forcing the words out through the tightness in my throat. "I know he is."

Maggie's eyes narrow slightly, studying me, dissecting the layers of defense I've built. "And what makes you so sure?"

The room feels smaller, the walls closing in as I look at Maggie, the calm in her eyes both a comfort and a challenge. "He's alive," I whisper again, gripping onto the lie as if it's the only thing that can save me. "He has to be."

When I get home, the silence is a breath of fresh air; Marlo's things are gone. It's like a weight has been lifted, an oppressive presence finally exorcised from my life. Ever since my speech at the candlelight vigil two days ago, she's been a ticking time bomb, ready to go off at the slightest provocation.

"It was true, everything I said was true, Marlo," I insisted as we trudged into the house, the night heavy with lingering tension.

"I don't care! That was not the time or place to divulge my son's transgressions. No one will care about finding him now," she spat, each word dripping with vitriol and contempt. I knew then that she had a point, and that point could very well work to my advantage. My motivations were far from noble; I spoke out to shift the blame onto Lilah, to deflect any suspicion from myself. Jasper had likely been talking to the cops, and I knew he'd likely told the detective about our night together, every detail painting me in a bad light. I had braced myself for Marlo to storm off to a sterile hotel room that night, expecting her to seek refuge in some anonymous corner of the city.

But instead, she locked herself in the guest room, a silent storm brewing behind that door. Now, as I stand there, I see that her suitcase is gone. No note, no traces of her lingering fury, just the delicious confirmation that she's finally gone. The guest room, free of her irritating presence, feels expansive. I soak in the emptiness, a quiet thrill coursing through me.

I shut the door and walk back into the kitchen, the stillness wrapping around me like a comfortable old sweater. I pour myself a celebratory glass of wine, savoring the crispness as it slides over my tongue. The blinking red light of my voicemail catches my eye, a small interruption in my bubble of newfound freedom. I press play, and Detective Wells' voice crackles through the speaker. "Mrs. Stratton, I'd love to talk to you whenever it's convenient. I'd like to ask you some more questions about Dean. Call me back immediately, thanks."

Short and sweet, with an edge that sends a chill down my spine. I tap my fingers on the counter, knowing Jasper's loose lips have been at work. I rummage through my purse, pulling out my address book, thumbing through the thick paper until I find Jasper's number. My fingers dial it, and a smile tugs at the corners of my mouth when he picks up on the first ring. "Hello?" His voice is cautious, a deer sensing the hunter.

"Hi, sweetie, it's Satara," I say lightly.

"Satara. Hello."

I lean against the counter, savoring the anticipation. "Are you busy later? I'd love to explain…well, you know."

There's a weighty silence, each second a drop of honey stretching out forever. "You lied to me," he finally says, the words hanging like smoke in the air.

"I didn't lie, silly," I reply, swirling the wine in my glass. "I just withheld the truth."

"That's the same thing."

"Listen, Jasper," I say, my voice taking on a coaxing tone. "I'd love to talk about this in person. I don't like speaking on the phone about this." Another silence stretches out.

"Okay," he concedes.

I beam, feeling a triumphant thrill course through me. "Excellent. Meet me in an hour at the drive-ins."

"The drive-ins? What is this, a date?" He laughs, disbelief coloring his tone.

"I thought it'd be nice. You *did* say you wanted to take me out on a date, right?"

"Yeah, but that was before—"

"Just meet me there in an hour. Please," I say, cutting him off and hanging up before he has a chance to protest further. I take another sip of my wine, feeling the sweetness settle inside me.

I pull into the drive-in theater, one of the few relics still standing in Orange County, and arguably the best one. There's one car off to the side, just before the entrance, parked so close to where the hill slopes away, revealing a skyline dotted with city lights. I pull up next to it, my instincts sharp as ever—it's Jasper. Even through the darkening twilight and from behind his rolled-up window, I can see how handsome he is, the contours of his face softened yet highlighted by the dim glow of the dashboard. I gestured for him to lower the window, and he obliged, his expression a mixture of anticipation and something close to regret. "Am I coming to you or are you coming to me?"

"I'll come to you," I respond with a breezy enthusiasm, grabbing my bag and hopping out to join him in his car. "I brought refreshments," I say as I slide into the passenger seat. He grins, a flash of genuine amusement breaking through his guarded demeanor. "Whiskey, right?" I say, pulling out a generous bottle of the same whiskey we'd drunk at the bar that night, its familiar label catching the dim light.

"Wow," he chuckles, shaking his head. "You're smooth, aren't you?"

I pull a glass out my bag and pour him a measure, watching as the amber liquid sways. "Only for you, Jasper," I say with a smile, offering him the glass. His eyes lock onto mine, the amusement fading into something more complex, a shift I can almost feel in the air between us. His fingers graze mine as he takes his glass, and the connection sends a little thrill through me. This is a game of truth and manipulation, and I intend to play it masterfully. "I'm sorry I didn't tell you I was married, Jasper," I say, tilting my head to catch his eyes. "I figured you wouldn't want to speak to me if you knew. Even though I was planning on leaving him."

Jasper takes a long swig of his drink, his eyebrows twitching up in a moment of contemplation. "I saw you, on the news. They talked about your missing husband and flashed a photo on the screen, a picture of you two together. They talked about the candlelight vigil. I was in complete denial. I had to show up. I had to see for myself," I don't say anything, I just wait for him to continue because I know he's not done. "And… you're right, I probably *wouldn't* have wanted to speak to you if I knew you were married," he says flatly, but then his gaze softens, drifting over my face and pausing at my lips. "But to say I didn't enjoy kissing you that night would be a lie."

A smile tugs at the corners of my mouth. "I enjoyed kissing you too." I look at him through the dimly lit interior, the whites of his eyes glinting.

"Your husband is missing, Satara. That's not a big deal to you?"

"Of course it's a big deal! I've been worrying *sick* about him every single day. Even though he cheated on me I still want him to be okay."

Jasper bows his head and then looks up at me, his eyes searching mine. He shakes his head. "Your husband is an idiot for cheating on you."

"I agree," I say. "Did you speak to the cops?" I slip in, casual and serpentine. "What did you tell them? You spoke to the detective, right?"

"Not yet," he says, his shoulders tensing. "He chased me down. I told him not now. I'm planning on speaking to him tomorrow, actually."

"You don't have to tell him anything."

Jasper looks at me, shock and dismay clouding his features. "Why are you so concerned? Unless you…" His face softens, confusion giving way to a sudden, unsettling calm. His eyes search mine, trying to decipher the script of my intentions.

"Come here," I say breezily, taking the now empty glass out of his hand and dropping it to the floor. I pull his face toward mine and our lips crash together, an electric collision of desperation and desire. We move to the back seat, a tangled rush of limbs and breath, the confined space closing in around us. We shed our clothes, and I ride him, first slowly, and then quickly. The leather squeaks beneath us, the night folding over us like a conspiratorial curtain. Every touch, every movement is charged, a heady mix of lust and something darker, something waiting in the wings.

I close my eyes and savor it. Our first and last time. As we finish, I see the shift in his eyes, the sudden drop of his lids, the sluggish way his hands try to grasp at the air. Jasper starts to look confused, his face paling, his breaths coming in ragged heaves. "I feel…strange…" he murmurs, his voice a fading whisper. He starts gurgling, and I sit back as he starts to convulse.

"I poisoned you, Jasper," I say lightly, almost offhandedly, as if commenting on the weather.

His eyes widened in disbelief, darting between my face and the whiskey bottle. "Why…?" He croaks, the word barely making it past his lips as his strength ebbs away. His mouth foams up, his eyes bulge. I watch him struggle, a detached empathy flickering in my gaze. I reply, my tone is almost gentle. "I couldn't risk you torpedoing everything I've worked for."

He convulses for another minute, struggling to speak, until his body finally slumps, heavy and defeated. His eyes, once so full of suspicion and longing, now dim as consciousness slips away. The drive-in theater is a silent witness, the glowing screen flickering with stories that are not ours. I look at him one last time, the weight of inevitability settling over me. I collect the tainted bottle of whiskey and step out of the car, my engine echoing in the night as I drive away.

* * *

I'm at my desk, the fluorescent lights humming overhead as I plow through the mundane tasks that mark the rhythm of my days when he strolls up, casual, hands in his pockets, and leans against the edge of my desk. "Are you going to take a lunch?"

I glance up, pasted on smile in place. "I wasn't planning on it. I don't have much of an appetite." My fingers fidget with a stack of papers, a flimsy veil for my anticipation.

He lingers, and I continue my charade of busyness, waiting for him to break the silence. "Well, I was just going to grab some Chinese food around the corner. I could use some company," he says, eyes searching mine.

I meet his gaze, feigning uncertainty even though my decision had already been made the second he walked up. "Okay," I say, standing up and reaching for my coat.

The walk to the little hole in the wall Chinese restaurant is filled with easy conversation and the crisp bite of autumn air. We find a table near the window, the city life streaming by, invisible to us from inside our bubble. The food arrives steaming, fragrant, and we dive in, chopsticks clattering against plates. Chris picks up a long, glistening noodle with his chopsticks, twirling it playfully before extending it toward me. "Open wide," he teases, a crooked grin lighting up his face.

I laugh, a sound that feels foreign yet welcome, and lean forward to take the noodle, the warmth and savory flavor filling my mouth. "Delicious."

Being with Chris felt surreal, as if I'd stepped into an alternate timeline where the stains of my reality hadn't yet seeped through. Just a few weeks ago he would barely meet my eyes, all polite nods and sidelong glances. Now here we were, tangled in laughter at a tiny, forgettable restaurant, his chopsticks lifting delicate swirls of noodles to my lips.

The memory of killing Jasper still clung to my skin, a film of guilt and inevitability. It wasn't how I preferred to kill people. I liked to believe that I only reserved murder for those who really deserved it. Jasper's death felt different. It was messier, marred by selfishness. More an act of self-preservation than justice. It didn't feel clean, but it was done. The cyanide ensured that.

The night unfolded like a dark ballet—meeting with Jasper, the whiskey, the tainted glass. His realization too late, his betrayal etched onto his features as certainty turned to confusion, then fear. Chris leans in, his breath mingling with mine, and our lips meet in a tentative, electric kiss. For a moment, the world stops, the chaos outside ceasing to exist. But then, reality snaps back, harsh and unyielding. Chris jerks back, eyes wide with panic. "I'm sorry," he stammers, standing up abruptly. "I shouldn't have…I have to go."
He bolts from the table, out of the restaurant, leaving me there with the warmth of his kiss still tingling on my lips. The world outside our window continues, oblivious to the new fracture carved into my day.

After work, I drive to Chris's house. I'm frustrated with how slow his falling for me was. Just a few more days, a few more moments alone with him, I knew I was going to wear him down.

I crouch behind the Azalea bushes, their flowers like silent witnesses to my madness. Chris's kitchen window frames the domesticity I've never grown tired of watching, a perverse sort of television with stakes that could unravel everything. Inside, Lizzie is at the stove, her apron stained with the casualties of a family dinner.

Chris sits at the dining table, looking like someone might if they were waiting for a bus that never comes. He looks miserable, like every second in that kitchen is another notch in his invisible collar. But then Sophia, their little whirlwind, propels herself into his lap, and something inside him softens. He becomes a different man—

he's silly with her, making faces, his laugh a low, authentic rumble that drowns out the clanking of pots and pans. Sophia jumps down, eyes wide and urgent, the bathroom presumably her destination as she seems squirmy, dancing on tiptoes before her little legs take her off down the hall. And that's when it happens. Chris turns, maybe for no reason at all, and his eyes lock onto where I'm half-hidden by the bushes. For a heartbeat, there's nothing but the space between us, an electric tension snapping across the distance. My breath catches, deep in the back of my throat. He knows I'm here. I can see the recognition blooming in his eyes, and suddenly, it isn't just my own desperate fantasy anymore. It's real and tangible, as palpable as the evening pressing in around us.

SUGAR

* * *

That evening when I get home, there's a brown Cadillac Deville haphazardly parked in my driveway, and I don't have to guess whose it is because Detective Wells hops out as soon as he sees me pull up. He's wearing a tweed grey suit and those big, obnoxious sunglasses that shield his eyes. The stern set of his face says he means business.

I steady my breathing, plaster a smile on my face, and glide out of the car. I've been avoiding him to devise my next move. Anticipating this unwelcome visit wasn't high on my list of premonitions, though maybe it should have been. Detectives and cops showing up unannounced is practically a genre trope, especially when your significant other is a missing person.

"Detective Wells, what a pleasure to see you," I say, walking up to him with my heels clicking hard on the pavement like a countdown to some inevitable ending.

He pulls his sunglasses off, his eyes assessing me with a precision that feels like a scalpel. "*Is it* a pleasure to see me?" His voice is flat as a sheet of unmarked paper. "You've been avoiding me."

I tilt my head, feigning innocent surprise. "Oh, nonsense! I wasn't doing it on purpose. I've just been very busy getting my affairs in order. You know…money, finances. Since…well, since Dean is missing, I needed to figure out how I was going to pay the bills since he was the primary breadwinner."

His eyes narrow just a fraction, a tell-tale sign he's dissecting every syllable I offer. "Did you get it figured out?"

I produce my best smile. "Yes. His hospital is releasing his last paycheck to me. They're reprinting it so it has my name on it, then I can cash it." I had spoken to a very stern-sounding lady in accounts payable for the hospital over the phone this morning. It was a dance of persuasion and desperation—turning on the waterworks, pleading that I've already gone through enough, and now she was about to make me homeless. She took pity on me, saying that because I was his spouse she could do it. Now I have a sizeable check in my name arriving in the mail any day now.

Wells stands there, weighing my words as if they might just tip the scales of justice one way or another. "That's good to hear," he finally says, though there's no reassurance in his tone. "I still have a few more questions."

I nod, letting my posture relax just enough to seem compliant but not surrendering my ground. "Anything you need, detective. Anything at all," but as he steps closer, his shadow merging with mine under the evening sun, I can't help but think he sees right through this carefully constructed act. "Would you like to come in?" I lead the way, not waiting for an answer. When we get inside, I see Detective Wells take in the décor.

"Beautiful home, Mrs. Stratton," he says, his tone neutral, but there's a hint of genuine appreciation there.

"Thank you, Detective Wells," I reply, grateful he doesn't question the overwhelming pink of it all. "Would you like some tea?"

He nods. "Sure."

I lead him to the kitchen, each step betraying a casualness I don't feel. He follows at a measured pace, his eyes scanning everything. The aroma of herbal tea fills the room as I prep the kettle, resisting the urge to add a special ingredient. Detective Wells is a different beast; I couldn't kill the detective that was investigating my husband's death—I might as well just turn myself in if I did that. I can't help but wonder if he knows about Jasper yet. Surely someone's found him by now. I left his car where discovery was inevitable. Jasper deserved to be found, to be mourned in his own way. I had prepared a story, fabricating truths to appear unassailable.

"Mrs. Stratton, I wanted to ask you more about your husband's affair," Wells says, causing my hands to still for only a fraction of a second. I keep the smile on my face, though it feels like it might crack. "You said during the candlelight vigil that he was sleeping with Ms. Patrick, correct? When did you find this out?" His voice is almost a whisper, an echo of compassion, and I exploit it, conjuring tears on cue.

"I found out a few days before he went missing. I... I hadn't even confronted him yet." My voice trembles, the perfect pitch of a wounded wife.

Wells takes out his notepad and scribbles something. "I see."

"I wanted to figure out what my next move was before I said anything. I had just been preparing to contact a divorce lawyer to draft the papers. But then he...he just disappeared." My words drop into the rising steam like stones as I cut off the boiling kettle before it can shriek.

"I see," he murmurs again. "And, Mrs. Stratton, are you aware that Ms. Patrick suspects you of doing something to your husband?"

My hands freeze once more, and I can feel the heat rising to my cheeks, but I manage to maintain my composure, wiping away a tear that falls like a well-rehearsed cue. "I wouldn't hurt a fly," I say with a soft, incredulous laugh. "Especially my husband. I loved him. Yes, he cheated, but I would never do anything to hurt him." I let the tears fall freely now, an avalanche of rehearsed grief.

Detective Wells's gaze pierces me. "Do you know a Jasper Sanchez?"

I meet his stare, my expression carefully crafted to be casual, almost indifferent. "The name doesn't ring a bell," I say, pouring hot water into both cups, watching the steam rise and dissipate.

"Well, he was at your husband's candlelight vigil."

I furrow my brows, pretending to sift through a fog of distant memories. "You know that name does actually ring a bell. He was one of my husband's friends, I believe. Yes...*Jasper*. They sometimes played golf together on the weekends." The lie tastes like iron on my tongue. Dean had never touched a golf club in his life.

"I see," Wells responds, but his voice has taken on an edge. "He was found dead at the drive-ins yesterday morning."

I lift a hand to my mouth in a gesture of orchestrated shock. "Oh dear," I whisper. "What the hell is happening in this town? It used to be safe."

"I've been wondering the same thing, Mrs. Stratton," Wells' eyes are relentless, probing for the slip-up that will unravel my tightly wound narrative. "We found your phone number in his address book," Wells continues, his voice a scalpel now, precise and cutting. "It was just labeled 'S,' and I couldn't figure out if it stood for your first name, or your surname, which obviously, was also Dean's."

I shake my head, summoning fresh tears like an actress digging deep on opening night. "Well, I'm sorry I can't be of any more help when it comes to Jasper," I say, eyes soft and compliant. "I never met him, but from what Dean told me, he was a fine gentleman. When is his funeral? I'd love to attend. Pay my respects."

Detective Wells takes a sip of his tea, considering. "No arrangements have been made yet, since his mother and father are both deceased, and his siblings are scattered across the country. But I'll keep you posted."

"Please do."

A couple more minutes pass by in a haze of banalities, general questions about Dean. Then, with a resolute flip, he closes his notepad and stuffs it into his suit pocket. "Well, I have got to get going. It's getting late, and I don't want to take up too much of your evening."

"Thank you, Detective Wells," I say with a smile, wide and bright as an open wound. His blue eyes meet mine, filled with an inscrutable something that teeters on the edge of understanding but remains opaque.

"Thank you for the tea," he says as I usher him to the door. My lips curl into a polite farewell, but inside, my heart is thrumming a symphony of frenetic energy as I hear his car start up and drive away. As soon as he's gone, my blood boils over the pot, morphing from anger into a hot, molten determination. With swift, steady fingers, I dial the number I forced into my memory. The phone rings, and rings, and my breath quickens until Millicent Garcelle's silky smooth voice wafts through the receiver, as if conjured from some dark, velvety night.

"Hello?"

"I have another job for you. I'll come by tomorrow afternoon."

Millicent doesn't ask questions. She understands the unspoken language of desperation and determination. I hang up, the resolve crystallizing in my chest like a protective shell. I eye the teacup Detective Wells was drinking out of, his wad of bright blue gum disgustingly hanging off the side of my beautiful floral teacup.

* * *

I knock on Millicent's door, the sound echoing my resolve, and I hear her yell, "Come in!" I push the door open, hoping she'd be alone this time, unlike my last visit. She emerges from the back wearing a fabulous purple gown as if she were headed out for a glamorous night out. She seems flustered, fastening a giant bejeweled earring onto her ear, her movements precise but hurried.

"Am I interrupting?" I ask, a raised brow hinting at amusement.

"If you were interrupting, I wouldn't ask you to come in I'd politely tell you to fuck off," she says as she puts on the other earring. "How's what's his name... Chris?"

"Fine. Slow but fine."

Millicent smiles. "Patience is a virtue, darling," she purrs, and then her eyes shift to my hands. "What's that?"

I step further into her apartment, holding the photo of Lilah up. I took it at the barbecue that Dean and I hosted last summer. To say she looked beautiful that day was an understatement, white halter dress and perfect sugar red lipstick. I hold up the photo. "Do you know this woman?"

Millicent's eyes flick from mine to the photo again. She snatches it out of my hand, studying it with a critical eye. "I've never met her," she says finally. "Pretty girl, though. Is that who we're putting the spell on?" Amusement dances in her eyes, a glimmer of dark mirth.

"No," I say, each word weighted with bitterness. "That's the woman who was fucking my husband behind my back," the darkness in my voice is palpable, a storm gathering just beneath the surface. Millicent's eyebrows arch in surprise. "I figured that you helped her put a spell on him. It was the only logical explanation seeing as she is an absolute bitch," I say, my words cutting like a knife.

"Oh, well I don't know her," she says dismissively, gliding over to her plush, extravagant sofa. "Who's the lucky bloke we're doing the spell on then?"

I sit across from her, placing the other item I brought down on her coffee table with a calculated precision. "A detective," I say. "A detective investigating my husband's disappearance," I point to the chewing gum stored in a Ziploc bag like a macabre trophy. "That's his chewing gum."

She stares at me, her expression shifting from curiosity to something more calculating. "You killed him, didn't you?" I don't respond. Her green eyes pierce mine, searching, probing. "You killed your husband for poking the little redhead lady, didn't you?"

"She wasn't just some lady. She was my best friend."

Millicent sits back, a slow, dangerous smile curving her lips. "I understand," Millicent says. "Doing what I do, you have to have some sort of darkness inside you." She leans in slightly, as if to draw me into her orbit. "Making people fall for someone else against their will," she continues slowly, each word a seductive drip, "requires a touch of the sinister."

I stare at her, my curiosity mingling with a wary respect. "Have you killed people?"

Millicent's eyes glint with a dark amusement. "I've had my fair share of lovers who have scorned me," she says, her voice dropping an octave, becoming almost velvety with menace. "And you know what they say. Hell hath no fury like a woman scorned," her laugh is soft, almost musical, but it carries an edge that makes my skin prickle. She sinks back into the plush depths of her sofa, the picture of languid elegance, but now her presence feels like a coiled serpent. "You see, darling," she continues, her eyes never leaving mine, "magic isn't just about power. It's about control. Manipulation. Knowing where to twist the knife, metaphorically speaking, of course." She waves her hand airily, the giant jewels on her earrings catching the low light. I don't say anything, I just smile, mesmerized.

"So... who did you kill? Who scorned you?"

Her expression turns melancholic. "Ten years ago," Millicent begins, her voice a soft murmur, "I put my first love spell on a man who I believed was my everything. His name was Daniel," She hesitates, as if tasting the name after so long leaves a bitter tang in her mouth. "He was magnetic, funny, and made me feel seen in ways I hadn't before," she continues, her eyes far away. "But as the years passed, the spell started to weaken, due to my lack of experience at the time, though I didn't know it at first. But the magic frayed slowly. I didn't see the signs until it was too late," I lean in, captivated by the rawness in Millicent's tone. "Daniel became restless," Millicent says, a tremor in her voice. "He began talking about leaving, about moving on. The day he told me he was done, that he was going to leave me, the spell was barely a whisper. I felt something snap inside me."

Her eyes harden, the storm of that memory flashing through them. "I shot him," she admits, her voice a mix of defiance and regret. "Panic and rage blurred my vision. I couldn't let him go, not after everything." Millicent pauses, regaining her composure. "I kept him in my basement, his body decaying until he was just bone. I couldn't let go."

The room feels colder, the reality of Millicent's confession hanging heavy between us. She rises from her seat, moving with a strange grace to her altar, a small wooden bench right underneath her window. With gentle hands, she lifts up the skull that was perched there, cradling it like a precious artifact. "This," she says, her voice almost tender, "was Daniel. My first love," She kisses the top of the skull with a reverence that borders on sanctity. "I keep it to remember him. To remind myself of the depth of my love—and the darkness it holds."

I watch, in awe. Keeping the skull of my lover never occurred to me. I've kept other small mementos— but have never thought of keeping a skull. It seemed too risky. But Millicent is fearless. Keeping her lover's skull on her altar, displaying it proudly for everyone to see. I feel a pang of recognition. I see myself reflected in Millicent's actions, in the desperate, consuming need to hold on to love, no matter the cost. "We're alike, you and I. Driven by our desires, willing to cross lines others wouldn't dare approach," I whisper.

Millicent turns to me and her smile returns after sharing her story about her lost love. "I've been thinking the same thing since I first met you," she whispers. "Kneel darling," she instructs. "Let's make sure the good detective is properly enchanted."

* * *

It's almost midnight when the phone rings, the sound slicing through the quiet as I lay in bed with my feline companions snuggled close. Avocado sprawls comfortably on my stomach, and I gently maneuver him off, his protest a lazy meow. I lift the receiver to my ear and breathe out a guarded, "Hello?" There's a long stretch of silence.

And then, his voice cuts through. "Satara, it's Chris."
My body locks up, heart pounding. He saw me the other night. Saw me peering through his window, caught in a trance of longing. My mind races through scenarios, the delicate balance of fear and hope teetering dangerously. Would the spell soften his anger? I'd felt the inevitability of this moment all week, so much so that I'd taken two days off work, sheltering myself from a run in with him. Luckily, when your husband goes missing, people give you more grace than usual.

Take all the time you need, my boss said. So, I did, retreating into my cocoon of avoidance. I push down the fear rising in my throat. "Hi, Chris," I manage, struggling for a casual tone, but my voice trembles.

"We've missed you at work." He doesn't sound angry.

Relief unfurls in my chest, and I lean against the counter, a hint of a smile tugging at my lips. "We?"

He breathes out a soft laugh. "Okay, just me," he admits. "But Sebastian's been asking about you too. Says the office is dull without you."

"Oh, bless his heart." My smile broadens, warmth spreading through me. Maybe things are okay.

"I... saw you the other night," he says. I hold my silence, letting him carry the weight of the conversation. "It's okay, though. I didn't mind."

"No?"

He sighs, and it's a sound full of weariness and honesty. "No, I'm flattered, honestly. I'm glad you saw how miserable I am."

I bit my lip. "I did see how miserable you are."

He clears his throat, a rustle on the line as he shifts. "You're probably wondering why I'm calling so late."

"The thought did cross my mind."

There's a hush of background noise, his voice dropping to a whisper. "Satara, I can't stop thinking about you," he whispers. I beam, performing a quiet, triumphant dance, my pink nightgown a blur of motion in the dim light. "I don't know how or why, but you're in my head. No matter what I do, I can't shake the thought of you. I think... I think I'm falling for you."

The words reverberate in my mind, heady and intoxicating. I've never felt such happiness, not even on my wedding day. My entire body thrums with excitement. "Oh," I say, voice smooth and confident now. "Is that so?"

"Yes. You've completely taken over my thoughts, and I can't ignore it anymore," he confesses.

A broad smile breaks across my face. "I'm glad," I say, allowing the joy to overflow, my tone dipped in the sweetness of triumph. Chris is mine now, reeled into my orbit, a fact sealed with his late-night confession. "Do you want to come over?" The words tumble out before I can second guess them. It doesn't take more than five seconds for him to answer.

"Yes."

When Chris arrives, the air between us is charged, humming with raw need. The moment he steps inside, we collide in a tangle of limbs and urgent kisses. Our encounter is feverish, intense, breaking down barriers we'd both carefully maintained. His touch ignites something in me, a fire that burns away the ghosts of the past.

It's the best sex of my life, a blur of passion that leaves me breathless and exhausted. When Chris finally slips out at four a.m., he plants a lingering kiss on my lips, one that feels more like love than a one-night stand. The weight of his departure settles in, my head a swirl of emotions. In those few hours with Chris in my bed, nothing else mattered. Not Dean, not Lilah, not the looming threat of discovery for my crimes—only him.

As the first light of morning cracks through the blinds, I dress for work, trying to cloak myself in the guise of a grieving wife. But it's a struggle; my heart is still fluttering from last night. I practice my grief-stricken expression in the mirror, summoning the shadows under my eyes and the drop of my lips. Colleagues approach with quiet condolences, their words buzzing around me like harmless insects.

Each expression of pity and sympathy lands softly, evoking the appropriate nods and murmured thanks. I move through the motions, a carefully orchestrated performance of sorrow. Then Chris walks in, casual yet visibly marked by sleeplessness. His eyes, though slightly weary, glitter with a secret joy. A tiny, unreadable smile playing on his lips. Our eyes meet, and he offers a slight nod and a subtle raise of his eyebrows. The gesture is understated, almost dismissive, but beneath the surface lies a shared understanding. I force myself not to react, not to let the heat of our secret betray me. As the day drags on, I find myself replaying every touch, every whisper of the night before. In the moments of quiet, when the office hum fades to a background murmur, I steal glances at Chris. Each exchange, no matter how trivial, is a small thrill, a reminder of the night's bliss. My longing for him is a current beneath the surface, powerful and all-consuming.

SUGAR

* * *

I'm humming to myself as I bake, savoring the silky voice of the male singer crooning on the radio. The kitchen fills with the comforting scent of vanilla, and I'm feeling amazing. Detective Wells has requested another meeting with me this evening, and I'm confident the spell will work its magic once more. It will be so easy to twist him around my finger, get him to divulge secrets he'd never share under normal circumstances.

Chris and I can't seem to stay away from each other. Since that night, it's been a heady mix of passion and secrecy. We've quickly turned his office into our private sanctuary, making love on his desk, our laughter filling the gaps between words and moans. His touch is intoxicating, a daily need I can't deny.

I glide a knife through the ripe strawberries, cutting them meticulously. The rich smell of vanilla cake mingles with the tartness of fresh fruit, a sensory feast that mirrors the sweetness and acid of my plans. Each slice of strawberry nestles perfectly atop the frosted cake, a piece of art in its own right. I smile, satisfied with my work. I place the cake on a polished platter, the final touch to my deception, and make my way to Lilah's.

Lilah's house is modest, a testament to the life she's pieced together on a single mother's schoolteacher salary. She never liked to open up about her husband's death, offering only the terse explanation of "a terrible accident," that pained her to mention. Knowing her all these years, I've learned to just avoid the subject, respecting her privacy.

Since the six years I've known Lila, she's only been on a few dates with a handful of unimpressive men. I used to admire her independence, her ability to be content without a partner. It seemed almost magnificent to manage life alone. But now, that admiration is stained with betrayal. The knowledge that she was sleeping with Dean claws at me. I want to know everything—when it started, if there was love, or if it was just sex. But today, I bite down on my questions, mask my true intentions with a smile, and focus on the semblance of reconciliation I'm here to present.

I ring her doorbell, and almost instantly hear the unmistakable, heavy-footed thumping of someone dashing down the stairs. It's Danny, her son, no doubt. The door swings open, and I'm met by his expectant gaze. Danny is a handsome boy, his copper brown hair and freckles mirroring his mother's features, but his soft brown eyes and protruding nose aren't Lilah's. It's a shame he never got to meet his father. Though my hatred for Lilah is all consuming I still feel some empathy for her child—or what little empathy I could muster up. But it is there, faintly. Danny is at that awkward teen phase, caught in the no-man's-land between childhood and maturity. "Hi, Danny. Is your mother home?"

His eyes fixate on the cake, not me. "Is that for us?" he mumbles, clearly entranced by the dessert.

"Yes, it's not just for you it's also for your mother, so you can't eat all of it, alright?" I say with a sly smile, trying to engage him. He just stands there, looking down at the ground. One thing I've learned about teenagers is that they carry a world of feelings but seldom express them. Conversations with Danny require me to keep the dialogue going, a skill I've fine-tuned over our brief interactions. "May I come in?" I prod gently.

Danny steps back, opening the door wider. "Mom! Satara is here!" She suddenly appears in the living room; I hadn't even heard her come down. Lilah's stare is intense, her expression fierce and unyielding. But she forces a smile onto her face, the corners of her mouth twitching up mechanically as she turns to Danny. "Go to your room, Danny," she says flatly.

Danny's eyes flicker back to the cake, a momentary distraction from the tension between us. "Can I have cake?"

"Later. After dinner," Lilah says, her tone leaving no room for negotiation. She turns her attention back to me, grabbing the cake from my hands with swift aggressiveness. The silence stretches thickly between us, an awkward void that neither of us wants to fill. Finally, she breaks it. "Tea?"

I nod. "That would be lovely, thank you." I follow her to the kitchen, and she sets the cake down on the counter, her movements deliberate and composed. As Lilah busies herself with the tea, I try to read the lines of her face, the tautness of her jaw, the flicker of emotions in her eyes.

With her back turned to me, I allow my eyes to wander over the familiar surroundings—the simple, mismatched cabinets, the worn countertops, the little trinkets that speak of her quietly lived life. The kettle whistles, and Lilah deftly pours hot water into two cups, placing one in front of me. She leans against the kitchen counter, dipping her teabag in and out of her cup. "You know everyone calls me a whore now," Lilah says flatly. "Ever since your little speech at the candlelight vigil."

I raise an eyebrow. "Sorry about that."

Lilah lets out a dry, humorless laugh. "Sure, you are, Satara," she straightens up, squarely facing me. "The other teachers at my school look at me like I've murdered him," she takes a sip of her tea. I mirror her, taking a sip as well. "But that was your goal, right?" Her green eyes are unwavering, drilling into me.

I shrug. "No," I say, maintaining my calm. "Not particularly."

"Even my son asks me questions, and I have no idea what to tell him," Lilah says, her voice heavy with fatigue.

"Tell him the truth honey," I say lightly, almost breezily. "Tell him you fucked my husband."

Lilah closes her eyes, and I watch as a tremor passes through her. She shakes her head slowly, a wave of emotion crashing over her. "I just don't know…" her voice trails off, and for a moment, she seems utterly defeated. The tiredness racks her beautiful face, lines of exhaustion marring her features. "Forget it," she mutters more to herself than to me.

I lean against the counter across from Lilah, studying her. "What's the matter, Lilah? Can't handle the fallout of your choices?"

Her eyes snap open, a flicker of anger reigniting behind the haze of exhaustion. "This isn't just about me, Satara," she says, her voice low but firm. "Danny is innocent in all of this. He didn't ask for any of it."

"Neither did I," I counter smoothly. "But here we are."

She looks at me, and for a moment, I see a flicker of something— maybe regret, maybe a shred of guilt. It's almost pitiful. She gets dangerously close to me, staring at me intently. I ignore the feeling that rises up inside me. "You're right," she says quietly. "Here we are. And what good does it do to keep fighting?"

We stand there. My eyes flit down to her lips and back up to her eyes. I lean in, and she leans in. We don't move. Just stand there, our faces mere inches away from each other. It feels like a short moment, but it also feels like an eternity. She finally backs up, her chest heaving up and down. I continue the conversation as if it didn't just happen. "Maybe it doesn't do any good, but it's the only thing keeping me going."

Lilah sighs. "What are you going to do, Satara? What's your endgame?"

I smile, a cold, calculated smile. "That's for me to know and for you to worry about."

"You hate me, so why are you here?" Lilah says, her patience clearly worn thin. "Let's cut the bullshit, Satara."

I shake my head gently. "I don't hate you, Lilah," I say, trying to inject a note of sincerity into my voice. "I came here to apologize for my speech at the candlelight vigil. I brought the cake as a peace offering."

Lilah's smile is condescending, almost mocking. "If you think I'm ever going to eat anything you make again…" she says darkly, her voice fading off. My eyebrows furrow at her accusation. Does she really think I'm trying to poison her? The absurdity of it almost makes me laugh. Poisoning her now would be ludicrous, undermining my goal to pin Dean's disappearance and subsequent death on her. If she suddenly dropped dead, I'd undoubtedly be the prime suspect. Does she really think I'm that stupid?

"Don't be ridiculous, Lilah. It's just a regular cake."

But Lilah's stare is steely. In a sudden, cold act of defiance, she picks up the cake and slams it facedown into the sink. Frosting flies everywhere, smattering against the walls, getting into her hair and onto her face. She looks unhinged, her calm facade shattered.

I stare at her in surprise, struggling to maintain my composure. The sight is both shocking and almost laughable. "Well, that was rude," I say flatly, holding back the urge to smirk at her outburst. "I worked really hard on that cake."

Lilah's expression twists with a mix of anger and disgust. "Get out," she says, her voice trembling with barely restrained fury.

I rise slowly from my chair, making sure to keep my movements measured and unhurried. I look at her, *really* look at her, and see the raw edges of a woman pushed to her limits. "Fine," I say, my voice cool. "But know this, Lilah—whatever happens next, you brought it upon yourself." I can feel her eyes burning on my back as I make my way to the door.

She follows me out the door. "You know I'm going to prove it! I'm going to prove what you did Satara," she yells wildly as I walk away. I don't say anything back. She's red and furious. "Fuck you!" She screams. I smile inwardly as some of the neighbor's watch, their heads peeking from behind their doors, some peering out their windows, getting a front row seat at how easy it was for Lilah Patrick to lose her temper.

Exactly as I planned.

Behind me, Lilah is left to clean up the mess—both the physical wreckage of the cake and the lingering wreckage of our confrontation. And I walk away, my mind already spinning new threads, laying new traps, certain that in the end, I will be the one to win.

SUGAR

* * *

Cynthia arrives first for the book club, cheese platter in hand and all smiles. She looks beautiful, of course, wearing a stunning midnight blue dress with billowy sleeves, her hair perfectly curled, eyes sparkling with an affectation of warmth that's more for show than anything else. "How are you doing, sweetheart?" she asks me, it seems Cynthia had forgiven me for essentially blackmailing her. There isn't an ounce of anger in her tone when she greets me. Her eyes sweep over my face with what seems like genuine concern. It's ironic, really, the layers of pretense we cloak ourselves in.

"Doing well, thanks, despite everything." I force a smile just wide enough to match hers. Lizzie arrives next. She's a mess, and the sight of her struggling brings a smile to my face. Her hair is disheveled, her skin is dull and lifeless. She had already suspected me having an affair with her husband, but I wonder if she knows for certain now.

I understand the contradiction of being furious with Lilah for fucking my husband and me doing the same to another woman, but it's different; Lilah was my best friend. It's a matter of principle. Lizzie and I are merely acquaintances, nothing more.

Cheryl and Dawn arrive together, Cheryl greeting me with her usual air of arrogance, a queen presiding over her subjects. She hugs me and I silently roll my eyes, noting the audacity it takes to act so high and mighty when she put a spell on her husband to make him fall in love with her. She's no better than me, and that secret knowledge brings me quiet joy. Dawn has another purple bruise on her neck, suspiciously shaped like a hand mark. She's covered it up well with makeup, but I can still see it. She gives me a sentimental smile, one that tries to reach her eyes but falls short. It's a mask, but then, aren't we all wearing masks tonight?

As they settle in, I brush all their comments about Dean aside, their sympathetic gazes, and their surface-level apologies like flies too insignificant to swat. "I can't believe it's already been two months since..." Cheryl trails off, looking at me with pity that feels like bile in my throat.

"Time flies," I say coolly, pouring wine into glasses and handing them out as distractions. "Who wants to start the discussion?"

The night wears on with forced laughter, strained smiles, and the hollow sound of glasses clinking. Cynthia goes on about the book, her voice a dull drone as I zone out. The sound of laughter and wine-fueled conversation gradually dissipates as the group trickles out, and I notice Dawn lingering, leaving her and I in the room. The remnants of the evening—a few empty wine glasses, crumbs from hors d'oeuvres, and discarded napkins—scatter the surfaces of my home. I watch Dawn, noting the way her hands fidget like restless birds as she helps me clean up, her eyes dart nervously around the room, never resting on one spot for too long. "Satara, can I talk to you for a moment?" she asks, her voice a fragile tremor, the sound barely breaking through the muted calm that has fallen over the room.

"Of course, Dawn," I reply, curiosity mingling with the tension coiling in my stomach, transforming my voice into something softer, more careful. Dawn's fingers twist the hem of her rust-colored blouse that does not go well with her coloring, and I can see the fabric wrinkle and stretch under her anxious grip. Her gaze flickers around the room like a skittish moth before finally settling on mine. There's a raw edge to her eyes, a mix of fear and determination that sends a shiver down my spine.

"I... I think you made Dean disappear," she says, each word dropping between us like a stone into a still pond, sending ripples of shock outward. My breath catches, but I force my face into a mask of calm, though the air between us feels charged; electric.

"Dawn, I don't know what you're talking about," my voice is steady but cautious. "Why would you think that?"

Her gaze doesn't waver, and for a moment, I'm trapped in her stare, a mute witness to the storm of emotions swirling behind her eyes. "You have to understand," she continues, her voice cracking like dry branches. "I can't live like this anymore. Richard... he's..." Her voice trails off, the words unsaid hanging heavy in the air, almost visible in the dim light.

There's a desperation in her that's raw and palpable, and it makes me wonder just what kind of hell she's been living through. "Dawn, I'm sorry you're going through this, but I can't help you."

Dawn's shoulders sag, and for a moment, she looks utterly defeated. The tension in her frame seems to deflate, leaving her looking smaller, more fragile. "I just thought... maybe you could..." she whispers, her voice trailing off into uncertainty.

The weight of her words and the implications they carry are almost too much to bear. "No," I say firmly, breaking the silence. "You need to leave my house now."

She nods, a strange mix of resolve and resignation washing over her face before she turns towards the door. Her movements are slow, almost reluctant, as though she's dragging herself through quicksand. Just as she reaches the threshold, something inside me wrenches, compelling me to call her back. "Dawn, wait," She pauses, turning back with that last sliver of hope still glimmering in her eyes. "Buy a gun. Stop being so fucking weak."

* * *

As I am busy preparing for Detective Wells' visit, the interaction with Dawn keeps needling in my mind. What made her ask me that question? What made her so certain that I had killed Dean? Sure, she could be speculating, but there was something in her eyes, something in the way her voice cracked like ice under pressure. It was almost as if she knew. Which isn't plausible. Dawn and I aren't very close. The possibility of her knowing puts me on edge, but there's no time to ruminate. I step into a hot, steamy shower.

The water pounds against my skin, washing away all traces of the evening. I let the steam envelop me, breathing deeply, but the questions cling like stubborn cobwebs in my mind. Post-shower, I redo my hair and makeup with precision, then slip into a knee-length mini dress, black with fringe. I slip into my highest black pumps and stare at myself in the mirror. I stare at myself as I slip an acid tab on my tongue. A brief, foolish wish rises in me: I wish Chris could see me right now. I'd love for him to take me out to a fine five-star restaurant, fill my glass with the best wine, and then take me home and ravage me. I grimace at the thought, pushing it aside before I got too turned on. One day, once all this blows over, Chris and I will be together properly.

The other day, during one of our rendezvous in his office, I had asked him if he wanted to be together, *really* be together. He told me without a doubt that he did, he just needed time to tell Lizzie, to get things situated before moving out. I had even suggested he could slowly start bringing his things over to my house. "I have an extra room for Sophia on the weekends," I said with a smile, and Chris loved that. I knew he would.

The truth was, I didn't care about having Sophia come over on the weekends. If Chris were to give up all parental rights to Lizzie, I'd be very happy. But I know that will never happen. What I really wanted—and what made my heart flutter—was to start anew with Chris. To get married, to have our own family. Sophia would just be a reminder of his past, a reminder of his last relationship. And I didn't want that. My heart flutters at the thought of starting a family with Chris. But tonight, I must charm Detective Wells; play my part.

When he knocks at my door, the atmosphere shifts like the calm before a storm. I open the door, a glass of wine delicately balanced in my hand, its deep crimson color almost glowing in the soft light of the hallway. The detective's reaction is immediate; his eyes widen slightly, and his breath seems to catch at the sight of me. His eyes flicker up and down, taking in every detail, and I revel in the effect. "Detective, please come in," I say, a smile stretching across my face that blends warmth and amusement, just a shade shy from being too inviting. He hesitates for a fraction of a second before stepping inside, the solidity of him filling the entryway.

"Thank you, Mrs. Stratton."

"Wine?" I offer, gracefully gesturing with the glass in my hand.

"Oh no, thank you. I'm on duty," he replies, but his blue eyes betray him as they flick momentarily towards the glass, the rich liquid catching the light.

"Oh, come on now," I coax, "one glass won't hurt, will it? Consider it a gesture of hospitality."

He wavers, the tension in his shoulders betraying the inner conflict, trying to fight the spell from taking hold. "All right, just one," he finally concedes, the words more a surrender than agreement. I pour him a glass, the glug-glug sound like a countdown. As I hand it to him, our fingers brush together ever so slightly.

We settle on the sofa; I sit so close to him that our knees almost touch. I glance down at his hands, taking in the small details like a painter eyeing his canvas. No wedding ring, just a pale, ghostly tan mark where one used to be. That makes things much easier for me; the space where the ring had been a silent cry for connection was a vulnerability I can gently exploit. I'll have him wrapped around my finger in no time. I take a deliberate sip from my glass, the cool liquid a sharp contrast to the warmth radiating between us. "So, Detective, what brings you here tonight?" I ask, my voice laced with curiosity and just a hint of playful challenge.

Detective Wells tries to maintain his composure, but his gaze falters, his lips pressed into a thin line before he clears his throat. "I, uh, I spoke with Lilah yesterday," he begins, a note of frustration creeping into his tone. "She mentioned seeing you invite a man into your house about a month ago."

I let out a soft, incredulous laugh, shaking my head in mock disbelief. "Lilah is lying, detective. She's crazy. She showed proof of that today when I brought her a cake as a peace offering."

His brow furrows in confusion. "A cake?"

I nod, leaning in a bit closer, my voice dropping to a conspiratorial whisper. "I brought her a cake this morning, just as a friendly gesture. She freaked out and screamed obscenities at me like wild banshee. You can even ask her neighbors—they witnessed everything."

Detective Wells rubs the back of his neck, taking a large gulp of his wine. He clearly isn't a regular wine drinker, I can tell by the way he gulps it down as if he's drinking a beer. "I know Lilah can sometimes be... unreliable." I place a gentle hand on his knee, feeling the heat radiating through the fabric of his trousers.

"Exactly, Detective. She's untrustworthy. Whatever she says she saw, it's simply not true."

He nods slowly, the edges of doubt crumbling under the weight of my words and the persuasive pull of the wine. "So…there was no man?" I shake my head, my eyes meeting his. I watch as he squirms under my stare. "You're right. I should have known better than to take her word at face value."

"She was sleeping with my husband, Detective. She is not a good person," He doesn't say anything back, and his face goes red. I wasn't sure if it was the wine, or me. I give his knee a reassuring squeeze before retracting my hand, the physical contact brief but lingering in its effect. "I appreciate your diligence, Detective. Truly. But I hope you can see now that Lilah is not a reliable source."

He finishes his wine, the glass now empty and abandoned on the coffee table and he abruptly stands up, almost as if he has just realized what he was doing. "Thank you for your time, Mrs. Stratton. And for the wine."

"Leaving so soon?" I try to hide my smile as he makes his way to the door.

He looks at me and then down at his watch. "I have to get going. Thanks again."

"Anytime, Detective. Anytime."

As the door closes behind him, I smile wide. It's amazing, really, how easy it all is. The entire interaction with Detective Wells unfolded like a well-rehearsed play. His eyes never once questioned my performance, his mind too clouded by the spell. Not once has he asked me how I met Dean. He hasn't even investigated it at all. It's as if the surface of my curated life was enough to convince him, the layers underneath too dark and twisted for him to fathom. But if he did, one peek beneath the mask, one look into that history, and the cards might come crumbling down.

The image I've so meticulously constructed could shatter, jagged pieces revealing the truth. The fact is no one knew how I really met Dean. No one knows about that chapter of my life shrouded in institutional grey and fluorescent lights. No one knows that Dean was one of the orderlies at the mental institution I was in. That sterile, loveless place where the days morphed into each other, each one marked by the ticking of clocks and the distant hum of fluorescent lights. He couldn't see the threads of fate that wove Dean and me together; couldn't see past the smoke and mirrors I so expertly placed before him. No one knew the truth.

SUGAR

1971

Waylon's memory was like a stone shackled to my ankle. I thought killing him would bring relief, but it only unearthed a ravenous hunger I couldn't seem to quell. It turns out that once you step into darkness, it's impossible to find the exit. So, there I was, roving the seedy alleys of the city, lurking outside dingy clubs and bars, waiting for trouble. But the funny part is that when you go looking for trouble, it has the gall to play hide-and-seek.

One night I walked into a popular disco club called The Clubhouse, the music thumping so deep it felt like it might shake my darkest sins loose. The floor shimmered with reflections of colored lights, casting kaleidoscopic shadows on faces of strangers cloaked in sweat and desire. The air was heavy with the cloying scent of cheap perfume and spilled drinks. Resting against the bar, I let the rhythm of the music steady the tempest inside me. It wasn't long before a man approached, eyes glistening with the predatory glint of intoxication. His shirt clung to his chest, soaked from the damp heat of too many bodies packed too closely together. He did a once over of me. "Can I buy you a drink?" he asked, voice slurring slightly. I looked him over, calculating. The desperation in his eyes was so conspicuous it bordered on tragic.

"Yes," I said, forcing a smile. It was not a friendly smile; it was more of a grimace. But of course, he was a man, so he didn't notice this. We traded small talk, his words fumbling to fill the space between us while mine stayed sharp, circling the kill. He pushed a shot towards me; and I let the glass sit there for a minute before I threw the vodka back down my throat in one quick action. I had expected him to slip something in my drink. I wanted so badly to wake up naked in his bed, foggy brained and smelling of sex, not remembering how I got there. Unfortunately, it didn't happen. It never happens when you want it to.

I learned his name was Kirk and he sold vacuums and loved poker. Boring. The entire time we were talking Kirk's eyes flicked to the curves of my body, barely concealed by the thin fabric of my dress. After a while my patience frayed to the edge of snapping, I couldn't bear it any longer. "Cut to the chase."

He blinked, confusion shadowing his features. "What?"

"I know you just want to fuck me, so just cut the bullshit and take me to your car."

He laughed and shook his head. "I know this is going to sound crazy, but that's not my goal. I want to get to know you first." I rolled my eyes and grabbed his hand and slipped it under my short dress. His expression twisted in a mixture of disgust and surprise. "What's wrong with you?" he hissed, yanking his arm from my grip as if my touch burned him. He stood up, taking a step back, shaking his head as though to clear the very thought of me. Anger surged, hot and blinding, as I watched him slink back into the crowd. I didn't wait for my heartbeat to slow; I stalked off, shoulders set like granite. No one rejects me. He'd learn that soon.

I found my car and lit a cigarette, the smoke curling around my face and I waited. Time stretched, elastic and torturous. Finally, he emerged, looking around as though checking for threats that weren't there—or so he thought. Headlights off, I followed him, keeping a respectable distance. His apartment was not far, and I parked down the street, the engine's idle a low growl as he fumbled with his keys at the entrance. I slipped out of the car, following the shadows, every step a crescendo of anticipation. He disappeared inside, and I counted to ten—no more, no less—before making my way to the door. It would be unlocked; childless unmarried men were essentially careless and had nothing to live for. If he had a wife or girlfriend I'm sure he'd lock the door then—or she'd be the smart one to make sure all the doors were locked, and the house was secure. Just as I thought, the door clicked open softly. I stepped into the dimly lit hallway, the scent of stale fast food and unwashed linens mixing with the lingering beat of disco from the club.

As I stood there, listening to him take a shower, the anger I had earlier simmered and turned into a cold calculation. Not tonight. I made a note of his address, committing the aging apartment complex to memory. This man, this rejector, was going to be my next project, my next obsession. It started with daily surveillance, as I trailed him, shadowing the mundane rhythms of his life.

I watched him head to work; I followed him as he met with friends at diners and picked up takeout. On a quiet Sunday afternoon, I followed him to a local grocery store. I was ready for another day of mundane surveillance when something unexpected unfolded. A girl, no older than twelve, got out of his car. She was a mirror to my own past, to the wounds inflicted by Michael, the thief of my innocence. My heart pounded, an ugly revelation taking shape. This man wasn't just a rejector; he was a predator.

In that moment, my purpose solidified, gaining the edges of righteous anger. The fucker. Suddenly, there was no trace of guilt left within me—I had real cause to kill him now. Inside the grocery store,

I wove through the aisles until I found them in the meat section, his hand settled possessively on her back as they scrutinized packages of steak. The sight made my vision blur, blood roaring in my ears, the past and present colliding in a nauseating whirl. I saw him turn his head and whisper in her ear, his lips pursed. His lips brush across her cheek. It was subtle, but I saw it. I was high as hell, my head swimming from the acid I took earlier. But I knew this wasn't a hallucination. This was real.

I walked towards them, an undeniable force propelling me forward. Rage seethed through my veins, and with it, a cold clarity. "You fucking creep," I said, my voice low and dark.

They both turned to look at me. "What did you just say?"

"You heard me," I hissed, stepping closer, invading his space with the purpose of someone who has nothing left to lose. "How dare you lay your hands on her, you vile piece of shit."

His eyes darted around as fury had unchained my restraint. Customers nearby began to look over, sensing the undercurrent of violence, but I had tunnel vision—focused solely on him. "You don't know what you're talking about lady," he protested.

"I know exactly what you are," I said, my voice dripping with cold assurance. "And I promise you, I'm going to make you pay for every moment you've stolen from her."

The girl, frozen with indecision, looked between us, unsure if I posed a real threat. He would learn that I was darkness incarnate, that my purpose was a maelstrom that once unleashed, would show no mercy. Rage seethed through my veins, and with it, a cold clarity. "I can save you," I said to the girl, my voice as steady as my resolve. Before she could react, I grabbed her arm. Her yelp was sharp and sudden.

"Get your hands off her, you crazy bitch! You're that woman from the club, I knew you looked familiar! You've been following me, haven't you?" he shouted, a mixture of panic and anger tainting his words. With a surge of determination, I pulled the girl, who couldn't have weighed more than a hundred pounds, toward the entrance. A chorus of *"Hey!"* and *"Ma'am!"* erupted from the shoppers and employees as I forcefully dragged her outside.

"Let me go!" she screamed, her voice cracking with both fear and confusion. "You're hurting me!"

"I'm saving you!" I insisted, my grip tightening.

"I don't need saving! He's, my dad!" she screamed, her words tearing through my conviction like a blade. Stunned, I let go of her arm. Within moments, the police arrived, their lights casting a disorienting wash of red and blue over the scene. The man blurted out his accusations.

"This crazy woman followed me and tried to kidnap my daughter!" he shouted, pointing at me with a trembling finger. I stood there, frozen, the cacophony of the scene washing over me. The din of voices, the blaring hum of streetlights, and the distant wail of a siren forming a disorienting symphony. I shook my head. All of this for an attempted kidnapping, it seemed unnecessary. I would have felt different if I took her, but she was safe. No need for the entire police force to come running, but here they all were, regardless.

A male officer stared at me, pen and notepad in hand. "Can you tell me what happened?" he asked, his tone stern but not unkind. I attempted to explain, tried to string together my thoughts into a coherent narrative, but my words were jumbled frantic.

"I saw them together, and I thought… I saw him kissing the little girl. I was trying to save her," I pleaded, my voice breaking.

"You saw him kissing her or you *thought* you saw it ma'am?"

I blinked, taking myself back to the moment. Him leaning down, his lips just mere inches from her ear as he whispered, his mouth traveling to the corner of her lips. It was subtle, but I saw it. I didn't imagine it. "No. I saw it…I definitely saw it." I said, my voice tinged with a sense of uncertainty. The cop heard it too. He raised his eyebrows as he stared at me.

I turned and listened to the man from a few feet away as he told his version of events to another officer. "I met her at a club last weekend," he said. "I think she was trying to get revenge on me for rejecting her. She's crazy, officer. I want her locked up for stalking me and trying to kidnap my daughter."

The officers exchanged looks, a silent conversation passing between them. One of them gently but firmly placed a hand on my shoulder. "Ma'am, for your own safety and the safety of others, we think it would be best if you came with us. We're going to take you to a facility where you can get some help."

I shook my head violently. "No, *you don't understand!*" I cried, trying to pull away as a police officer grabbed me. "I'm not crazy. *Please,* you have to believe me!" But my pleas fell on deaf ears. To them, I was just another unhinged woman lost to her delusions. The truth I had seen, the darkness I had tried to combat, was eclipsed by their preconceived notions. They escorted me to the squad car, the chill of the handcuffs biting into my wrists. I stared out the window, the blur of streetlights and shadows intertwining in my mind. Reds, blues, oranges and yellows streaked my vision. I was still incredibly high on acid when they took me to the psych ward, which didn't help my case of me not being insane as I watched one of the orderlies transform into a dog right before my eyes. "Her pupils are extremely dilated," she barked, shining a light into my eyes. "She's not well."

At the psych ward the nurses and doctors spoke to me in soft, measured tones, asking questions I couldn't quite process. They nodded sympathetically, their eyes never quite meeting mine, convinced of my madness. Days bled into nights, and I became another name on a long list of the forgotten. They truly believed I was crazy, that my ramblings were nothing more than the product of a fractured mind. The more I tried to protest, the deeper I sank into their narrative, trapped in a place that echoed with the cries of the misunderstood.

Conversations with nurses and doctors were a loop of condescension and misunderstanding, their questions probing the depths of my mind, trying to unearth a reason for my perceived insanity. Then one day, Dean arrived. He was a new orderly, tall and thin and unassuming, with kind eyes that seemed out of place in the sterile, clinical environment. His first day in the ward was nondescript—that is, until he approached me, his expression curious yet nonjudgmental.

"Hello, I'm Dean Stratton," he introduced himself with a genuine smile as he handed me my medication cup. His voice was warm, lacking the usual pitying tone I had grown accustomed to.

"Hi," I replied, my voice tinged with suspicion. "I'm... no one, really."

He chuckled softly, shaking his head. "I've been here for just a few hours, and I can already tell you are definitely someone, even if you don't think so."

There was an honesty in his words that caught me off guard, and for the first time in a long while, I felt a flicker of hope. Over the next few days, Dean made an effort to speak to me during his rounds, never prying too hard but always showing a genuine interest in what I had to say. One afternoon, as we sat outside in the small, enclosed courtyard, he finally broached the subject that had landed me in the facility. "So, they say you tried to kidnap a girl," his tone is gentle. "But I sense there's more to your story."

I took a deep breath. "I saw someone I thought who preyed on children. I was just trying to save the girl."

He nodded, his eyes never leaving mine, and for the first time, I felt a flicker of understanding from someone. "I believe you," he said simply, his words soothed my wounded soul. For weeks, Dean and I talked whenever we had the chance. He listened as I recounted my past, the abuse I had endured as a teen under the guise of love, the darkness I had fought against. He never judged, never doubted, always offering a shoulder and a kind word. I felt a surge of emotions I hadn't allowed myself to feel in years—hope, trust, and something deeper, something frighteningly vulnerable. As my time in the facility seemed to stretch on interminably, Dean approached me with a gleam of excitement in his eyes. "I have a surprise for you," he said, his smile wide.

I raised my eyebrow, curiosity piqued. "What kind of surprise?" I asked, a smile playing on my lips.

He leaned in closer, lowering his voice to a conspiratorial whisper. "You're getting out tomorrow."

A surge of emotion hit me like a tidal wave—elation, disbelief, relief. "Really?" I breathed, not daring to believe it.

"Really," Dean confirmed, his eyes brimming with warmth. "I saw your release papers earlier this morning. You're free to go."

The next morning, my release papers were processed, and I stood on the threshold of the facility that had been both my prison and my sanctuary. Yet amidst the joy of regaining my freedom, there was a gnawing sadness deep within me—a fear that I might never see Dean again. As I prepared to leave, I found Dean waiting for me by the entrance. "Am I still going to see you?" I asked, my voice barely above a whisper, dread clawing at my insides.

Dean glanced around, ensuring no one else was watching, and then his lips were on mine, soft and warm. "Just know, I broke all the rules for you," he murmured. "I was not supposed to fall for a patient like this, but I couldn't help it."

Returning to my old life was surreal. I was surprised to find that I still had my job at Weinman and Weinman. My colleagues welcomed me back with hesitant smiles and cautious words, their curiosity palpable but unspoken. Life changed swiftly after that. Dean and I started seeing each other outside of the facility.

Our love grew rapidly, a whirlwind romance that seemed to defy the constraints of time. After a few blissful months, Dean popped the question in the most unexpected way. We were at a quaint little café, sharing a quiet breakfast when he slid a small velvet box across the table. I was on cloud nine, deliriously happy. I had finally found true love, someone who understood and cherished me for who I was. After a miserable couple of years—after Waylon, finally there was a sense of completeness, a feeling that I had been made whole again.

The months turned into years. Dean left the mental institution shortly after I did and began his residency to become a doctor, which was always his plan from the beginning. It was a new chapter in his life, full of promise and endless hours at the hospital. Initially, I was ecstatic for him, proud of his dedication and ambition. But it didn't take long for me to realize that his demanding schedule would affect our relationship more than I had anticipated. The late-night shifts and endless rounds at the hospital consumed Dean's time and energy. Last year is when it got even worse, and we stopped being intimate, and he started to become nasty, and controlling. We had once defied the odds, but now it seemed those odds were catching up to us.

PRESENT DAY

I push open the heavy door to the beige-bricked building where Dr. Maggie and I have our weekly excavation of my soul, feeling unusually buoyant. Inside, the waiting room is oppressively quiet, the sort of silence that feels like an impending storm. I sit in one of the russet chairs, flipping through magazines, and wait as the minutes stack up, one on top of another, like a Jenga tower about to topple over. She never comes out, and it's already 4:30—half an hour past our appointment.

I rise, confused, a jittery feeling gnawing at my stomach. A man I recognize drifts into my line of sight. He's another therapist who works in the building, his face a familiar but name-unknown kind of way. I seize the moment and intercept him. "Excuse me, have you seen Dr. Maggie? We had a four o'clock."

He stops, and a shadow passes over his face, something close to horror tinged with sorrow. "You didn't hear?" His voice is soft, but it slices through the air like a scalpel. I just look at him, my head shaking in slow-motion disbelief. He hesitates, glancing at the floor where dusty sunlight pools, then meeting my eyes again, his own fraught with sadness. "Dr. Maggie was found dead yesterday morning."

The words land on me like a physical blow. "Pardon?" It's a reflex, like if I hear it again, it might somehow change.

"She was stabbed at her home last night," he elaborates, his tone gentle but unyielding. "Such a terrible loss. She was a lovely lady."

I swallow hard, the world narrowing down to a single point of understanding, jagged and sharp. "Thank you," I manage, my voice barely more than a whisper. I pivot hurriedly, each step down the stairs feels like falling, and by the time I push through the double doors and out onto the street, the cold air hits me, bringing with it a slurry of disbelief and sorrow. I drive home, my vision blurred by tears of confusion and the surreal weight of disbelief. The mantra repeats in my head like a broken record:

I didn't kill her. It wasn't me.

When I pull up to my street, something out of a nightmare greets me— flashing lights, an ambulance, and a cluster of police cars corralling the house next door like vultures. Mr. Hanson—the quiet, bent man who's been my neighbor for years—stands on his lawn, his face contorted in grief, streaked with tears that carve lines through the grime of his age. He's hysterical, crying out in strangled gasps.

My curiosity overrides my caution, and I drift closer, my feet moving as if through molasses. There's yellow tape encircling the Hanson home, a glaring ribbon of tragedy. Through the open door, I catch glimpses of frantic activity—officers trying to console Mr. Hanson.

And then, amidst the chaos, I see her. Mrs. Hanson lies sprawled on the living room floor, an almost surreal splash of gore against the drab carpet. Her stomach is an open, visceral wound, blood still glistening like some macabre painting. I step back, my breath coming in jagged bursts. This can't be real. Today isn't real. But it becomes all too tangible when Detective Wells emerges from the house, his gaze locking onto mine with an intensity that freezes me in place. His eyes reveal a cocktail of horror and suspicion.

I didn't do it I mouth, my eyes wide, pleading, as the gravity of his glare weighed on me like an accusation. Without waiting for a response, I turn on my heel and run, each step back to my house louder and more desperate. I slam the door behind me, my breath erratic, sharp as shattered glass. Inside, the rooms feel alien, warped by the day's events. I didn't kill them. I collapsed against the door, trembling. But a cold, insidious doubt worms its way into my mind. Did I?

SUGAR

1977

The only woman I've ever killed was my mother.

It happened a year ago, in a perfectly ordinary setting—the elderly home where she's lived out her life for the past three years. At only sixty years old my mother had developed dementia, her mind a fragile web of frayed connections. I watched her slip further away each visit, her eyes losing their focus, words tumbling out in meaningless clusters. She often didn't recognize me but greeted me with a blank, polite smile reserved for strangers.

One morning, while I was busy making breakfast for Dean, I got a call from a nurse at the senior home. The woman's voice was low and tinged with concern. "Mrs. Stratton, you need to come see your mother. She's having some sort of episode."

I froze, the spatula motionless in mid-air. I hadn't visited in a week, and apparently in that one week her condition had worsened. "What sort of episode?"

The line rustled with nervous static. "Well, she keeps repeating something very concerning."

I could tell by her tentative tone that she was young and inexperienced, probably thrust into this role by someone with a higher pay grade. My patience thinned like ice over a thawing pond. "Please get to the point. What is my mother saying, ma'am?"

There was a heavy silence, each second dragging out like a lifetime. Then she said it, her breath shaky and uncertain. "She keeps saying, *my daughter is a killer.*"

My stomach dropped, an icy dread seeping into my bones. I had to sit down, the kitchen tilting ominously. I glanced over at the stairs. Luckily, Dean was in the shower getting ready to leave for work. He couldn't hear this. He couldn't see me unraveling.

"She keeps repeating it over and over and…" the woman trailed off, waiting for me to respond, perhaps hoping I'd offer some reasonable explanation.

"I'll be there this afternoon," I said, cutting her off.

"Thank you." I hung up the phone with a trembling hand. The drive to the facility was a blur, the world outside a grey smear of asphalt and bare trees. Memories of my mother before the illness crowded my mind—her laugh, her stern but loving eyes, the way she used to stroke my hair and hum softly. But those memories were tainted now by her illness.

When I arrived, an orderly directed me to my mother's room, her eyes averted. Through the window I see my mother sitting in her rocking chair, staring out the window at the winter-bare garden below, her lips moving in a silent litany. "We don't know why she keeps saying it, but it's scaring everyone," she explained, her voice hushed as though my mother might hear through the closed door.

"I'm so sorry. Her mind really is gone," I shook my head, forcing a note of grief into my voice. "Sometimes she says the most nonsensical things."

"Well do you have any idea why she could be saying that?" The woman asked.

I searched her face; it was etched with concern. She was a pretty woman, no more than twenty, with big blue eyes and bouncy brown curls. She was a short little thing, probably not even five feet tall. I wondered if she was the one who called me. I couldn't tell from her voice. "Well, I did eat my twin in the womb. Mother never quite got over that."

She stared at me horrified.

It was the truth. Mother was devastated once she found out she had lost one of her babies. When she was pregnant with us, my father had died in the war, and she never wanted to bare someone else's child, she said it would be a betrayal to my father. Ironic, isn't it? I was a killer before I was even born.

The orderly twisted her mouth, concern shadowing her face. "If you could maybe talk to her, get her to stop saying that we would all be very grateful." It comes out more like a demand than a request, the edge in her voice clear.

I nodded once. "I'll sure try," I said with a tight smile. The woman stared at me for far too long, her eyes searching mine as if excavating some buried truth. I held her gaze until she relented, pulling open the door. both of us step inside. "May I have some time alone with her, please?" I asked, my tone clipped.

The girl's face turned sour, but she nodded and stalked out of the room, leaving me alone with my mother. I turned around and slowly made my way over to her. "Mother, it's me," I said, stepping into her line of sight. She turned slowly, and for a moment, a flicker of recognition crossed her face before it clouded over again.

"My daughter is a killer," she whispered, her voice hoarse and raw, as if she'd been saying it for hours. I felt my breath hitch, my hands trembling.

"It's not true," the words tasted bitter on my tongue. I sat next to her, her eyes faraway and staring into nothingness. But she just looked through me, her eyes distant and unfocused. The rest of the afternoon passed in a haze, my attempts to calm her and distract her proving futile. The words haunted me, lingering long after I'd left her behind.

I drove home, my stomach in a twist. How could she know? Had she somehow seen through the fog of her disease, glimpsing the dark truth I carried? Each visit after that felt like a tiny death—me dying a little more inside, her repeating those damn words like a broken record. The nurses watched me with concern, their eyes following me down the hallways, whispers trailing in my wake. Every other day, I returned, forced through the ritual by some unnamable guilt.

And then one day, fed up, I decided to bring tea.

Mother always loved tea. I brewed it just as she liked it, but that day, there was a special ingredient—cyanide. I offered the cup to her, my hands unsteady, but she swatted it away, her mind too tangled to remember how she loved it. Frustration ate at me. I couldn't force her without her screaming and alerting the nurses.

"Come on, mother, let's get you to bed," I whispered. She didn't say anything back except for those same five words:

My daughter is a killer.

I guided her to bed, her frail body compliant, and pulled a pillow from beneath her head. I hesitated, the weight of what I was about to do crashing down on me, but the memory of her words—the accusation—burned like acid. I placed the pillow over her face, closing my eyes, refusing to look. She didn't even struggle, her body too weak to fight. I held it there until she went limp, my own breath ragged and uneven, tears streaking down my face. I go home and wait, the minutes stretching into hours, dragging the shackles of guilt behind each one. Finally, the call came. The voice on the other end is somber but concise. "Your mother has passed."

Part of me wondered if they suspected I had killed her. They were sick of her, scaring everyone with her daily mantra. They *had* to know. But they never said anything.

They wanted it to stop, too.

I hung up, letting the phone slip from my fingers. The words echoed in my skull. My mother's death was the only one I ever truly mourned. There was something so devastating about it, a unique sorrow that pierces deeper than any other loss. Losing your mother means losing the person who gave you life, who formed the core of your world. For all her faults, for all the hurt and confusion, she was still my mother. She was the one who held me as a child, who kissed my scraped knees, who once knew me better than I knew myself.

The finality of her death was like a gaping wound, a raw emptiness that nothing could fill. I had taken her life, not out of malice but out of a twisted sense of mercy and desperation. Yet, the act left me hollow, burdened with an unbearable grief that would never truly leave me. In the end, it was not just her physical death I mourned but the loss of everything she had been and could never be again. Her death ripped from me the last fragile threads of my own humanity, leaving behind a cold, relentless void.

PRESENT DAY

I didn't kill them. I couldn't have. The thought is a pinball ricocheting through the corridors of my mind, each bounce sending panic coursing into my veins. The air feels thicker, the walls closer, an invisible jury judging from every corner. Unless—I catch myself grasping at the memory, a broken thread in a web of half-forgotten nights—unless I blacked out during an acid trip.

But no, I've never completely blacked out like that before. The darkness in my recollection feels more like sleep than oblivion, even if it was painted in the hallucinatory hues of acid. I've been doing acid long enough that I never lost my agency on it. Never woke up in some grim twilight zone with blood on my hands and someone's life snuffed out behind me. The trips, while wild, always had a tether, a filigree of control woven through the madness.

Because...why them? Especially Mrs. Hanson. It doesn't make any sense. I remember how she looked at me that one day, that look of detest in her eyes. As if she knew what I did to Dean. But no. She was my neighbor. I knew well enough that killing my neighbor would only put more suspicion on me. And what about Dr. Maggie? Did I drive to her home, sneak in unnoticed and stab her to death all on an acid trip? I don't know. *No.* I didn't wake up covered in blood. I squeeze my eyes shut, trying to remember…. remember *anything*. The fragments of memories slip through my fingers like grains of sand, each thought scattered by the wind. My mind feels like a maze twisted upon itself, every corner leading to another dead end.

The phone rings and I jump. I slowly walk over to the phone and put the receiver to my ear, the sound of my heartbeat pounding in the silence. Expecting Detective Wells to be on the other end, ready to dive into a cross-examination that would root out the truth from the rubble of my mind, I brace myself. "Hello?"

"It's Chris." My whole body relaxes, the tension melting away at the sound of his voice. It always does that, strangely enough—smoothed the rough edges of my panic, wraps me in a fleeting calm. "I uh... Lizzie kicked me out."

I blink, gripping the phone tightly. "She did?"

"Yeah, she's really upset at me. Can I stay at your place, just for the night until I can figure out what I'm going to do long term?"

Air catches in my throat. I look out the window. It's been a few hours since the pandemonium next door. Everything was calm, only a singular cop car was left outside. The tension from before feels like a coiled spring, temporarily released, but ready to snap back at any moment. I was relieved that Detective Wells left, never walking over to my house from next door to speak to me. Now is not a good time for Chris to stay here.

What if I blacked out again and killed Chris in the middle of the night? But…I can't say no to him. He's everything to me—my anchor in this tumultuous sea of doubt and fear. His presence might be the only thing keeping me tethered to some semblance of normalcy. "Bring your things," I say, the words sounding distant by the time they leave my lips.

Every part of me wants to stop him from coming over, from this night turning into another mystery for which I might be the unwilling and unwitting star. But the thought of his voice, his presence close enough to touch, drowns out the echo of all my fears. There's a softness in the way the evening light filters through the curtains, a deceptive tranquility. I take a deep breath, preparing for Chris's arrival, hoping desperately that tonight will be one of the good nights, one where my mind stays whole, and the darkness doesn't pull me under again.

SUGAR

* * *

I've decided to make lasagna from scratch. I layer the pasta sheets, smoothing over each layer with sauce, cheese, meat. It's methodical, almost meditative. By the time Chris arrives, the house smells like a cozy Italian bistro. He walks in with a duffel bag slung over his shoulder, a tired but grateful smile on his face. We exchange a quick kiss, and he drops his bag on the sofa. "It's nice here," he says, letting out a pleased sigh. "Smells amazing."

We sit down to eat, and I try to push away the thoughts gnawing at the edges of my conscience. Between mouthfuls of lasagna, I casually mention, "My neighbor was murdered today."

Chris doesn't even bat an eye. "That's sad," he says, his voice muffled by a forkful of food. "Do they know who did it?"

"No. They don't know who did it."

My nerves are a tight, fraying wire. The normalcy of his reaction feels bizarre, like we're actors in a play that's taken a dark and unscripted turn. After we finish eating, Chris gets up and gently pulls me into his lap at the dinner table. His warmth seeps into me, melting some of the tension. "Let's go to bed," he whispers, his breath tickling my ear. We don't fuck, we make love, and for a while, everything feels right. But that night, nightmares torment me. Mrs. Hanson's stomach, a gaping wound, blood pouring out—an image tattooed onto my mind. I don't see colors like I did when I was awake, I just see blood. A deep dark red; almost black. I wake up in a cold sweat, my mind foggy, disoriented. Different snippets of another strange dream mesh together—Chris whispering in the hallway to someone, shadows moving about the house. I feel the weight of his body on the bed at one point again. I hear him whisper in my ear, *fucking crazy murderous bitch.* The words linger like a haunting echo. I feel myself teetering on the edge of madness.

219

Morning arrives like an unwelcome guest. Tiredness racks me, but I'm relieved to find Chris in the kitchen, shirtless, making breakfast. The mingling scents of coffee and bacon fill the air, adding a comforting layer to the morning haze. "Good morning," he says lightly, his demeanor cheerful. "I'll make you a cup of coffee. You look tired."

I sit at the table, watching him as he moves around the kitchen. His presence is soothing, even though a twinge of last night's dream lingers in my mind.

Fucking crazy murderous bitch.

"Will we be taking separate cars to work this morning?" I ask, my voice wary.

He pours me a cup, setting it in front of me. "We have to."

I warm my hands with the coffee mug. "Just for a bit, right? Since you and that insufferable bitch Lizzie are over, maybe we can start telling people about us soon."

Chris looks at me, his eyes sharp, glaring. "Me and Lizzie are not over until we divorce. And *do not* call her a bitch."

I stare at him, shocked by his response. He's only supposed to love me, why was he getting defensive about Lizzie? His face softens as he realizes the impact of his words.

"I'm sorry," he says, leaning down, kissing my face and neck, smothering me with affection. I smile. It feels good to be loved.

"I won't say anything until I have your approval," I reply, trying to sound obedient. "But people will see you leaving my house. They'll see your car outside my house."

Chris sighs, a heavy sound filled with resignation. "I don't care about your neighbors knowing. I just don't want this to affect work. So, let's keep it professional when we're there, okay?"

I nod, sipping my coffee. His words play in my mind on a loop, each repetition making them more surreal. How easily he compartmentalizes, shelves one life while living another, perhaps that's something I must strive to do too. My thoughts trail back to Mrs. Hanson and Dr. Maggie, and a cold lump of dread settles in my stomach. I just need to hold on, keep everything together. For now.

Chris spends another night at my house. We curl up with a bottle of wine, the glow from the living room lamp casting soft shadows on the walls. His presence brings a semblance of comfort, a distraction from the gnawing unease that's been clinging to me. I take a sip of wine, letting the warmth blur my edges. Then a thought hits me.

Where are my cats?

I furrow my brow, my fingers tightening around the wine glass as I try to remember the last time I saw Avocado and Whiskers. My heart races, the sudden spike of anxiety making it hard to think clearly.

"Is something wrong?" Chris asks, his gaze sharpening with concern.

"I..." I hesitate, wary of sounding crazy, but the feeling is too urgent to ignore. "I don't know where my cats are."

Chris stares at me, a flicker of worry passing over his face. "Well, they must be here somewhere. Do they hide?" he asks, glancing around the room, and then bending down to look under the slight crack of the sofa like they can fit under there.

"I just can't remember the last time I saw them," I say, my voice thinning, nearly cracking with suppressed panic.

"Well, I'll help you look for them." He gets up and grabs my hand to lift me off the sofa. The touch is grounding, a necessary tether. We start on the first floor, checking all the nooks and corners where they might have curled up. I call their names, my voice echoing through the quiet house. But there's no answering meow, no soft padding of paws.

"Let's look upstairs," Chris suggests. We search my room, moving through the repetitive ritual of lifting sheets, moving around furniture, and calling out into the sterile silence. We check the bathroom, peering into the tub and behind the shower curtain. No cats. Chris points to the door of the guest room. "I bet they're in here," he says.

I doubt it. I almost never open the guest room door. There was no way they were in there. But I shrug, the nagging worry driving me onward. "Maybe."

Chris opens the door, and we're immediately hit by a smell so foul it makes both of us gag. It's a rancid, putrid odor that seems to reach out and slap us in the face, clinging to the back of my throat. "Oh god, what is that?" Chris says through his hand that's tightly cupped over his nose.

Panic creeps up my spine, each note of that foul scent amplifying my dread. I call out desperately, "Whiskers? Avocado?" My voice shakes, the need to find them overtaking any thought of what might be causing the smell. Chris approaches the door to the closet, the source of the stench becoming unmistakable. The reality crystallizes, cold and sharp. He opens the door slowly, and both of us jump back in horror. It's Marlo. Dead.

* * *

No. This doesn't make any sense. I cup my mouth with my shaking hands. Marlo is gray and decaying, her mouth open as if she's screaming. My heart pounds in my chest like a frantic drum. I stare at Chris, who seems unnervingly calm, his expression unreadable. "I... I didn't do this," I whisper, my voice breaking.

Chris stares at me and nods, slowly backing away. "Okay, I believe you," he whispers. "We should call the police, though."

"No!" I say loudly, the urgency in my voice making him blink.

"Um, okay...why?" he asks, a mix of confusion and concern in his eyes. "We need to tell someone, Satara." He's edging out of the room, his movements cautious, as if he's unsure of what I might do next.

"The police are going to think I did it." There's a tremor in my voice, the paranoia tightening its grip around my lungs.

Chris shakes his head, trying to reassure me. "We'll explain. I'll back you up. You won't get in trouble."

I shake my head vigorously, my entire body vibrating with fear. I notice Chris sweating, or is he crying? I can't tell. The lines between reality and my worst fears blur, creating a disorienting haze. I move closer to him, my desperation palpable. He backs away, and I let out a loud guttural noise from the back of my throat. "Please," I cry. "Do you love me, Chris?"

"Of course." There's a hesitant edge to his voice.

"We're going to be together, right? We can't be together if you call the police." My voice is low. It shakes.

"Well, what do you want to do, Satara?"

Tears spill down my cheeks as I make my desperate plea. "You have to help me bury her."

He swallows hard, his eyes wide with a mix of emotions I can't quite read. "What?"

Panic racks through my body. "Please you have to help me bury her!" I scream, my voice cracking.

He stares at me, his eyes still wide. He lifts his hands up as if trying to calm me down. "Okay," he whispers. "Okay."

And so, we bury Marlo in the backyard under the lemon tree, right where I buried her son a few months earlier. The soil is cool and damp, the night air thick with the scent of earth and citrus. Chris is silent as we dig, but he keeps looking over at me with a strange, pained expression. I can feel the spell wearing off. I remember Millicent saying something about the spell wearing off on some people if their emotions were too conflicting. Maybe that's what's happening. Chris should be happy to help me bury her. He shouldn't be looking at me that way. He shouldn't be thinking terrible things about me.

After the deed is done, we head back inside, our silence heavy and oppressive. Chris sits at the table, and I stand across from him, leaning against the kitchen counter. The distance between us feels like an endless chasm. "Why are you looking at me like that?"

"Like what?" he asks, trying to sound casual but failing.

My hands shake uncontrollably. "You think I killed her," I whisper, my fear turning into a chilling certainty. Chris swallows, the tension in his throat visible. I wonder if he saw me grab the knife off the counter as his head was bent down.

"No, I don't," he replies, but his voice is almost a whisper, lacking the conviction I need it to have. We stare at each other for what feels like an eternity, the silence growing thicker, more unbearable.

Then, in a flash, Chris bolts for the door.

Panic floods through my veins as I chase after him. "Chris, wait!" But it's too late. I reach for him as he dashes for the door, my fingers just barely grabbing hold of his shirt. He trips, his body falling hard to the ground with a sickening thud. "You're supposed to love me!"

I scream, my voice echoing off the walls. The desperation in my voice sounds foreign, even to my ears. I ignore the deep gash the knife made to my side as I pull it out from my waistband; it's a dull pain. The cold steel of the blade catches the dim light, and I press it to his throat. "You're not going anywhere," I say, my voice icy and determined.

Chris's eyes widen in terror, and he begins to plead. "Okay, okay, please just don't kill me!" he screams, his face contorted in fear.

"Get up," I command, still pointing the knife at him. My heart pounds in my chest, adrenaline coursing through me like wildfire. Chris moves slowly as he gets up, his movements hesitant, eyes never leaving the blade. I keep the knife trained on him as I guide him back to the center of the house, away from the door and back into the kitchen. We move together, a macabre dance of terror and control. I yank a length of rope out from a drawer and tie his hands tightly behind his back, securing him to a chair in the corner of the kitchen. His breaths come quick and shallow, the sound mixing with my own harsh panting.

"Please, Satara, don't do this," he whispers, his voice breaking. Ignoring his pleas, I finish tying his ankles to the chair. His face is a mask of dread, his eyes pleading with me as if trying to reach some last glimmer of humanity within me. "We can talk about this, Satara! You don't have to do this!" Chris pleads, the desperation in his voice clawing at my sense of control.

"I'm doing this for us. We *will* be together," I say, my voice eerily calm. I drag the chair to the hallway closet, with him bound to it, across the floor. It takes more effort than I anticipated, his resistance making every moment more taxing. But the desperation fuels me, overriding any fatigue. With a final, strenuous heave, I get him into the closet.

"Please, we can talk about this, Satara! You don't have to do this!" Chris pleads, the desperation in his voice clawing at my sense of control. Backing away from the closet, I turn and leave, closing the door behind me. My hands shake with adrenaline. Chris's muffled cries grow fainter, obscured by the distance and the thick walls of the closet. I sink into the couch, the tension slowly sapping my strength. The bottle of wine we were sharing earlier in the night sits on the coffee table, half-empty, an eerie reminder of how quickly things spiraled out of control.

SUGAR

* * *

As soon as dawn hits, I rush out to my car, speeding through the quiet morning streets, panic-stricken, the shadows of my actions lingering like ghosts. Millicent's building comes into view. I bang on her door relentlessly, my fist aching but my urgency unrelenting.

"Jesus, what's your issue?" Millicent says as she finally opens the door, her eyes narrowing in irritation. She's wearing a purple satin robe, and her hair is all messed up. It's the first time I haven't seen her perfect and camera-ready. Before she can say more, I push past her, the air heavy with my desperation.

"The spell," I say, my chest heaving, breaths coming in sharp. "It's not working anymore."

Millicent's confusion is evident, her brow furrowing. "What do you mean?"

I pace back and forth, each step amplifying my sense of dread. "It... it's worn off or something. Chris, he's... he's not..." My voice fades, unable to find the words to encompass the betrayal, the fear.

"Calm down and tell me what's happened. Where is Chris?" she asks.

I stare at her, my emotions boiling over. "You told me he would be in love with me!" I scream, my voice raw.

Millicent raises her hands, palms out, trying to soothe my hysteria. "Satara, please. Just tell me, where is Chris?"

I swallow hard, my throat dry. "At my house."

"Alive?" she asks, her question piercing through my panic.

I look at her incredulously. "Does it matter?" I snap.

Millicent shrugs. "I want to make sure he's okay."

I shake my head in disbelief. "Why are you acting all self-righteous? You don't care about people! You told me yourself you've killed before." My voice is rising again, fueled by frustration and fear.

"We're not talking about me right now."

Her cold demeanor only fuels my anger further. I let out a loud scream, the sound echoing in the confined space of her living room.

"Just do the spell again!" I scream, my voice cracking. I rifled through my purse, finding the Ziploc bag with Chris's hair that I cut off this morning. I hurl it at her, my desperation palpable. "And do it correctly this time."

"So, he's alive," she says slowly, picking up the bag, her eyes flickering with some unreadable emotion. "And why are you covered in dirt?"

"Yes!" I scream, the word tearing from my throat. "He's alive. Is that what you want to hear?" My voice is raw, eyes burning with unshed tears. Millicent stares at me, her green eyes boring through mine, assessing, calculating.

"Okay," she says finally, her voice calm, almost too calm. She moves through her house with an eerie grace, gathering the items she needs for the spell. I watch her, my heart pounding, every second feeling like an eternity. She sets up the small altar, lighting the candles, the flickering flames casting shadows that dance menacingly on the walls.

"Sit," she instructs, her voice commanding but devoid of emotion. I comply, my body rigid with tension, my eyes never leaving her hands as she works. Millicent lit candles and begins the incantation, her words a chant that reverberates through the room, weaving the spell. I clutch the edges of the chair, my knuckles hurting, my breath bated. The air grows thick with the heavy scent of incense and herbs, a heady mix that makes my pulse race. She pauses, her eyes locking onto mine. "Remember, Satara, magic is not foolproof. There are forces beyond our control," she says, her tone a warning.

"I don't care. Just make him love me again."

She continues the ritual, her voice rising and falling in a melodic cadence. The room's atmosphere grows thicker, heavier, as if the very air is charged with power. My heart pounds in my chest, the anticipation almost too much to bear. Finally, she finishes, the spell cast, the magic hanging in the air like a living thing. She turns to me, her face unreadable. "It's done."

I feel a mix of relief and trepidation. Part of me wants to believe that everything will be alright now, that Chris will love me again, that things will finally be as they should be. But deep down, a gnawing fear remains. The fear that even magic might not be enough to mend what's been broken. The fear that perhaps, some things are beyond our control, beyond any spell's power. As Millicent extinguishes the candles, the smoke curling into the still air, I can only hope that her magic is strong enough to bring Chris back to me. And as I leave her house, the dawn's light creeping over the horizon, a cold certainty settles in my bones.

* * *

I've made a casserole for us tonight, a kind of dinner shaped by childhood memories. I dish out a generous helping for Chris, the metal spoon clinking against the ceramic, and move towards the dining table.

"Okay, dinner is served!" I announce. Chris stares back at me, his expression a wall of indifference. My smile fades like condensation on a mirror. "It's okay," I murmur, almost to myself. "You'll love me again soon enough."

Chris wriggles in his chair, the ropes cutting into his wrists, his muffled grunts piercing the suffocating quiet.

"I suppose I can take the tape off your mouth now. But you're going back in the closet if you scream, okay?" I widen my eyes, my voice teetering between threat and plea. Chris just continues to stare, a silent war in his gaze. I laugh, the sound brittle, fragile. "You're so handsome," I say, peeling the tape from his mouth, watching his lips turn raw from the adhesive. I sit down at the table across from him. "Silly me. Your hands are tied up—you can't eat on your own," With a warped tenderness, I feed him a forkful of the casserole. "Open wide."

"People are going to start wondering where I am," he says flatly, his voice a faraway echo. "You can't just hold me hostage forever."

I freeze, the fork hovering mid-air between us. The hollow truth of his words gnaw at the edges of my sanity. He's right, of course. I grab the phone off the receiver, the cord stretches taut as I bring it over to him. "You're going to call everyone important that you know, including your wife." I hold the phone out to him.

"And tell them *what?*" His voice is a canyon, empty and echoing.

I smile, a twisted parody of the girl-next-door cheer. "That you're living with me now, silly. And you won't be coming back."

"What about work?" he asks, a hint of defiance creeping into his tone. I stare at him, my eyes sharp; cold.

"You'll go back to work eventually. Just call and say you need a few days off."

I didn't have much of a plan, but I was hoping once the second love spell kicked in, he would do anything I asked him without force. Chris takes a deep breath, the weight of the moment pressing down like a vice. The silence stretches, thick and suffocating. "If you don't comply, I will kill you," my words cut through the quiet like a blade, leaving no room for doubt, no space for hope. He tries to hold onto defiance, but it slips from his grasp. "And then I'll go to your house," I add, "and I will kill your beautiful wife and child."

Panic blazes in his eyes, replacing the dull resignation.

"No!" he yells, his voice cracking under the pressure.

"Trust me, I don't want to do it, Chris!" I scream.

"You can't force someone to love you...to be with you." His whisper is a gut punch. I stare at him, the fragments of my composure slipping away.

"I have before, and I can now."

"Who?" he breathes, eyes wide, innocent in their fear.

"My husband," I say, the words bitter on my tongue. "He tried to leave me, too. Tried to leave a few weeks before he disappeared. I told him there was nowhere to run or hide. That no matter where he goes, I would hunt him down and kill him. He knew I would do it. So, he stayed."

My voice grows darker, a storm of memories crowding in. I think back to that fateful night. He had been packing his bags, his resolve like a physical barrier between us. My threats had been the tidal wave that crashed through that barrier, and he had stayed—his love twisted into a chain that bound us both. Chris's eyes remain on me, a silent challenge, daring me to continue, to unravel all the tightly wound strings. "I killed him," I whisper, the admission pulling steel strings from my vocal cords. "He cheated on me with my best friend."

"You shouldn't have done that."

I shake my head, grief racking my entire body. "Unfortunately, there are no laws against cheating. So, I got justice on my own."

"Satara," he whispers.

"I was jealous," I continue. I sniff, tears are falling free now. "It took me a long time to finally accept this…" My voice falters. I stare at him, my eyes stinging. "I was jealous of my husband, not my best friend."

Chris blinks. "What do you mean?"

Something blooms inside me. the need to admit everything. To put everything out on the table for Chris. The man I was going to be with for the rest of my life, deserved to know. And once the spell kicks in, I know that he'll keep my secret. "I was jealous that my husband got to be with Lilah," he stares at me, willing me to keep talking. "I had feelings for her," I croak out, the words tasting like acid. "I was in love with her."

He's eerily calm. I shake my head and continue. "The feelings had always been there, I think. I just wanted to deny them, I willed them to go away. Because it felt wrong. I was not supposed to be in love with a woman. It's not…*normal*. So, I told myself that…that I had killed Dean because I was in love with him, and I was angry that he cheated. But in reality, I was angry that Lilah chose him over me," I swallow hard and continue. "I was supposed to have a family. The kids. The perfect loving and devoted husband. The beautiful traditional home. I was not supposed to be a *lesbian*."

"So, you—"

"And I know she felt it too! I *know* she did, Chris. I saw the way she looked at me. The way she touched me during that threesome, the way she kissed me…it *was real*. We could've…no it wasn't possible. We could have never been together." The words rush out quickly.

Chris stares, the emotional chasm between us widening by the second. "You've killed before him, haven't you?" He's piecing together the jagged edges of a puzzle that should never have existed.

"Michael, my first love. He was my first kill," I admit, a dark pride mingled with sorrow. "A man in Los Angeles, who tried to rape me. A pastor in North Carolina, Waylon. A sweet man named Jasper who didn't deserve it," my voice falters, shaking under the weight of my own darkness. "And…" the next words are like shards in my throat, "My mother."

Chris's eyes remain emotionless, a mask of horror barely held in check. "I smothered her with a pillow." Sobs break through my resolve like fissures in a dam. I gather myself quickly, brushing away tears, the vulnerability too dangerous to linger in.

"And what about the woman in your closet? That was your mother-in-law, right?"

I shake my head. "I didn't kill her. Or my next-door neighbor. Or Dr. Maggie."

"Dr. Maggie?"

"My therapist. She was stabbed."

"So, who killed them, Satara?"

"I don't know." I say, my voice rising, splintering.

"Satara…" he starts, a note of suspicion creeping in.

"I didn't kill them!" I scream slamming my fist on the table, my voice reverberating off the walls. He stares at me, doubt etched in every line of his face.

"She was in your closet," he whispers.

I shake my head, denial wrapping around me like a shroud. "No. No, no, no, I didn't *kill them.*"

Just then, the sharp sound of the doorbell rings through the tension-soaked air. I turn towards the door, each step heavy with fear and dread. At the threshold of my chaotic world and the one outside,

I hesitate, knife tucked hidden in my palm. The sudden sound of the doorbell sends a jolt of fear through me; my heart races, the echo of our conversation still hanging in the air like a dark cloud. Chris looks towards the door, his eyes wide with a new kind of terror, but he's rooted to the chair, bound to the fate I've thrust him into. "Don't make a sound." I untie his hands, which is a risky move, but I have no choice.

My mind races as I approach the door, the knife still gripped tightly in my hand. I hide it behind my back. Every step feels like an eternity, the creaking floorboards announcing my approach even louder than my pounding heart.

With a deep breath, I open the door slightly, peering through the narrow crack. A uniformed police officer stands there, his face serious but non-threatening. "Good evening, ma'am," he says, his tone professional. "I'm Officer Jenkins. We've had reports of a disturbance in this household."

My blood runs cold. "What kind of disturbance?" I struggle to keep my voice steady.

"Neighbors reported hearing screams," his eyes narrow slightly as he tries to peer past me into the house. "Is everything alright in here?"

"Yes, everything's fine," I stammer, my mind racing for an explanation. "Just a little argument with my boyfriend. But we've sorted it out now."

He raises an eyebrow, clearly not convinced. "I'm going to need to have a quick look around, ma'am. Just to be sure."

Panic claws at my insides. I step back, opening the door reluctantly but keeping a tight hold on the knife hidden behind my back.

"Of course, Officer. Please, come in."

As he steps inside, I can see Chris's face pale. His eyes dart from me to the officer, silent cries for help seemingly reflecting in his wide eyes.

"Is someone else here right now?" Officer Jenkins asks, stepping further into the house, his hand resting on his belt, ready for any sudden move.

I force a smile, trying to remain calm. "Yes, my boyfriend is still here. This is Chris," I point at him. "Like I said, we had a little argument, but we're fine now."

Officer Jenkins moves past me, his gaze fixed on Chris, who is seated rigidly at the kitchen table. "Sir are you alright?" he asks, his voice full of concern.

Chris looks at me, his face a mixture of fear and defiance, and then turns to the officer.. "I'm fine," he says flatly, choosing his words carefully. "Just a misunderstanding that got a bit loud. We'll be alright."

The officer doesn't seem entirely convinced but nods slowly. "Okay, but if you need any help, don't hesitate to call. We're just a phone call away."

I nod, the tension almost unbearable. "Thank you, Officer. We appreciate it." He gives Chris one last thoughtful look before turning to leave. I follow him to the door, every instinct urging me to watch his every movement until he's out of sight.

"Take care, ma'am," he says with a final glance around, seemingly satisfied but still wary. He steps back outside, and I close the door behind him, my heart racing, my breath coming in short, panicked gasps. I turn back to Chris, my hands trembling. The knife remains in my grip, a cold reminder of how close we were to the edge. "See?" I say, my voice barely above a whisper. "Everything's under control." I force a smile on my face in order to keep from breaking down entirely.

Chris looks at me, his expression a turmoil of emotions. Fear, defiance, and something almost like pity flicker across his face. "Satara, you can't keep doing this," he says softly as I begin to tie his hands to the back of the chair again, the weight of his words pressing down like a heavy shroud. But before I can respond, the house feels even colder, the severity of the late afternoon dawning on me. The spell Millicent helped cast, the spiraling web of lies and desperate attempts to hold onto love—everything feels like it's teetering on the brink of collapse.

"Maybe it's time to leave this place, Chris. We can start over somewhere else," I say, almost pleading as I tie his hands behind him again, my fingers trembling. He didn't ask for help. He didn't try to run. Maybe he *did* want this as badly as I did. "We can be happy. Just you and me."

His eyes never leave mine. "Satara, you need help. This isn't love, it's—"

"Don't say it," I cut him off, my voice sharp. "We can be happy. We *will* be happy." His silence is answer enough, the despair deepening in my chest. I can't shake the feeling that the shadows within are growing, darkness creeping ever closer, threatening to swallow us both. Just then, the doorbell rings again, setting my nerves ablaze, every chime a hammer on cracked glass. "Don't say anything," I hiss, my voice thin, a wire stretched too tight. Walking to the door, every step feels like a descent into dread. I open it, my shock electric when I see Lilah standing there, her smile a shard of cruelty in the dim light. She doesn't give me a moment. Her fist crashes into my face, detonating stars behind my eyes. I fall back, gravity a vicious lover, my head hitting the floor with a sickening thud. Dizzy, knocked halfway into unconsciousness, the room spins in a surreal tilt-a-whirl. Lilah stands over me, her breath shallow; triumphant.

"You don't know how long I've been waiting to do that." Her voice is dark, laced with venom. Before I can respond, she starts kicking, her blows a relentless barrage against my stomach, my ribs—a symphony of pain.

"Stop! This is all going way too far!" Chris yells, his voice cracking through the fog. I look over at him, searching for clues in the chaos. What did he mean? What did any of this mean? Lilah freezes, her foot hovering mid-kick. "We got the full confession," Chris says, his voice steadier now. "Now come over here and untie me."

Lilah stops kicking me and rushes to Chris, her fingers fumbling in haste as she undoes the ropes. I lift my head as much as I could. Chris and Lilah—they know each other? I watch through hazy eyes as Lilah pulls a tiny black tape recorder from underneath the kitchen table. It had been taped there for God knows how long. Probably since Chris had asked to stay over.

"What took you so long? Were you going to just let me die?"

"Shut up, Abdul. I needed to send the cop over first to confirm you were in danger. Camille told me you were here but—"

"Bullshit, you wanted a full confession first."

The room spins, my sense of reality crumbling.

Abdul? Who is Abdul?

The door flies open, the suddenness of it a gunshot.

"Where is he?" A panicked voice calls out, threading through my fragmented perception. I recognize it—it's Millicent. She runs in, her arms wrapping around Chris, pure relief etching her features before she hugs him.

"I'm so glad you're safe," she breathes.

"It's over. It's finally over," Chris says, the weight of victory in his words.

What's over? Someone else rushes in—Cynthia. "Did she confess? *Why* is she not in handcuffs?"

"It's okay, Stacey punched her lights out. She's down for the count."

The next figure that runs in is a ghost turned flesh—Dr. Maggie—alive, sobbing, her question frail with hope. "Is it over? Is it really over?"

"Yes," Lilah answers calmly, "Good job, everyone."

ONE HOUR LATER

Being Lilah Patrick has been a blast. I got to be this classy, sophisticated woman. I lived in a cozy, modest home—nothing too flashy, just the simple life I had wanted. Being undercover for six years ain't a walk in the park. It took a lotta backstory and a ton of commitment. But you know what? It's been a wild ride. I've carefully cooked up this story, and I've had some top-notch help from folks playing their parts to perfection. It gave me a real kick knowing that I finally got to slap the cuffs on this psycho broad.

Now I'm staring at Satara through the glass of a questioning room. She's handcuffed, her expression completely emotionless. Detective Wells walks over and stands right next to me. He looks back and forth between me and Satara. "Well, you did it. I doubted you there for a minute, but you did it. Good job, Stacey."

I nod at Detective Wells and give him a thin smile. "I just couldn't go home until I caught her. I know you wanted me to give up and get off the case—"

"I asked you to give up years ago. The chief wasn't happy."

"Well, I bet the chief's smiling now," I say, grinning. "I just caught a freakin' serial killer. A *woman* serial killer. This'll make history, won't it?"

Detective Wells doesn't answer me, just tips his hat and gives me a wink. "Have fun talking to her. Don't get too violent." He walks off, leaving me to my moment.

I place my hand on the cold metal door and push it open. Standing at the doorway, I stare at her. She's been pretty much catatonic since we arrested her. Real steely and silent, her eyes got that faraway look. "How does it feel?" my voice echoes in the cold room. She slowly turns her head to look at me, just turns her head, her body still. She's got dark circles under her eyes, looking real tired. "How does it feel to know that your whole life was a lie?"

She just stares, not a word coming out of her mouth. I sit down in the cold chair across from her, cross my legs, and sling my arm over the back of the chair. "There was no Love Witch. It was just an idea I came up with, knowing you'd be dumb and desperate enough to believe it."

Still, no reaction.

"Her real name is Camille, and she's Abdul's cousin. I hired her as an informant because Abdul kept hounding me, saying how perfect she was for the role when I told him my idea. Oh, sorry, you know Abdul as Chris," I let out a chuckle. "You see, I hired Abdul first. He came on what, like, two years ago? Your place of employment was privy to the investigation the entire time. They were happy to accommodate Abdul and Cynthia and give them fake roles in the company. You ever seen Abdul working? He wasn't doing shit but keeping an eye on you. He had some drug charges, and we made a deal with him to drop em' if he worked for me as an undercover informant. His role was to make you fall for him, get you to let your guard down, and confess your deepest, darkest secrets. And mess with your emotions a bit." a smile twitches at my lips.

There's a flicker in her eyes. Maybe it's anger, maybe it's despair. Either way, I got her. This six-year operation was a masterpiece, and now it's time to relish my success. Finally, she speaks. "Tell me," Satara says, almost whispering. "Tell me everything. I need to know what was real and what was not," her voice is hollow. "Did Dean ever love me?"

I smile, keeping my voice steady. "Yes, at first," I say. "But once he found out what you were…he stopped."

She looks at me, desperate. "When did he find out?"

"The Big Bear trip a year ago."

"Tell me. Tell me how."

I stare at her for a moment, then nod. "Alright."

So, I do.

I wish Dean hadn't found out I was undercover. He ain't no criminal or cop, so lying and keeping his cover was tough for him. He was just trying to be a good husband. Satara was making breakfast for everyone, and Dean, thinking he was being helpful, grabs my suitcase, thinking it was hers, to pack up her things. That's when he found my notepad—all the little notes and clues I had written down about Satara. I was in my room when I saw Dean at the doorway, holding my little notepad.

Dean's brow furrowed as he was flipping through the pages filled with my handwriting. His eyes got as big as saucers with each line he read. "Lilah, what the hell is this?"

I froze for a second, my heart pounding in my chest. I quickly peeked my head out the door and glanced around, making sure Satara or anyone else wasn't within earshot. I grabbed his arm and pulled him into my room and shut the door. "Keep your voice down," I hissed. "We can't talk about this here."

He looked panicked, confused. "Lilah, what's going on? What's all this about Satara? She *killed* someone?"

I took a deep breath, trying to keep my own nerves at bay. "Meet me tomorrow evening after we get home. Somewhere private. We'll talk then."

He shook his head, still trying to process everything. "What am I supposed to tell Satara?"

"Tell her something, anything. Say it's a work dinner, I don't give a shit. Just cover for me and don't say *anything* about this, Dean. I'm telling you; this is way bigger than you think."

He hesitated, looking back at me like he might throw up all over. Finally, he nodded, albeit reluctantly.

"Okay. Tomorrow evening. I'll see you then."

"Good," I said, my voice steady, trying to convey more confidence than I felt. I didn't have much hope for him. Dean was weak. "And Dean… *act normal.* We can't afford to tip her off."

He swallowed hard, nodding again, and slowly left the room, still in disbelief. We both knew there's no going back now.

Dean was acting weird the rest of the night. I could tell he wasn't gonna hold up too well. But I kept an eye on him, trying to distract Satara as much as possible. Even resorted to flirting with one of Dean's friends all night—knowing Satara would eat it up, focusing on me instead of her husband. Things were going smoothly until we started playing charades and she lost it over something Dean said. I watched as she got up and stormed to her room, slamming the door so hard the whole cabin shook. I shot Dean a look, narrowing my eyes to let him know he fucked up. What an idiot. Now I had to fix it.

My feelings for Satara were complicated. I had grown attracted to this woman I was hunting, but I had to stuff those feelings down. Because the thing was, as much as I had feelings for her, I also hated her. *God,* I hated that woman with every fiber of my being.

I suggested a threesome. I needed to make her feel like everything was fine, that Dean really wanted her. Luckily, Dean played along, focusing most of his attention at Satara instead of me. Good boy. Kept the crazy broad pacified for a little while. I didn't want to admit it at the time, but now I know that part of that night was also for me. But I don't say that out loud.

After I'm done with the story, I lean forward in my seat. "He wanted to get away from you. He tried everything to get you to hate him. See, he was smart enough to know he couldn't be the one to leave—nah, he knew you'd explode like a goddamn volcano," I scoot my chair closer to her before continuing, my voice steady, low. "So, he became controlling. Started telling you what to wear, what not to wear, calling you a fat cow when you ate too much, never sexually satisfying you. It was all a ploy to get you to leave. But no matter what he did, no matter how much of a goddamn asshole he was to you, you just wouldn't stop loving him because you're a silly pathetic fucking woman with no dignity," I stare at her, my eyes like razors. She stares back, her eyes wide. A single tear falls. "You're probably wondering about Cynthia and the book club, right? You see, that was all for fun, if I'm being honest. Well, *most* of it. Lydia Ramirez is also a criminal informant. You know her better as Cynthia. A couple years back she stole thousands of dollars' worth of merchandise from a designer store. It was easy to get her to become an informant, bitch cried the entire time in the questioning room, pleading for us not to send her to prison."

"You see, Lydia—Cynthia—was your close friend. She wasn't your *best* friend, of course—that was me. But Lydia was the confidant you felt most comfortable telling embarrassing things to because you cared less about what she thought about you. You didn't love her like you did me. Lydia was a confidant who didn't really offer reasonable solutions but can give you the answers you *wanna* hear. I knew she'd be the one I would choose to tell you about the Love Witch, and you'd believe her. And guess what? You ate that shit *right up*," I chuckle. "You *really* believed she had a Love Witch put a spell on Jeff Bailey—by the way, have you ever seen them together? Think. *Really* think. The answer is no, right? She's not married to fucking Jeff Bailey," I lean back in my chair. "Anyways, the other girls in the group are who they say they are. Cheryl is Cheryl. And Dawn is Dawn. We *did* bring Dawn into the fold by the end though. Poor woman was scared to ask you to kill her husband. I'm honestly surprised you didn't take the bait. I told her we'd lock that fucker up for putting her hands on her and their eight-year-old daughter if she helped us. Let's just say, her husband was a real nasty son of a bitch. Anyways, before that none of the other women knew anything about what we were doing. All except for the woman who played Lizzie, of course," I laugh.

"That woman gave us issues. Her real name is Farrah Collins. We picked her up for arson around the same time as Abdul. We offered her a deal, and she became Lizzie Stiles, easy peasy. Told her she could bring her little one with her too. She's a real cute kid, ain't she? Well, anyway, Farrah was upset because she missed her loser boyfriend and wanted to go home. I told her either she stayed and played her role, or she went to jail. She *hated* being an informant. Every day, she would call me up on the phone and say, 'Just kill me off! Stage a burglary or a hit and run, please. I'm not even a major character in the story!'"

I laugh, thinking about those frantic calls I got from her in the middle of the night. "She got paranoid and upset when you made a scene at the book club about her not knowing her own husband's likes and dislikes. Remember that? Anyway, she calls me up and is like, 'She knows I'm not his wife, I messed up, I'm dead, she knows I'm a fraud, *blah blah, blah*," I stare at Satara, who's still got that faraway look, but I know she's listening. I see the look in her eyes, the way her mouth twitches, a slight little response to something I said.

"By the way, Dr. Maggie is a real therapist. But she's been my informant since you started seeing her," I say. "She cared about you. She really did. But she knew you were dangerous from the start, so when I came to her and asked her to be my informant, she agreed. You gave poor Dr. Maggie a real scare that day you followed her, you know that right? She told me she saw you sitting in your car. She said she looked *right* at you. But you're so delusional that you genuinely believed you were getting away with it."

"Why did you make me believe she was dead?"

"It was her idea to kill herself off. She didn't wanna do it anymore. Said she felt unsafe around you, so we told that nice male therapist that we were conducting an investigation and to inform you that she was stabbed and killed at her home, so she'd never have to have a session with you again," Satara blinks but doesn't say anything else. I smile as Detective Wells pops in. "Hell, you even thought you had Wells under your spell! He didn't even have to *try,* and you believed it. Isn't that right, Joe?"

"Chief wants to see you," he says.

"I'll be out in a minute."

He closes the door, and I turn back to her. "Anyway, you wanna hear something funny? Your neighbor—Mrs. Hanson, you know the one you killed? —saw you hauling a big suitcase in your truck that night. We were already certain you killed Dean, but I wanted a full confession before we arrested you. That was my call, and I made a lot of people upset about it. But the other people you killed needed justice too, not just Dean. *Every* single one of them." I lean in closer. "We're gonna need you to lead us to his body at first daylight by the way."

"I didn't kill Mrs. Hanson, or Marlo."

I stare at her and purse my lips together. "Sure, sweetie keep telling yourself that. You were probably high as a kite."

"It's true," she whispers. She opens her mouth to say something else, and then hesitates. I sit and watch until she works up the gumption to say whatever she was gonna say. "What about Jasper?"

I shake my head. "You got to him before we did. He never knew about anything."

She seems to be thinking about something, her eyes shifting. "Jasper really liked me. We…we could've…" her voice trails off.

"It's a shame, ain't it?"

I tell her the story about the night before she killed Dean, how he called me on the phone that night, scared out of his mind. He started yapping before I even got a chance to say hi. "I'm nervous about tonight," he said.

I rolled my eyes but tried to sound like I cared. He was such a pain in my ass. "It'll be fine, Dean. Calm down. It's just a night out getting drinks and sushi."

I heard shuffling on the other end. "So, you don't think it's strange? Her inviting you out to dinner? The three of us? We've never done that before."

Of course it was strange, but I don't tell him that. I needed him to hold it together, or he'll screw everything up. "Dean, it'll be okay. Just don't tip her off."

"So, when are you going to arrest her?"

"Soon, Dean. I promise."

"She's getting crazier by the day. I don't know how long I can keep doing this."

He kept droning on. The truth is, I couldn't care less if Dean was murdered. In fact, it'd help my case if she offed him. More evidence. I hadn't nailed her yet, but if we could get her to confess, she would rot in prison forever.

"You know, yesterday she randomly brought home two cats. And I couldn't say anything, I just had to go along with it."

"Cats? Where'd she get them?"

"No idea, she probably stole them."

I sighed loudly. "I'll get the cats outta there, okay?"

"This isn't about the cats, goddamn it! Do you get that my life is in danger, Stacey?"

"Do not call me Stacey. Call me Lilah."

He was quiet for a moment. "I just want this to be over so I can get out of this living nightmare where I have to sleep with one eye open every night. You *know* I can't leave; she already threatened my life if I did. And if she finds out what we're doing she'll surely kill me."

"Just be ready for dinner. Now hang up before she catches you talking to me."

I knew right off the bat Dean was in trouble the moment we parted ways from our dinner. The way her demeanor changed, how her back stiffened and she got less talkative—it was a dead giveaway. I don't think Dean noticed, but after almost a decade as an undercover cop, I've got a Ph.D. in reading people. It was probably the way he kept glancing at me pitifully throughout the night.

Idiot.

Something tipped her off, alright, and I had a bad feeling about it. But I decided not to warn him. He was just a pawn in my perfectly constructed plan, after all.

"That's what the big dummy gets for marrying a woman he met at a looney bin. Oh, and I got the cats back to their owner by the way. Judy Smithson, the sweet lady down the street? I don't even want to know how you got 'em."

"Don't call him a dummy," she says under her breath, unmoving.

"Do you even feel bad at all?" I ask. "Do you feel bad for takin' the lives that you did? Or are you that fucked up in the head?"

She stares, her expression steely. Then she moves her eyes to meet mine. "Cunt."

I raise an eyebrow. "That make you feel better?"

We lock eyes, the room filled with silence. This is the bare, ugly truth out in the open, no more games or lies to hide behind. She breaks the silence.

"Why?" Satara asks. "Why fabricate my whole life and torture me like this? *Why?*" Her voice shakes.

It's the question I've been wanting her to ask since I walked into the room. "Michael Messino. Who I believe was your first victim," I see her expression change, the blood draining from her face. "You killed him. And I found him four hours later. He was supposed to meet me for dinner, and he never showed up," I feel my emotions rising, trying not to think about that moment. I watch as her expression changes as she finally understands. "Michael was my fiancé."

Her eyes widen, no longer distant. Now they're full of shock, maybe even realization. "Yeah," I continue, my voice a bit steadier despite the lump in my throat. "We were gonna start a family. Danny is his by the way, I was already pregnant with him when you killed him. He's a good actor ain't he? He kept his conversations with you short for a reason. That was his idea. Smart boy he is," I say. "We had plans. A whole life ahead of us. But you took that away. You ended it before it even began. There's no coming back from that."

I can tell she's struggling with her own emotions now, the weight of what she did finally settling in. It's a small, bitter victory for me, knowing she understands the depth of her actions, but it won't bring Michael back. Nothing can. Anger bubbles up and I try to keep my composure, but I can't. I just can't. I stand up and pace the room. I look at her.

"You want to know why I did all this? Well, there's your answer. Revenge, plain and simple. I wanted you to feel what I felt. Your future with Chris Stiles was never a possibility. *He never existed.* Your life is turned upside down, your reality is shattered, everything you thought you knew, *gone.* Now you know. Now, you finally understand."

She looks up at me from her seat, her eyes boring through me. "Six years. Six fucking years you pretended to be my friend…all because you were angry at me for getting revenge on the man who raped me when I was fifteen?" She shakes her head, her eyes growing even darker. "I think it was something else keeping you here… I think it was me."

I shake off the accusation. "I have no idea what you're talking about. I was just doing my job, biding my time waiting for you to slip up. And it doesn't matter what happened to you in the past, you had no right to *kill* him."

"You felt it. I know you did."

"I didn't—"

"You had feelings for me. You stayed for six years because you never wanted to leave me, admit it right now, Lilah!" She screams, her voice ragged, tears streaking her face.

My heart thumps in my chest as I stare at her. "My name is Stacey."

"You didn't date a man for six *fucking* years."

The silence stretches on, tortuous and long. "I was still grieving over Michael. He was my first true love. And you took him away from me." My voice is dark; ragged.

Satara's face is streaked with tears. "All I ever wanted was love," she whispers.

I stop pacing and sit back in my chair, watching the devastation wash over her. The game's over, and neither of us came out unscathed. But at least now, there's some semblance of closure. "You thought you had everyone wrapped around your little finger, when the whole time I was the one pulling the strings," I stare at her, my gaze unwavering. "I won."

SUGAR

EPILOGUE

It's been three years since Satara was arrested. The media storm was a whirlwind after that. It had never been done before, a six-year undercover sting operation. It made waves. It made history. And sadly, that meant Satara made history.

They call her the Lovesick Killer.

It's ridiculous, giving her a nickname. But I know that's how it goes now. Edmund Kemper, the Co-Ed Killer; David Berkowitz, the Son of Sam; and so on, and so forth. And now Satara Stratton, the Lovesick Killer, is part of that list. It disgusts me how many people idolize her. Women writing her letters of support saying they understand why she did what she did. Men writing her ten-page letters professing their love for her.

There were even rumors that she had an army of men—apparently, she called them devotees—that would do anything for her. I had no idea if it was true or not, I read it in some gossip rag a couple months ago.

Satara got what she wanted in the end…love.

People idolized her. She was America's first convicted female serial killer that had acted alone. Up until this point there had been female serial killers, but they always had a male accomplice. Satara was praised for acting alone without a man's help. Her face was everywhere, taunting me. On the news. On magazines and newspapers. Once the trial ended and the case was closed, I moved back to Chicago and bought a ranch house for Danny and me out in the country. Got some chickens and pigs. I've lived a quiet life, away from the media, away from seeing her face. One day she wrote me a letter. I didn't even bother to read it. I ripped it up into little pieces, threw it away, and spat on it.

She's still trying to appeal to this day, saying someone set her up with two killings, still claiming her innocence for the murders of Marlo Stratton and her neighbor, Glenda Hanson. But no one believed her, not after the taped confession about all the other killings.

It went exactly as I planned. You see, I killed them for a good reason.

I went over to talk to Satara a couple days after the vigil, but she wasn't home. Marlo answered, and immediately started accusing Satara of killing Dean. She was hysterical, crying, yelling, all that. And then I told her. I told her I was undercover, and we were gonna prove she killed her son; we just needed a bit more time. That was a big mistake, but I thought it would calm the broad down, reassure her that everything was gonna be okay. Well, it did the opposite. She screamed and yelled some more, saying that I knew what she was the entire time, and I let her kill her son. She threatened to go to the police, she threatened to sue the department. After that, it was all a blur. I picked up a hammer that was in a kitchen drawer and cracked it over her head. She fell and never got back up. I figured I'd hide her in the closet of the guest room. So, I moved her, grabbing her by the feet, and dragging her up the stairs. It wasn't easy, but I did it. I grabbed all her things, throw 'em in her suitcase, and carry it outside. And that's when I froze, because Mrs. Hanson was standing right there, a couple of feet from the doorway, her face twisted in horror and confusion. I blinked and looked down at the suitcase, then back up at her.

"I heard screaming," she said.

I laughed. "Oh, that was nothing, me and Marlo were just having a chat."

She stared at me. "Is that your suitcase you're carrying, or someone else's?"

I cocked my head and looked at her. I stop using my fake little prissy voice and use my real voice, which is probably one or two octaves lower. "Go back inside, Mrs. Hanson," I said. She looked at me in horror and then she did. Went right back inside. I knew I had to handle her soon. She knew I did something.

Getting to Mrs. Hanson was tricky though, 'cause she and Mr. Hanson never went anywhere, and they were never separated. It took me a while to get to her until I got an idea. I called the Hanson household and asked Mr. Hanson if he could help me with my broken refrigerator. That's what he did before he retired—he was a handyman. Of course, my fridge wasn't actually broken, so I had to break it, which was real hard. Sometimes breaking something on purpose is a lot more difficult than doing it by accident.

He came right over that same afternoon I called him, happy to help me and have something to do besides sitting on his recliner and watching *Taxi* all day. While he was preoccupied working on my fridge, I told him I needed to go to the grocery store for some bread and slipped out, heading down the street to his house. Mrs. Hanson answered the door and when she saw me, I could tell she was real scared. She tried to hide it, but I could see it. I pushed her further into the house and closed the door behind me. She fell back to the ground screaming, and I walked to the kitchen and picked out the biggest knife they had. When I came back Mrs. Hanson was still on the ground, on account of her being old and decrepit as shit. God rest her soul.

Anyway, I started stabbing her in the stomach and kept stabbing until she stopped screaming. And then—this part was hard, but I had to do it—I used my hands to open up one of the stab wounds on her stomach. Blood and guts were all over my hands, and the squishing and squelching sound didn't make it any easier. I stared down at the cavernous hole of gore that I made in Mrs. Hanson's stomach and smiled. I *needed* to do it to make Satara look like a monster. A fuckin' depraved woman who deserved to be locked up forever.

It worked. She's in prison for life now. I think back to that moment in the living room with Mrs. Hanson and her guts exposed. I don't know why, but it makes me smile. Maybe I had become the very person I was hunting for all those years. But Satara never slashed anyone's stomach open and pulled out their guts for fun; she never did anything as sick as that. Maybe I was worse. It doesn't matter anymore. That's all behind me now.

Now I'm hummin' in the kitchen as I prepare a beef stew for Danny and me. I call him. *"Danny!* dinner is ready, get your butt out here."

He emerges from his room. He'll be going off and starting a life of his own soon. He's grown a lot over the past three years— physically and emotionally. I was proud of him, not many kids could survive living a lie for so long in order to catch a serial killer and come out alright. But Danny was brave and resilient, just as his father was.

I stop stirring the pot of stew and point to the white rectangular box in his hands. It has a red bow wrapped around it. "What's that?"

Danny sits at the kitchen table. "Our neighbor gave it to us. Said it was a late birthday gift for you."

We only had one neighbor that lived close to us—his name was Tom. He owned a horse ranch. Sometimes he'd pop by just to say hello. It was clear he had a thing for me. I laugh to myself. He also wore a cowboy hat. Who would've thought.

Danny sets the gift down and slides it across the kitchen table. He eyes it. "Can I open it?"

"Well, it's for me, not you," I say with a laugh.

"I think it's chocolate," he says plainly.

I rest my hand on my hip, watching him eye the box. I can't say no to him. "Alright, fine, you can open it.

He smiles wide and unties the red bow wrapped around the box. Sure enough, it was a chocolate assortment. Tom was a chocolatier. He worked out in the city running a little candy shop. I've gone there a few times to pick up some sweets whenever I was craving sugar. His chocolate was some of the most delicious chocolate I had ever tasted.

"You can have just *one*," I say. "I don't want you to spoil your dinner."

He excitedly grabs a piece of chocolate and pops the whole thing in his mouth.

"Jesus, Danny. You are a monster!" I laugh.

He laughs along too, his tongue and teeth coated in chocolate. I grab the box, ready to put it away, but I couldn't help grabbing a piece for myself, taking a little bite before placing it back. Of course it was delicious, with a cherry center, my favorite. But then something catches my eye. It's a tiny piece of paper tucked under one of the chocolates. I pull it out. Maybe he left a secret note for me.

I smile and open it.

"Mom…"

I look up, and the sight before me makes my stomach drop. One of Danny's eyes is swollen and bulging, blood seeping from the lid, forming a dark, sticky trail down his cheek. It pops out, hanging by the delicate nerves, swaying slightly as his body twitched erratically, movements sharp and unnatural, reminiscent of a marionette with tangled strings. His mouth began to foam, a thick, white spittle collecting at the corners before spilling over as he gasps for breath. It was a sound that sent chills down my spine, a frantic, desperate noise. "Danny?" I manage, my voice trembling as panic gripped me tightly.

The blood drains from my face, leaving only a cold sweat behind. I can feel the rhythmic thumping of my heartbeat in my ears. Every beat echoed my rising dread. All I can do is stare, frozen in shock, as Danny continued to twitch; the horror of the moment consuming every ounce of rational thought. I look down at the piece of paper in my hands and read it:

Game. Set. Match. -S

ABOUT THE AUTHOR

Mia Ballard has been writing stories since she was ten years old. She loves all things horror and writing stories about unhinged women. She is the author of the poetry collection *Delicate Thoughts*. SUGAR is her debut novel. She currently resides in California with her partner John and adorably anxious Springer Spaniel.

Instagram: @Galaxygrlmia
Mballardwrites@gmail.com

Printed in Dunstable, United Kingdom